HALF BAD

HALF
BAD

SALLY GREEN

VIKING
An Imprint of Penguin Group (USA)

VIKING

Published by the Penguin Group
Penguin Group (USA) LLC
375 Hudson Street
New York, New York 10014

USA ★ Canada ★ UK ★ Ireland ★ Australia ★ New Zealand ★ India ★ South Africa ★ China

penguin.com
A Penguin Random House Company

First published in the United States of America by Viking, an imprint of Penguin Group (USA), 2014.
Published simultaneously in the UK by Penguin Books Ltd

LIBRARY OF CONGRESS CATALOGING-IN-PUBLICATION DATA
Green, Sally.
Half bad / Sally Green.
pages cm. — (The half bad trilogy ; 1)
Summary: In modern-day England, where witches live alongside humans, Nathan, son of a White witch and the most powerful Black witch, must escape captivity before his seventeenth birthday and receive the gifts that will determine his future.
ISBN 978-0-670-01678-5 (hardback)
[1. Witches—Fiction. 2. Good and evil—Fiction. 3. Family life—Fiction. 4. Toleration—Fiction. 5. Fathers and sons—Fiction. 6. Prisoners—Fiction. 7. England—Fiction.] I. Title.
PZ7.G826323Hal 2014   [Fic—dc23   2013041190

Printed in U.S.A.

1   3   5   7   9   10   8   6   4   2

Designed by Nancy Brennan   Set in Fournier MT

For my mother

CONTENTS

PART ONE: *THE TRICK*

The Trick 3

The Cage 4

Push-ups 5

Ironing 13

The Trick Doesn't Work 16

PART TWO: *HOW I ENDED UP IN A CAGE*

My Mother 23

Jessica and the First Notification 24

My Father 29

My Mother's Suicide 30

The Second Notification 31

Jessica's Giving 39

A Long Way off Seventeen 47

Thomas Dawes Secondary School 51

More Fighting, Some Smoking 64

The Fifth Notification 76

My First Kiss 83

BW 94

Post-Trauma 104

The Story of the Death of Saba 110

Mary 116

Two Weapons 129

The Sixth Notification 136

PART THREE: *THE SECOND WEAPON*

The Choker 153

The New Trick 156

The Routine 158

Lessons about My Father 162

Fantasies about My Father 173

Thoughts about My Mother 176

Assessments 178

Punk 179

A Hunter 190

Gran 197

Visitors 199

Codified 205

PART FOUR: *FREEDOM*

Three Teabags in the Life of
Nathan Marcusovich 229

Nikita 238

Cobalt Alley 245

Money 253

Jim and Trev (Part One) 255

Jim and Trev (Part Two) 265

Hunters 274

Arran 279

PART FIVE: *GABRIEL*

Geneva 289

Gabriel 299

The Roof 313

PART SIX: *TURNING SEVENTEEN*

The Favors 323

The Eagle and Rose 334

Trusting Gabriel 340

Annalise 353

The Fairborn 359

Back to Mercury 369

Three Gifts 384

Running 393

❦

"There is nothing either good or bad,
but thinking makes it so."

Hamlet, William Shakespeare

HALF
BAD

PART ONE

THE TRICK

The Trick

There's these two kids, boys, sitting close together, squished in by the big arms of an old chair. You're the one on the left.

The other boy's warm to lean close to, and he moves his gaze from the telly to you sort of in slow motion.

"You enjoying it?" he asks.

You nod. He puts his arm round you and turns back to the screen.

Afterward you both want to try the thing in the film. You sneak the big box of matches from the kitchen drawer and run with them to the woods.

You go first. You light the match and hold it between your thumb and forefinger, letting it burn right down until it goes out. Your fingers are burnt, but they hold the blackened match.

The trick works.

The other boy tries it too. Only he doesn't do it. He drops the match.

Then you wake up and remember where you are.

The Cage

The trick is to not mind. Not mind about it hurting, not mind about anything.

The trick of not minding is key; it's the only trick in town. Only this is not a town; it's a cage beside a cottage, surrounded by a load of hills and trees and sky.

It's a one-trick cage.

Push-ups

•.•••.•

The routine is okay.

Waking up to sky and air is okay. Waking up to the cage and the shackles is what it is. You can't let the cage get to you. The shackles rub but healing is quick and easy, so what's to mind?

The cage is loads better now that the sheepskins are in. Even when they're damp they're warm. The tarpaulin over the north end was a big improvement too. There's shelter from the worst of the wind and rain. And a bit of shade if it's hot and sunny. Joke! You've got to keep your sense of humor.

So the routine is to wake up as the sky lightens before dawn. You don't have to move a muscle, don't even have to open your eyes to know it's getting light; you can just lie there and take it all in.

The best bit of the day.

There aren't many birds around, a few, not many. It would be good to know all their names, but you know their different calls. There are no seagulls, which is something to think about, and there are no vapor trails either. The wind is usually quiet in the predawn calm, and somehow the air feels warmer already as it begins to get light.

You can open your eyes now and there are a few minutes to savor the sunrise, which today is a thin pink line stretching along the top of a narrow ribbon of cloud draped over the smudged green hills. And you've still got a minute, maybe even two, to get your head together before she appears.

You've got to have a plan, though, and the best idea is to have it all worked out the night before so you can slip straight into it without a thought. Mostly the plan is to do what you're told, but not every day, and not today.

You wait until she appears and throws you the keys. You catch the keys, unlock your ankles, rub them to emphasize the pain she is inflicting, unlock your left manacle, unlock your right, stand, unlock the cage door, toss the keys back to her, open the cage door, step out—keeping your head down, never look her in the eyes (unless that's part of some other plan)—rub your back and maybe groan a bit, walk to the vegetable bed, piss.

Sometimes she tries to mess with your head, of course, by changing the routine. Sometimes she wants chores before exercises but most days it's push-ups first. You'll know which while still zipping up.

"Fifty."

She says it quietly. She knows you're listening.

You take your time as usual. That's always part of the plan.

Make her wait.

Rub your right arm. The metal wristband cuts into it when the shackle is on. You heal it and get a faint buzz.

You roll your head, your shoulders, your head again and then stand there, just stand there for another second or two, pushing her to her limit, before you drop to the ground.

one	Not minding
two	is the trick.
three	The only
four	trick.
five	But there are
six	loads of
seven	tactics.
eight	Loads.
nine	On the look-out
ten	all the time.
eleven	All the time.
twelve	And it's
thirteen	easy.
fourteen	'Cause there ain't
fifteen	nothing else
sixteen	to do.
seventeen	Look out for what?
eighteen	Something.
nineteen	Anything.
twenty	N
twenty-one	E
twenty-two	thing.
twenty-three	A mistake.
twenty-four	A chance.

twenty-five	An oversight.
twenty-six	The
twenty-seven	tiniest
twenty-eight	error
twenty-nine	by the
thirty	White
thirty-one	Witch
thirty-two	from
thirty-three	Hell.
thirty-four	'Cause she makes
thirty-five	mistakes.
thirty-six	Oh yes.
thirty-seven	And if that mistake
thirty-eight	comes to
thirty-nine	nothing
forty	you wait
forty-one	for the next one
forty-two	and the next one
forty-three	and the next one.
forty-four	Until
forty-five	you
forty-six	succeed.
forty-seven	Until
forty-eight	you're
forty-nine	free.

You get up. She will have been counting, but never letting up is another tactic.

She doesn't say anything but steps toward you and back-hands you across the face.

fifty   "Fifty."

After push-ups it's just standing and waiting. Best look at the ground. You're by the cage on the path. The path's muddy, but you won't be sweeping it, not today, not with this plan. It's rained a lot in the last few days. Autumn's coming on fast. Still, today it's not raining; already it's going well.

"Do the outer circuit." Again she's quiet. No need to raise her voice.

And off you jog . . . but not yet. You've got to keep her thinking you're being your usual difficult-yet-basically-compliant self and so you knock mud off your boots, left boot-heel on right toe followed by right boot-heel on left toe. You raise a hand and look up and around as if you're assessing the wind direction, spit on the potato plants, look left and right like you're waiting for a gap in the traffic and . . . let the bus go past . . . and then you're off.

You take the drystone wall with a leap to the top and over, then across the moorland, heading to the trees.

Freedom.

As if!

But you've got the plan, and you've learned a lot in four months. The fastest that you've done the outer circuit for her is forty-five minutes. You can do it in less than that, forty maybe, 'cause you stop by the stream at the far end and rest and drink and listen and look, and one time you managed to get to the ridge and see over to more hills, more trees and a loch (it might be a lake but something about the heather and the length of summer days says you're in Scotland).

Today the plan is to speed up when you're out of sight. That's easy. Easy. The diet you're on is great. You have to give her some credit, 'cause you are super healthy, super fit. Meat, veg, more meat, more veg, and don't forget plenty of fresh air. Oh this is the life.

You're doing okay. Keeping up a good pace. Your top pace.

And you're buzzing, self-healing from her little slap; it's giving you a little buzz, buzz, buzz.

You're already at the far end, where you could cut back to do the inner circuit which is really half the outer circuit. But she didn't want the inner circuit and you were going to do the outer whatever she said.

That's got to be the fastest yet.

Then up to the ridge.

And let gravity take you down in long strides to the stream that leads to the loch.

Now it gets tricky. Now you are just outside the area of the circuit and soon you will be well outside it. She won't know that you've gone until you're late. That gives you twenty-five minutes from leaving the circuit—maybe thirty, maybe thirty-five, but call it twenty-five before she's after you.

But she's not the problem; the wristband is the problem. It will break open when you go too far. How it works, witchcraft or science or both, you don't know, but it will break open. She told you that on Day One and she told you the wristband contains a liquid, an acid. The liquid will be released if you stray too far and this liquid will burn right through your wrist.

"It'll take your hand off," was how she put it.

Going downhill now. There's a click . . . and the burning starts.

But you've got the plan.

You stop and submerge your wrist in the stream. The stream hisses. The water helps, although it's a strange sort of gloopy, sticky potion and won't wash away easily. And more will come out. And you have to keep going.

You pad the band out with wet moss and peat. Dunk it under again. Stuff more padding in. It's taking too long. Get going.

Downhill.

Follow the stream.

The trick is not to mind about your wrist. Your legs feel fine. Covering lots of ground.

And anyway losing a hand isn't that bad. You can replace it with something good . . . a hook . . . or a three-pronged claw like the guy in *Enter the Dragon* . . . or maybe something with blades that can be retracted, but, when you fight, out they come, *ker-ching* . . . or flames even . . . no way are you going to have a fake hand, that's for sure . . . no way.

Your head's dizzy. Buzzing too, though. Your body is trying to heal your wrist. You never know, you might get out of this with two hands. Still, the trick is not to mind. Either way, you're out.

Got to stop. Douse it in the stream again, put some new peat in and get going.

Nearly at the loch.

Nearly.

Oh yes. Bloody cold.

You're too slow. Wading is slow but it's good to keep your arm in the water.

Just keep going.

Keep going.

It's a bloody big loch. But that's okay. The bigger the better. Means your hand will be in water longer.

Feeling sick . . . ughhh . . .

Shit, that hand looks a mess. But the acid has stopped coming out of the wristband. You're going to get out. You've beaten her. You can find Mercury. You will get three gifts.

But you've got to keep going.

You'll be at the end of the loch in a minute.

Doing well. Doing well.

Not far now.

Soon be able to see over into the valley, and—

Ironing

•·.•·.•˙

"You nearly lost your hand."

It's lying on the kitchen table still attached to your arm by bone, muscle, and sinew that are visible in the open, raw groove round your wrist. The skin that used to be there has formed lava-like rivulets, running down to your fingers as if it has melted and set again. Your whole hand is puffing up nicely and hurts like . . . well, like an acid burn. Your fingers twitch, but your thumb is not working.

"It might heal so that you can use your fingers again. Or it might not."

She took the band off your wrist at the loch and sprayed the wound with a lotion that dulled the pain.

She was prepared. She's always prepared.

And how did she get there so quickly? Did she run? Fly on a bloody broomstick?

However she got to the loch, you still had to walk back with her. That was a tough walk.

"Why don't you speak to me?"

She's right in your face.

"I'm here to teach you, Nathan. But you must stop trying to escape."

She's so ugly that you've got to turn away.

There's an ironing board set up on the other side of the kitchen table.

She was ironing? Ironing her combat trousers?

"Nathan. Look at me."

You keep your eyes on the iron.

"I want to help you, Nathan."

You hawk up a huge gob, turn, and spit. She's quick, though, and snatches back so it lands on her shirt not on her face.

She doesn't hit you. Which is new.

"You need to eat. I'll heat up some stew."

That's new too. Usually you have to cook and clean and sweep.

But you've never had to iron.

She goes to the pantry. There's no fridge. No electricity. There's a wood-burning range. Setting the fire up and cleaning it out are also your chores.

While she's in the pantry you go to look at the iron. Your legs are weak, unsteady, but your head's clear. Clear enough. A sip of water might help but you want to look at the iron. It's just a piece of metal, iron-shaped, with a metal handle, old. It's heavy and cold. It must be heated up on the range to do its job. Must take ages. She's miles from anywhere and anything, and she irons her trousers and shirts!

When she comes back a few seconds later you're round

by the pantry door and you bring the iron down hard, pointed side against her head.

But she's so bloody tall and so bloody fast. The iron catches the side of her scalp and sinks into her shoulder.

You're on the floor clutching your ears, looking at her boots before you pass out.

The Trick Doesn't Work

•·•·•°

She's talking but you can't make sense of it.

You're back sitting at the kitchen table, sweating and shuddering a bit, and blood from your left ear is running down your neck. That ear won't heal. You can't hear at all on that side. And your nose is a mess. You must have landed on it when you fell. It's broken, blocked up, and bloodied, and it won't heal either.

Your hand is resting on the table and it's so swollen now that the fingers can't move at all.

She's sitting on the chair next to you and is spraying your wrist with the lotion again. It's cooling. Numbing.

And it would be so good to be numb like that all over, numb to it all. But that won't happen. What will happen is that she'll lock you back up in the cage, chain you up, and it'll go on and on and on . . .

And so the trick doesn't work. It doesn't work, and you do mind; you mind about it all. You don't want to be back in that cage, and you don't want the trick anymore. You don't want any of it anymore.

The cut on her scalp is healed, but there's the wide ridge of a black-red scab underneath her blonde hair and there's blood on her shoulder. She's still talking about something, her fat slobbering lips working away.

You look around the room. The kitchen sink, the window that overlooks the vegetable garden and the cage, the range, the ironing board, the door to the pantry, and back to the ugly woman with nicely pressed trousers. And clean boots. And in her boot is her little knife. She sometimes keeps it there. You saw it when you were on the floor.

You're dizzy so it's easy to swoon, sinking to your knees. She grabs you by your armpits but your left hand isn't injured and it finds the handle and slides the knife out of her boot while she grapples with your dead weight, and as you let your body sink farther you bring the blade to your jugular. Fast and hard.

But she's so bloody quick, and you kick and fight and fight and kick but she gets the knife off you and you've no kick and no fight left at all.

Back in the cage. Shackled. Kept waking up last night . . . sweating . . . ear still doesn't work . . . you're breathing through your mouth 'cause your nose is blocked. She's even chained your bad wrist, and your whole arm is so swollen that the shackle is tight.

It's late morning, but she still hasn't come for you. She's doing something in the cottage. Tapping. Smoke's coming out of the chimney.

It's warm today, a breeze from the southwest, clouds

moving silently across the sky so the sun is managing a series of appearances, touching your cheek and casting shadows from the bars across your legs. But you've seen it all before, so you close your eyes and remember stuff. It's okay to do that sometimes.

PART
TWO

HOW I ENDED UP IN A CAGE

My Mother

I am standing on my tiptoes. The photograph is on the hall table but I can't get hold of it properly. I stretch and stretch and nudge the frame with my fingertips. It's heavy and hits the floor with a clatter.

I hold my breath. No one comes.

I pick the frame up carefully. The glass hasn't broken. I sit under the table with my back against the wall.

My mother is beautiful. The photograph was taken on her wedding day. She is squinting into the sun, sunlight on her hair, a white dress, white flowers in her hand. Her husband is beside her. He is handsome, smiling. I cover his face with my hand.

I don't know how long I sit there. I like looking at my mother.

Jessica appears. I'd forgotten to listen for her.

She grabs hold of the frame.

I don't let go. I cling onto it. Tight.

But my hands are sweaty.

And Jessica's much bigger than me. She yanks it up, pulling me to my feet, and the frame slides out of my hands. She holds it high to her left and brings it down diagonally, slicing the edge of the frame across my cheekbone.

"Don't ever touch this picture again."

Jessica and the First Notification

•·•·•

I am sitting on my bed. Jessica is sitting on my bed too, telling me a story.

"*Mother asks, 'Have you come to take him away?'*"

"*The young woman at the front door says, 'No. Absolutely not. We would never do that.' The young woman is sincere and keen to do a good job but really naive.*"

I interrupt. "What's naive mean?"

"Clueless. Dumb. Thick. Like you. Got it?"

I nod.

"Good, now listen. *The naive woman says, 'We are visiting all White Witches in England to notify them of the new rules and to help fill in the forms.'*"

"*The woman smiles. The Hunter standing behind her has no smile. He is dressed in black like they all do. He is impressive, tall, strong.*"

"Does Mother smile?"

"No. After you are born Mother never smiles again. *When Mother doesn't reply, the woman from the Council looks concerned. She says, 'You have received the notification, haven't you? It's very important.'*"

"*The woman flicks through the papers on her clipboard and pulls out a letter.*"

Jessica opens out the parchment she is holding. It is a

thick piece, large, and the folds make a deep cross shape. She holds it delicately, as if it is precious. She reads:

> "*Notification of the Resolution of the Council of White Witches in England, Scotland, and Wales.*
>
> "'It was agreed that to facilitate increased protection of all White Witches, a record of all witches in Britain should be made and maintained.
>
> "'A simple coding system will be used for any witches and whets (witches under age seventeen) who are not of pure White witch parentage, using the references: White (W), Black (B), Fain/Non-Witch (F). Thus Half Codes will be recorded as (W 0.5/B 0.5) and Half Bloods recorded as (W 0.5/F 0.5) or (B 0.5/F 0.5). The mother's code will be the first code, the father the second. The 0.5 codes will be maintained for as little time as possible (and not past age 17) until an absolute code (W, B, or F) can be designated to the person.'

"Do you know what it means?" Jessica asks.

I shake my head.

"It means that you are a Half Code. A Black Code. Non-White."

"Gran says I'm a White Witch."

"No, she doesn't."

"She says I'm half White."

"You're half Black.

"*After the woman has finished reading out the notification, Mother still doesn't say anything but goes back inside the house, leaving the front door open. The woman and the Hunter follow her in.*

"*We're all in the lounge. Mother is sitting on the chair by the fire. But the fire isn't lit. Deborah and Arran have been playing on the floor but now they sit on either side of her on the arms of the chair.*"

"Where are you?"

"Standing right by her."

I imagine Jessica standing there with her arms folded, knees locked back.

"*The Hunter positions himself in the doorway.*

"*The woman with the clipboard perches on the edge of the other chair, her clipboard on her tightly clenched knees, pen in her hand. She says to Mother, 'It'll probably be quicker and easier if I fill the form in and you just sign.'*

"*The woman asks, 'Who is the head of the household?'*

"*Mother manages to say, 'I am.'*

"*The woman asks Mother her name.*

"*Mother says she is Cora Byrn. A White Witch. Daughter of Elsie Ashworth and David Ashworth. White Witches.*

"*The woman asks who her children are.*

"*Mother says, 'Jessica, age eight. Deborah, five. Arran, two.'*

"*The woman asks, 'Who is their father?'*

"*Mother says, 'Dean Byrn. White Witch. Member of the Council.'*

"*The woman asks, 'Where is he?'*"

"*Mother says, 'He is dead. Murdered.'*"

"*The woman says, 'I'm sorry.'*"

"*Then the woman asks, 'And the baby? Where is the baby?'*"

"*Mother says, 'It's there, in that drawer.'*"

Jessica turns to me and explains. "After Arran was born, Mother and Father didn't want any more children. They gave away the cot, the pram, and all the baby things. This baby isn't wanted and has to sleep on a pillow in a drawer, in an old, dirty onesie that Arran used to have. No one buys this baby toys or presents, because everyone knows it isn't wanted. No one gives Mother presents or flowers or chocolates, because they all know she didn't want this baby. Nobody wants a baby like this. Mother only gets one card but it doesn't say 'Congratulations.'"

Silence.

"Do you want to know what it says?"

I shake my head.

"It says, 'Kill It.'"

I chew my knuckles, but I don't cry.

"*The woman approaches the baby in the drawer, and the Hunter joins her because he wants to see this strange, unwanted thing.*

"*Even asleep the baby is horrible and ugly, with its puny little body, grubby-looking skin, and spiky, black hair.*

"*The woman asks, 'Does he have a name yet?'*

"'*Nathan.*'"

Jessica has already found a way of saying my name as if it is something disgusting.

"*The young woman asks, 'And his father . . . ?'*

"*Mother doesn't answer. She can't because it's too awful; she can't bear it. But everyone knows just by looking at the baby that its father is a murderer.*

"*The woman says, 'Perhaps you can write the father's name.'*

"*And she takes her clipboard to Mother. And Mother is crying now and she can't even write the name. Because it's the name of the most evil Black Witch there has ever been.*"

I want to say "Marcus." He's my father and I want to say his name, but I'm too afraid. I'm always too afraid to say his name.

"*The woman goes back to look at the sleeping baby and she reaches out to touch it . . .*

"'*Careful!*' *the Hunter warns, because even though Hunters are never afraid, they are always cautious around Black witchcraft.*

"*The woman says, 'He's just a baby.' And she strokes its bare arm with the back of her fingers.*

"*And the baby stirs and then opens its eyes.*

"*The woman says, 'Oh goodness!' and steps back.*

"*She realizes she shouldn't have touched such a nasty thing and rushes off to the bathroom to wash her hands.*"

Jessica reaches out as if she's going to touch me but then pulls her hand away, saying, "I couldn't ever touch anything as bad as you."

My Father

•.•*•.•

I am standing in front of the bathroom mirror, staring at my face. I'm not like my mother at all, not like Arran. My skin's slightly darker than theirs, more olive, and my hair's jet black, but the real difference is the blackness of my eyes.

I've never met my father, never even seen my father. But I know that my eyes are his eyes.

My Mother's Suicide

•··•·•

Jessica holds the photograph frame high to her left and brings it down diagonally, slicing the edge of the frame across my cheekbone.

"Don't ever touch this picture again."

I don't move.

"Do you hear me?"

There's blood on the corner of the frame.

"She's dead because of you."

I back against the wall.

Jessica shouts at me. "She killed herself because of you!"

The Second Notification

•.•·•.•

I remember it raining for days. Days and days, until even I am fed up with being alone in the woods. So I'm sitting at the kitchen table, drawing. Gran is in the kitchen, too. Gran is always in the kitchen. She is old and bony with that thin skin that old people have, but she is also slim and straight-backed. She wears pleated tartan skirts and walking boots or wellies. She is always in the kitchen and the kitchen floor is always muddy. Even with the rain, the back door is open. A chicken comes in for some shelter, but Gran won't stand for that, and she sweeps it out gently with the side of her boot and shuts the door.

The pot simmers on the stove, emitting a column of steam that rises fast and narrow and then widens to join the cloud above. The green, gray, blue, and red of the herbs, flowers, roots, and bulbs that hang from the ceiling by strings, in nets, and in baskets are blurred in the fog that surrounds them. Lined up on the shelves are glass jars filled with liquids, leaves, grains, greases, and potions, and some even with jam. The warped oak work surface is littered with spoons of all kinds—metal, wooden, bone, as long as my arm, as small as my little finger—as well as knives in a block, dirty knives covered in paste lying on the chopping board, a granite pestle and mortar, two round baskets, and more jars. On the back of the door hang a beekeeper's hat, a selection of aprons, and a black umbrella that is as bent as a banana.

I draw it all.

I'm sitting with Arran watching an old movie on TV. Arran likes to watch them, the older the better, and I like to sit with him, the closer the better. We've both got shorts on, and we've both got skinny legs, only his are paler than mine and dangle farther over the end of the comfy chair. He has a small scar on his left knee and a long one up his right shin. His hair is light brown and wavy, but somehow it always stays back off his face. My hair is long and straight and black and hangs over my eyes.

Arran is wearing a blue, knitted jumper over a white T-shirt. I'm wearing the red T-shirt that he gave me. He's warm to lean close to, and when I turn to look up at him he moves his gaze from the telly to me, sort of in slow motion. His eyes are light, blue-gray with glints of silver in them, and he even blinks slow. Everything about him is gentle. It would be great to be like him.

"You enjoying it?" he asks, not in a hurry for an answer.

I nod.

He puts his arm round me and turns back to the screen.

Lawrence of Arabia does the trick with the match. Afterward we agree to try it ourselves. I take the big box of matches from the kitchen drawer and we run with them to the woods.

I go first.

I light the match and hold it between my thumb and forefinger, letting it burn right down until it goes out. My small, thin fingers, with nails that are bitten to nothing, are burnt but they hold the blackened match.

Arran tries the trick too. Only he doesn't do it. He's like the other man in the movie. He drops the match.

After he goes back home I do the trick again. It's easy.

Me and Arran creep into Gran's bedroom. It smells strangely medicinal. Under the window there's an oak casket where Gran keeps the notifications from the Council. We sit on the carpet. Arran opens the casket lid and takes out the second notification. It's written on thick, yellow parchment and has gray writing swirling across the page. Arran reads it to me; he's slow and quiet as always.

"*Notification of the Resolution of the Council of White Witches in England, Scotland, and Wales.*

"In order to ensure the safety and security of all White Witches, the Council will continue its policy of Capture and Retribution for all Black Witches and Black Whets.

"In order to ensure the safety and security of all White Witches an annual Assessment of witches and whets of mixed White Witch and Black Witch

parentage (W 0.5/B 0.5) will be made. The Assessment will contribute to the designation of the witch/whet as White (W) or Black/Non-White (B)."

I don't ask Arran whether he thinks I'll be a W or a B. I know he'll try to be nice.

It's my eighth birthday. I have to go to London to be assessed.

The Council building has lots of cold corridors of gray stone. Gran and I wait on a wooden bench in one of them. I am shivering by the time a young man in a lab coat appears and points me to a small room to the left of our bench. Gran isn't allowed to come.

In the room is a woman. She's also in a lab coat. She calls the young man Tom and he calls her Miss Lloyd. They call me Half Code.

They tell me to strip. "Take your clothes off, Half Code."

And I do it.

"Stand on the scales."

And I do that.

"Stand by the wall. We have to measure you." They do that. Then they take photographs of me.

"Turn to the side."

"Further."

"And face the wall."

And they leave me there staring at the brush strokes in

the cream-colored shiny paint on the wall while they talk and put things away.

Then they tell me to put my clothes on, and I do that.

And they take me through the door and point at the bench in the corridor. And I sit back down and don't look at Gran's face.

The door opposite the bench is paneled dark oak and is eventually opened by a man. He's huge, a guard. He points at me and then at the room behind him. When Gran starts to get up he says, "Not you."

The assessment room is long and high, with bare stone walls and arched windows above head height along each side. The ceiling is arched too. The furniture is wooden. A huge oak table reaches across almost the full width of the room, keeping the three Council members to their far side. They sit on large, carved wooden chairs like ancient royalty.

The woman in the center is old, thin, gray-haired, and gray-skinned, as if all the blood has been drained out of her. The woman to the right is middle-aged and plump and has deep black skin and her hair pulled tight off her face. The man to the left is a bit younger and slim and has thick, white-blond hair. They are all wearing white robes made of roughly woven material, which has a strange sheen when the sunlight catches it.

There is a guard standing to my left, and the one who opened the door is behind me.

The woman in the middle says, "I am the Council Leader. We are going to ask you some simple questions."

But she doesn't ask them; the other woman asks the questions.

The other woman is slow and methodical. She has a list, which she works down. Some of the questions are easy— "What is your name?"—and some more difficult—"Do you know the herbs that draw out poison from a wound?"

I think about each question, and each one I decide not to answer. I am methodical too.

After the woman stops her questions the Council Leader has a go herself. She asks different questions, questions about my father, like, "Has your father ever tried to contact you?" and "Do you know where your father is?" She even tries, "Do you consider your father to be a great witch?" and "Do you love your father?"

I know the answers to her questions, but I don't tell her what they are.

After that they put their heads together and mutter for a bit. The blond-haired man tells the guard to bring Gran in. The Council Leader beckons her forward, as if she is reeling Gran in with her thin, pasty hand.

Gran stands beside me. We haven't eaten or drunk anything since early that morning, so perhaps that is why she looks so drained. She looks as old as the Council Leader now.

The Council Leader tells her, "We've made our assessment."

The woman has been writing on a piece of parchment and now she pushes it across the table, saying, "Please sign to confirm that you agree with it."

Gran moves to the table, picks up the piece of paper, and comes back to stand by my side. She reads the assessment out for me to hear. I like that about Gran.

"Subject:	Nathan Byrn
Birth Code:	W 0.5/B 0.5
Sex:	Male
Age at Assessment:	8 years
Gift (if over Age 17):	Not applicable
General Intelligence:	Not ascertained
Special Abilities:	Not ascertained
Healing Ability:	Not ascertained
Languages:	Not ascertained
Special Comments:	The Subject was uncooperative
Designation Code:	Not ascertained"

I am grinning for the first time that day.

Gran walks back to the table, picks up the fountain pen of the female Councilor, and signs the form with a flourish.

The Council Leader speaks again. "As you are the boy's guardian, Mrs. Ashworth, it is your responsibility to ensure he cooperates in the assessment."

Gran looks up.

"Come back tomorrow, and we will repeat the assessment."

I could go all year down the Not ascertained route, but the next day Gran says that I should answer some questions, though never the ones about my father. So I answer some questions.

They amend the form to show my General Intelligence as Low, and Languages as English. Special Comments says Uncooperative and Does not appear to be able to read. My Designated Code is still Not ascertained, though. Gran is pleased.

Jessica's Giving

It's Jessica's seventeenth birthday. Mid-morning and Jessica is even more full of herself than normal. She can't keep still. Can't wait to get her three gifts and become a true adult witch. Gran is going to perform the Giving ceremony at midday, so in the meantime we have to put up with Jessica pacing around the kitchen and picking things up and putting them down.

She picks up a knife, wanders about with it, and then stops beside me, saying, "I wonder what will happen on Nathan's birthday."

She feels the point of the blade. "If he has to go to an assessment he might not be able to have a Giving."

She's winding me up. I just have to ignore her. I will get three gifts. Every witch gets three gifts.

Gran says, "Nathan will receive three gifts on his birthday. That is the way it is for all witches. And that is the way it will be for Nathan."

"I mean, it's bad enough for a White whet if something goes wrong and they don't get three gifts."

"Nothing will go wrong, Jessica." Gran turns to look at her, saying, "I'll give Nathan three gifts, just as I'll give them to you and Deborah and Arran."

Arran comes to sit by me. He puts his hand on my arm and says quietly just to me, "I can't wait for your Giving. You come to mine and I'll come to yours."

"Kieran told me about a whet in York who didn't get three gifts," says Jessica. "He married a fain in the end and now works in a bank."

"What's this boy called?" Deborah asks.

"It doesn't matter. He's not a witch now and never will be."

"Well, I've never heard of such a boy," Gran says.

"It's true. Kieran told me," Jessica says. "Kieran said that it's different for Black Witches, though. They don't just lose their abilities. If Blacks don't get three gifts they die."

Jessica puts the point of the knife into the table in front of me and holds it there, balanced on its tip, by her index finger. "They don't die straightaway. They get sick, maybe last a year or two if they're lucky, but they can't heal and they just get weaker and sicker and sicker and weaker and then"—she lets the knife fall—"one less Black Witch."

I should close my eyes.

Arran gently wraps his fingers around the handle of the knife and moves it away, asking, "Do they really die, Gran?"

"I don't know any Black Witches, Arran, so I can't say. But Nathan is half White and he will get three gifts on his birthday. And Jessica, you can stop this talk of Black Witches."

Jessica leans close to Arran and mutters, "It would be

interesting to see what happens, though. I'd guess that he'd die like a Black Witch."

And I have to get out of there. I go upstairs. I don't break anything, just kick the wall a few times.

Surprisingly, Jessica hasn't chosen to have a big ceremonial Giving but a small and private one. Unsurprisingly, she has chosen to go so small and so private that although Deborah and Arran are invited, I am not. I heard Gran trying to persuade Jessica to invite me a few nights earlier, but it didn't work, and I don't want to go anyway. I have no friends to play with, so I'm left alone at home while Gran, Jessica, Deborah, and a glum Arran trudge to the woods.

Normally I'd be in the woods, but I can't leave the house because I don't want to be punished with one of Gran's potions. I don't want to go through twenty-four hours leaking yellow pus from boils the size of gobstoppers for the sake of Jessica.

I sit at the kitchen table and draw. My picture is of Gran performing the ceremony, giving Jessica three gifts. The gifts have just been passed to Jessica but she is dropping them, a sign of seriously bad luck. The blood from Gran's hand, the blood of her ancestors that Jessica must drink, drips bright red on to the forest floor, undrunk. And Jessica remains in the picture, horrified, unable to access her Gift, her one special magical power.

I like the picture.

All too soon the ceremonial group are back home, and it is clear that Jessica has not dropped a thing. She walks in the back door, saying, "Now that I'm no longer a whet, I need to find out what my Gift is."

She stares at the picture and then at me. "I'll have to practice on something."

And all I can do is sit there and hope that she never finds her Gift. And I hope that if she does find it, it's something ordinary like potion-making, Gran's Gift. Or that she has a weak Gift like most men. But I know there is no point hoping for that. I know she will have a strong Gift like most women, and she will find it and hone it and practice it. And use it on me.

I am lying on the lawn in the back garden watching ants building a nest in the grass. The ants look big. I can see the details of their bodies, how their legs move and march and climb.

Arran comes to sit by me. He asks me how I am and how school is going, the sort of stuff Arran is interested in. I tell him about the ants, where they are going and what they are doing.

Out of the blue he says, "Are you proud that Marcus is your father, Nathan?"

The ants carry on with their work, but I no longer care. "Nathan?"

I turn to Arran, and he meets my gaze with that open and honest look of his.

"He's such a powerful witch, the most powerful of all. You must be proud of that?"

Arran has never asked me about my father before.

Never.

And even though I trust him above anyone, trust him completely, I'm afraid to answer. Gran has drummed into me that I must never talk about Marcus.

Never.

I must never answer questions about him.

Any answer can be twisted or misinterpreted by the Council. Any indication that a White Witch sympathizes with any Black Witch is seen as treacherous. All Black Witches are tracked down by Hunters under the direction of the Council. If they are captured alive they suffer Retribution. Any White Witch who aids a Black is executed. I have to prove to everyone, at all times, that I am a White Witch, my loyalties are to Whites and my thoughts are pure White.

Gran has told me that if anyone asks me how I feel about Marcus I must say I hate him. If I can't say that, then the only safe answer is no answer.

But this is Arran.

I want to be honest with him.

"Do you admire him?" Arran presses.

I know Arran better than anyone, and we talk about most things, but we have never talked about Marcus. We have never even talked about Arran's father. My father killed his father. What can you say about that?

And yet . . . I want to confide in someone, and Arran is the best and only person I can trust with my feelings. And he is looking at me in that way he has, all kindness and concern.

But what if I say to him, "Yes, I admire the man who killed your father," or "Yes, I'm proud that Marcus is my dad. He is the most powerful Black Witch and his blood runs in my veins." What will happen?

Still he presses me, "Do you? Do you admire Marcus?"

His eyes are so pale and so sincere, pleading with me to share my feelings.

I have to look down. The ants are still busy, evacuees carrying huge loads to a new home.

I answer Arran as quietly as I can.

"What did you say?" he asks.

I still keep my head down. But I say it a little louder.

"I hate him."

At that moment a pair of bare feet appears by the ant's nest. Arran's feet.

Arran is standing in front of me and he is sitting beside me. Two Arrans. The one sitting down scowls and then transforms before my eyes back into Jessica, looking cramped inside Arran's T-shirt and shorts.

Jessica leans across and hisses at me, "You knew. You knew all along it was me, didn't you?"

Arran and I watch her stomp off.

He asks, "How could you tell it wasn't me?"

"I couldn't."

Not by looking at her anyway. Her Gift is impressive.

After that first attempt at using her Gift to trick me, Jessica doesn't give up. Her disguises are flawless, and her determination and persistence equal to them. But her problem is a fundamental one that she is incapable of understanding: Arran would never try to get me to talk about my father.

Still, Jessica keeps trying. And whenever I get suspicious that Arran is really Jessica I reach out to touch him, to stroke the back of his hand or take hold of his arm. If it's Arran, he smiles and grabs my hand in both of his. If it's Jessica she flinches. She never manages to control that.

One evening Deborah comes into our bedroom, sits on Arran's bed, and reads her book. It's just the sort of thing Deborah does; she crosses her legs like Deborah does, has her head to one side like Deborah does, but still I'm suspicious. She listens to Arran and me talk for a minute or two. She seems to be reading the book; she turns a page.

Arran goes to brush his teeth.

I sit next to Deborah, not too close. But I can smell her hair isn't right.

I lean toward her, saying, "Let me tell you a secret."

She smiles at me.

I say, "Your smell is so revolting, Jessica. I'm going to be sick if you don't leave. . . ."

She spits in my face and walks out before Arran comes back in.

I do have a secret, though. A secret so dark, so hopeless, so absurd that I can never share it with anyone. It is a secret story that I tell myself when I'm in bed at night. My father is not evil at all; he is powerful and strong. And he cares about me . . . he loves me. And he wants to bring me up as his true son, to teach me about witchcraft, to show me the world. But he is constantly persecuted by White Witches who give him no opportunity to explain. They hound him and hunt him but he only attacks them when he has no alternative, when they threaten him. It's too dangerous for him to risk having me with him. He wants me to be safe, and so I have to be brought up away from him. But he is waiting for the right time to come for me and take me away with him. On my seventeenth birthday he wants to give me three gifts and give me his blood, the blood of our ancestors. And I lie in bed and imagine that one night he will come for me and we will fly away through the night together.

A Long Way off Seventeen

•˙•●•˙•

We are in the woods near Gran's house. The air is still and damp; the autumn leaves lie thick on the soft, muddy ground. The sky is flat and gray like an old sheet laid out to dry over the black branches of the trees. Jessica is holding a small dagger, her hands flat in front of her. The blade is sharp and bright. Jessica is smirking and trying to catch my eye.

Deborah stands slightly hunched, but she is smiling and calm, her empty cupped hands held out in front of her. In Gran's hands are a brooch that had been her grandmother's, my mother's engagement ring, and a cufflink that belonged to Deborah's father. Gran slowly lowers her hands over Deborah's. Their hands touch. Gran carefully passes the gifts to Deborah, saying, "Deborah, I give you three things so that you can receive one Gift." Then Gran takes the knife and cuts the palm of her own hand into the fleshy pad below her left thumb. Blood runs down her wrist; a few drops fall to the ground. She holds her hand out and Deborah bends forward, puts her mouth round the cut, her lips tight on Gran's skin. Gran leans toward her and whispers the secret words in Deborah's ear, and Deborah's throat moves as she swallows the blood. I strain to hear the spell, but the words are like the sound of wind rustling leaves.

The spell ends. Deborah, eyes closed, swallows one last time before releasing Gran's hand and standing straight.

And that is it. Deborah is no longer a whet; she is a true White Witch.

I glance over to Arran. He looks solemn but smiles at me before turning to hug Deborah. I wait my turn to give my congratulations.

I say, "I am pleased for you." And I am. I hug Deborah, but there is nothing else I can say, so I walk off into the woods.

Another notification arrived that morning, before Deborah's Giving.

Notification of the Resolution of the Council of White Witches of England, Scotland, and Wales.

It is forbidden to hold a Giving Ceremony for a whet of mixed White Witch and Black Witch parentage (Half Code: W 0.5/B 0.5) or mixed White Witch and Fain parentage (Half Blood: W 0.5/F 0.5) without the permission of the Council of White Witches. Any witch disobeying this Notification will be considered to be working against the Council. Any Half Code accepting gifts or blood without permission of the Council will be considered to be defying the Council and corrupting White Witches. The penalty for all concerned will be imprisonment for life.

Gran read the notification out and then Jessica started to speak, but I was already heading out the back door. Arran grabbed at my arm, saying, "We'll get permission, Nathan. We will."

I couldn't be bothered arguing with him, and I pushed him away. There was an ax by the pile of wood in the garden and I hacked and hacked and hacked until I couldn't lift the ax any more.

Deborah came to sit with me among all the broken bits of wood. She put her head on my shoulder, resting her cheek on it. I always liked it when she did that.

She said, "You'll find a way, Nathan. Gran will help you, and so will I, and so will Arran."

I ripped at the blisters on my hand. "How?"

"I don't know yet."

"You shouldn't help me. You'd be working against the Council. They'll lock you up."

"But—"

I jolted her off my shoulder and stood up. "I don't want your help, Deborah. Don't you get it? You're so bloody clever, but you still don't understand, do you?"

And I left her there.

And now Deborah has received her three gifts and Gran's blood, and in three years Arran will go through the same ceremony, but for me . . . I know the Council won't let it happen. They are afraid of what I'll become. And if I don't become a witch I'll die. I know it.

I have to be given three gifts and drink the blood of

my ancestors, the blood of my parents or grandparents. But apart from Gran there is only one person who can give me three gifts, only one person who can defy the Council, only one person whose blood will turn me from whet to witch.

The woods are silent. It feels like they are waiting and watching. And suddenly I know that my father wants to help me. I know the truth of it so well. My father wants to give me three gifts and let me drink his blood. I know it like I know how to breathe.

I know he'll come to me.

I wait and I wait.

The silence of the woods goes on and on.

He doesn't come.

But I realize that it's too dangerous for him to come to me and take me away. So I must go to him.

I must go and find my father.

I'm eleven. Eleven is a long way off seventeen. And I have no idea how to find Marcus. I don't have a clue how to begin to find him. But at least now I know what I have to do.

Thomas Dawes Secondary School

•٠•٠•

Notification of the Resolution of the Council of White Witches of England, Scotland, and Wales.

Any contact between Half Codes (W 0.5/B 0.5) and White Whets and White Witches is to be reported to the Council by all concerned. Failure by the Half Code to notify the Council of contact is punishable by removing all contact.

Contact is deemed to have been made if the Half Code is in the same room as a White Whet or White Witch or otherwise within a close enough distance that they are able to speak to each other.

"Shall I go and lock myself in the cellar now?" I ask.

Deborah takes the parchment and reads it again. "Removing all contact? What does that mean?"

Gran looks uncertain.

"They can't mean removing contact with *us*?" Deborah looks from Gran to Arran. "Can they?"

I'm amazed at Deborah; she still doesn't get it. It can mean whatever the Council want it to mean.

"I'll just make sure that we keep a list of witches Nathan

has contact with. It's easy enough. Nathan hardly meets anyone and certainly not many White Witches."

"When he starts at Thomas Dawes school, there'll be the O'Briens," Arran reminds her.

"Yes, but that's all. It'll be a small list. We just have to make sure we follow the rules."

Gran is right; the list is small. The only witches I come into contact with are my direct family and those I meet at the Council Offices when I go for assessment. I never go to any festivals, parties, or weddings, as my name is always missing from the invitations that arrive on our doormat. Gran stays at home with me and sends Jessica, and, when they are old enough, Deborah and Arran as well. I hear about the celebrations from the others, but I never go.

White Witches from anywhere in the world are welcomed into witches' homes, but visitors to our house are thin on the ground. When anyone does stay with us for a night or two they treat me as either a curiosity or a leper, and I quickly learn to keep out of sight.

When Gran and I traveled to London for my first assessment, we turned up late in the evening on the doorstep of a family near Wimbledon, and I was left staring at the red paint of the front door while Gran was taken inside. When she reappeared a minute later, white in the face and shaking with anger, she grabbed my hand and dragged me away, saying, "We'll stay in a hotel." I was more relieved than angry.

* * *

Before going to Thomas Dawes Secondary School, I attend the small village school. I'm the slow, dumb kid at the back, the one with no friends. Like most fains the world over, the kids and teachers there don't believe in witches; they don't understand that we live among them. They don't see me as special—just especially slow. I can barely read or write and am not quick enough to fool Gran when I skip school. The only thing I learn is that sitting in class bored stiff is better than sitting anywhere else with the effects of Gran's punishment potions. From the start of each day, all I do is wait until it's over. I suspect secondary school is not going to be any better.

I'm right. On my first day at Thomas Dawes I'm wearing Arran's cast-off too-long gray trousers, a white shirt with a frayed collar, a stained blue-gold-black striped tie, and a dark blue blazer that is absurdly oversized, although Gran has shortened the arms. The one item I have been given that is not a cast-off is a cheap phone. I have it "in case." Arran has only just been allowed one, so I know that Gran expects there will be an "in case" situation.

I put the phone to my ear and my head is filled with static. Just carrying it around makes me irritable. Before I leave for school, I put the phone behind the TV in the lounge, which seems a good place, as that too has recently started to set off a faint hissing in my head.

Arran and Deborah make the journey to school and back bearable. Thankfully Jessica has left home to train as a Hunter. Hunters are the elite group of White Witches employed by the Council to hunt down Black Witches in Britain. Gran says they are employed by other Councils in Europe more and more as there are so few Blacks left in Britain. Hunters are mainly women, but include a few talented male witches. They are all ruthless and efficient, which means Jessica is bound to fit right in.

Jessica's departure means I can relax at home for the first time in my life, but now I have secondary school to worry about. I plead with Gran that I shouldn't go, that it is bound to be a disaster. She says that witches must "blend in" to fain society and should "learn how to conform," and it is important for me to do the same, and that I "will be fine." None of those phrases seem to describe my life.

Phrases that come to mind, phrases that I'm expecting to hear, to describe me are "nasty and dirty," "pond life," and the old favorite "dumb ass." I'm prepared to be teased about being stupid, dirty, or poor, and some idiot is bound to pick on me because I'm small, but I don't mind too much. They'll only ever do it once.

I'm prepared for all that, but what I'm not prepared for is the noise. The school bus is a cauldron of shouting and jeering, simmering with the hiss of mobile phones. The classroom isn't much better, as it is lined with computers, all emitting a high-pitched whistle that gets into my skull and is not reduced one bit by sticking my fingers in my ears.

The other problem, and by far the biggest, is that Annalise is in my class.

Annalise is a White Witch, and an O'Brien. The O'Brien brothers also go to my school, apart from Kieran, who is Jessica's age and has now left. Niall is in Deborah's year and Connor is in Arran's.

Annalise has long blonde hair that glistens like melted white chocolate over her shoulders. She has blue eyes and long pale eyelashes. She smiles a lot, revealing her straight, white teeth. Her hands are impossibly clean, her skin is the color of honey, and her fingernails gleam. Her school shirt looks perfectly fresh, like it has been ironed just a minute before. Even the school blazer looks good on her. Annalise comes from a family of White Witches whose blood has been uncontaminated by fains as far back as can be remembered, and its only associations with Black Witches are her ancestors who have either killed or been killed by them.

I know I should steer clear of Annalise.

The first afternoon the teacher asks us to write something about ourselves. We are supposed to fill one page or more with writing. I stare at the paper and it stares blankly back. I don't know what to write, and even if I did I know I wouldn't be able to write it anyway. I manage to print my name on the top of the page, but even that I hate. My surname, Byrn, is that of my mother's dead husband. It is nothing to do with me. I cross it out, scratching it away. My palms are sweaty on the pencil. Glancing around the room

I see the other kids are busily scribbling and the teacher is walking around looking at what they are writing. When she gets to me she asks if there is a problem.

"I can't think of anything to write."

"Well, perhaps you could tell me what you did this summer? Or tell me about your family?" This is the voice she uses for the slow ones.

"Yeah, okay."

"So, shall I leave you to it?"

I nod, still staring at the piece of paper.

Once she has moved far enough away and is bent over some other kid's work, I do write something.

i hava bordr and sisser my bordrs Arran
he is niss and Debsis clvrer

I know it's bad, but that doesn't mean I can do anything to improve it.

We have to pass our essays in, and the girl who collects mine stares at me when she sees my piece of paper.

"What?" I say.

She starts to laugh and says, "My brother's seven, and he can do better than that."

"What?"

She stops laughing then and says, "Nothing . . ." and almost trips over in her rush to get to the front of class to hand the papers in.

I look to see who else is sniggering. The other two at my

table seem to be fascinated by their pencils, which they are gripping. The table to my left are grinning away one second and then staring at their desk the next. The same happens with the kids on the table to my right, except for Annalise. She doesn't look at the table but smiles at me. I don't know if she's laughing at me or what. I have to look away.

The next day in maths I can't work anything out. The teacher, thankfully, has quickly realized that if I'm ignored I'll sit quietly and not be any trouble. Annalise is hard to ignore. She answers a question and she gets it right. She answers another, correct again. When she answers a third one, I turn slightly in my seat to glance at her and I am caught again by her looking at me and smiling.

On the third day, in art, someone brushes my arm. A clean, honey-toned hand reaches past me and selects a black rod of charcoal. As the hand moves back, the cuff of her blazer grazes the back of my hand.

"That's a great picture."

What?

I stare at my sketch of a blackbird that has been pecking at crumbs on the deserted playground.

But I have stopped thinking about the blackbird and the sketch. Now all I can think is, *She spoke to me! She spoke to me nicely!*

Then I think, *Say something!* But all that happens is *Say something! Say something!* booms in my empty head.

My heart is banging on my chest wall, the blood in my veins throbbing with the words.

Say something!

In my panic all I come up with is, "I like drawing, do you?" and "You're good at maths." Thankfully Annalise has wandered away before I say either of them.

She's the first White Witch outside of my family to smile at me. The first. The one and only. I never thought it would happen; it might never happen again.

And I know I should steer clear of her. But she has been nice to me. And Gran said we should "conform" and "fit in" and all that stuff, and being polite is part of those things too. So at the end of the class I manage to direct my body enough to walk over to her.

I hold out my picture. "What do you think? Now it's finished."

I'm prepared for her to say something horrible, laugh at it or at me. But I don't think she'll do that.

She smiles and says, "It's really good."

"You think so?"

She doesn't look at the picture again, but continues to look at me and says, "You must know it's brilliant."

"It's okay. . . . I can't get the tarmac right."

She laughs, but stops abruptly when I glance at her. "I'm not laughing at you. It's great."

I look at the picture again. The bird isn't bad.

"Can I have it?" she asks.

What?

What would she do with it?

"It's okay. That's a stupid idea. It's a great picture, though." And she sweeps her own drawing up and walks away.

From then on, Annalise contrives to sit next to me in art and to be on the same team as me in phys ed. The rest of the school day we are split into graded groups. I am in all the lowest ones and she is in all the highest, so we don't see a lot of each other.

We are in art the following week when she asks, "Why don't you look at me for more than a second?"

I don't know what to say. It feels like more than a second.

I put my paintbrush in the jar of water, turn to her, and look. I see a smile and eyes and honey skin and . . .

"Two and a half seconds at most," she says.

It felt a lot longer.

"I never thought you'd be shy."

I'm not shy.

She leans in close to me, saying, "My parents said I shouldn't talk to you."

I do look at her then. Her eyes are sparkling.

"Why? What did they say about me?"

She blushes a little and her eyes lose some of their shine. She doesn't answer my question, but whatever they said doesn't seem to be bad enough to put Annalise off.

Back at home that evening I look at myself in the bathroom mirror. I know I'm smaller than most boys my age, but not a lot smaller. People always say I'm dirty, but I hang out in the woods, and it's hard to keep clean, and I don't see what the problem with dirt is. Though I do like it that Annalise is so clean. I don't know how she does it.

Arran comes in to brush his teeth. He's taller than me but he's two years older. He's the sort of boy I imagine Annalise would like. Handsome and gentle and clever.

Debs comes in as well. It's a bit crowded. She's clean too, but not like Annalise.

"What you doing?" she asks.

"What's it look like?"

"It looks like Arran's brushing his teeth and you're admiring your beautiful face in the mirror."

Arran nudges me and smiles a frothy smile.

My reflection tries to smile back and puts toothpaste on its brush. I look at my eyes as I brush. I have witch's eyes. Fain eyes are plain. Every witch that I have seen has glints in their eyes. Arran's eyes are pale gray with silver glints; Debs's are darker green-gray with pale green and silver glints. Annalise has blue eyes with silver-gray shards in them that twist and tumble, especially if she is teasing me. Deborah and Arran can't see the glints and neither can Gran; she says it's an ability few witches have. I haven't told her that when I look in the mirror I don't see silver glints, but that my black eyes have dark triangular glints that rotate slowly and aren't really glints at all. They aren't shiny black, but a sort of hollow, empty black.

* * *

Annalise's brothers Niall and Connor have blue eyes with silver glints. They are also instantly recognizable as O'Brien brothers by their blond hair, long limbs, and handsome faces. I avoid Annalise at breaks and lunchtimes, as I know if her brothers see us together she will be in trouble. I hate it that they might think I'm afraid of them, but I really don't want to cause trouble for Annalise, and in this huge school it's easy to avoid people if you want to.

At the end of the first month it's drizzling that fine misty rain that quickly covers your skin to let you wash yourself clean. I'm round the back of the sports hall, leaning against the wall and considering the alternatives to an afternoon of geography when Niall and Connor turn the corner. From their smiles it seems that they have found what they are looking for. I don't move from the wall, but I return their smiles. This is going to be more interesting than the Mississippi delta.

Niall starts with, "We've seen you talking to our sister."

I can't understand when or where, but I'm not going to bother asking, and I give him one of my "so what" looks.

"Just keep away from her," Connor says.

They both hang back looking uncertain what to do next.

I almost laugh, they are so inept, and I don't say anything, wondering if that is it.

It may well have been but then Arran appears behind them and blusters in with, "What's going on?"

As they turn to him they change. They're not afraid of

Arran, and they're not about to let him see they have been a little cautious with me.

They say, "Piss off," in unison.

When he doesn't, Niall advances on Arran.

Arran holds his ground, saying, "I'm staying with my brother."

The bell marking the end of lunchtime starts to ring, and Niall shoves Arran on the shoulder, saying, "Piss off back to class."

Arran is forced to step back, but he then takes a step forward, saying, "I'm not going without my brother."

Connor is looking at Arran and has half turned away from me, and it is just too tempting seeing the side of his face like that. I hit him hard with my version of a left hook. Before Connor's body touches the tarmac I sink down low to the ground behind Niall and jab him hard in the back of his knee with my elbow. He falls too, and so dramatically that I only just get out of the way. I am still low, so I punch Niall twice in the face, but I know I have to be quick to go to cover Connor. I rise, kick Niall in the side as he rolls away from me, and get Connor with a boot to his shoulder as he is getting up. Niall, though, is more of a danger, being bigger and much the tougher of the two, and he knows enough to roll away again as I start a run at him. I don't connect my kick, though, as Arran has grabbed my shoulders, surprisingly powerfully, and is dragging me away. I don't resist much. I've done enough.

Arran's arm is round me as we walk back to the school building. He is holding me tight, pulling me to him, but as we near the entrance he shoves me away. It's an angry shove.

"What's the matter?" I ask.

"Why are you laughing?"

Was I laughing? I hadn't realized.

Arran carries on into school, his arms out as if he needs to fend me off. The door slams shut behind him.

More Fighting, Some Smoking

•··•·•°

I don't go back into school that afternoon. I go to the woods and from there make my way home, timing my arrival to coincide with Arran's and Deborah's. I wait for Arran to say something, but he is giving me the silent treatment. It goes on all evening. I think he will relent when we go to bed, but he is already tucked up and switching the light off as I come into the room. I put the light back on and stand with my back to the door.

"I'll tell Gran about the fight tomorrow."

The lump under the bedclothes doesn't respond.

"You know fighting's normal, don't you? Most boys do it. It would be weird if I didn't do it."

Still nothing.

"I laughed because we'd beaten them. I was relieved. Let's face it, I had you on my side; we were at a disadvantage."

He still doesn't react.

"It doesn't mean I'm the Devil."

Finally he stirs and sits up to face me. "You know they'll say you started it."

Of course I know. I know that even if I don't fight, even

if I avoid Annalise, even if I get on my knees and lick Niall's and Connor's boots, it will make no difference; they will do what they like and say what they like, and what they say will be believed. Arran still hasn't accepted that there is no hope for me. He looks miserable, though.

I sit on my bed and ask, "Do you get a lot of stick for being my half-brother?"

"I'm your brother." And he gives me that look of his, the most-gentle-person-in-the-world look.

"Do you get much stick for being my brother, then?"

"Not much."

He's pretty hopeless at lying, but I love him more than ever for trying.

"Anyway," he says, "I've lived with Jessica all my life. Those jokers are amateurs."

I wonder when Niall and Connor will come back at me. My main concern is that they will go for Arran, but they don't. Maybe they realize that is stupider than just getting their revenge on me.

After the fight I leave school at lunchtimes and hang out in the streets nearby, avoiding the O'Briens and everyone I can, but it's a miserable existence and within two weeks I've had enough of hiding.

I'm leaning against the wall in the same spot as for the first fight when Niall and Connor round the corner. I know they're going to be more prepared this time, but I think that if I get Niall down first I have a decent chance against them.

They run at me and I see that they *are* more prepared; Niall is holding a brick.

The best form of defense is attack. I've heard that somewhere. So I run at them, shouting as loud as I can—bad stuff, swear words.

Niall is surprised enough to hesitate and I push him away, swerve past him and land a poor punch on Connor, who is a pace behind. But somehow Niall reaches back and grabs my blazer. I pull away from him, but Connor gets his arms round me, pinning my left arm to my body. I try to punch him with my right, but it's all over.

Niall catches me on the side of the head with the brick and Connor is clinging on to me.

Then I get rammed in my back, which must be with the brick again. But still I'm okay.

Then

T

H

U

D

It reverberates down my spine and stops me dead.
I've been hammered into the tarmac like a nail.
Connor's hands push him away from me.
He's staring at me. He looks pale, mouth open. Afraid.

Then he isn't there.

And slowly, slowly the tarmac rises up to my face and I have time to think that I've never seen tarmac do that before and wonder how . . .

My body is cold . . . and lying on something hard. My cheek is squashed into something hard. I taste blood.

But I feel okay. Strange but okay.

When I open my eyes everything is gray and fuzzy.

I focus. Oh, right the playground . . . I remember . . .

I don't move. The brick is there, lying on the tarmac. It doesn't move either. The brick looks like it has had a bad day as well.

I close my eyes again.

I'm in the woods near home. I vaguely remember walking here. I'm lying on my back looking at the sky and aching everywhere. I don't sit up but feel my face with my fingers, millimeter by millimeter, slowly daring to work my way to the bits I know are bad.

I have a fat lip that is numb and a loose tooth, my tongue is sore for some reason, I have a bloody nose, my right eye is swollen, and a cut above my left ear is oozing blood and a sort of sticky mucus. A dome has grown on the top of my head.

Gran bathes my face and puts lotion on the bruises that have appeared on my back and arms. My scalp starts to bleed again and Gran shaves the hair around the cut and puts some of her lotion on that too. She does all this in silence once I've told her whom I've been fighting.

I look in the mirror and have to smile despite my fat lip. Both my eyes are black and there are other colors too—purple, green, and yellow—coming out. My right eye is swollen shut. My nose is puffy and tender but not broken. My hair is shaved above my left ear and the skin covered with a thick yellow lotion.

Gran allows me to miss school until my eye heals. Thankfully by then my bald patch has begun to grow over.

On my first day back Annalise sits next to me as I paint. She whispers, "They told me what they did."

I have been thinking about Annalise and her brothers a lot in my days at home. I know it would be sensible to ignore her, and I'm fairly sure that if I ask her to she will avoid me. I have a little speech about it worked out, something along the lines of, "Please, don't talk to me anymore and I won't talk to you."

But Annalise says, "I'm sorry. It was my fault."

And the way she says it—the way she sounds like she is sorry, like she is genuinely upset—gets me angry. I know it isn't her fault and it isn't even my fault. And I forget my crummy speech and all my crummy intentions and instead I touch her hand with my fingertips.

Annalise and I spend the art lessons whispering and looking at each other, and I build up to well over two and a half seconds. I want to stare in private, though, and so does she. We begin working out how we can spend time together, alone.

We devise a plan to meet at Edge Hill, a quiet place on Annalise's way home from school. But every time I ask if today is the day that we can meet, Annalise shakes her head. Her brothers are guarding her, sticking close to her whenever she is out of classes and out of school.

Annalise isn't the only one being guarded. Once I am back at school, Arran and Deborah make a point of staying with me from the bus to the classroom. Arran escorts me home and misses lunch to be with me.

School is becoming unbearable, despite Annalise. The noises in my head are still there, and although I do my best to ignore them, sometimes I want to rip them out of my head and scream in frustration.

A few weeks after my beating, my head is hissing. It is Computer Technology and I don't know what we're supposed to be doing, I'm not interested, I don't care. I make an excuse that I need the toilet, and the teacher doesn't seem to mind as I walk out of the classroom.

The quietness of the corridor is a relief, and with nothing better to do I amble to the toilet.

I walk in just as Connor is coming out of a stall.

I take less than a second to register my chance and launch at him, landing a flurry of punches, and when he sinks to the floor I put in a few kicks.

Connor does nothing but try to protect himself. He never even tries to hit me. My attack isn't stopped by him but by Mr. Taylor, a passing history teacher. He drags me off Connor and I am swamped in Mr. Taylor's sweaty chest, where he keeps me tight while Connor writhes on the ground, whimpering for all he's worth.

Mr. Taylor tells Connor, "If there's something seriously wrong with you, stay still. If not, get up and let's have a look at you."

Connor stays still for a few seconds before getting up.

He doesn't look too bad to me.

"Come with me. Both of you." It isn't a request or even an order, more of a resigned comment.

Mr. Taylor has a grip on my wrist so tight that blood is cut off from my hand. We head down lots of empty, squeaky corridors at speed and abandon Connor at a medical room I never knew existed. Then Mr. Taylor swerves me in the direction of the headmaster's office and we come to a carpeted stop in front of the secretary's desk.

Mr. Taylor explains the situation to the secretary, who nods, knocks on the headmaster's door, and disappears inside. We only have to wait a minute before she reappears and tells us we can go in.

Only when I am standing in front of Mr. Brown's desk does Mr. Taylor let go of my wrist and sit down heavily in the chair by me. The chair creaks.

Mr. Brown taps on his keyboard and doesn't look up.

Mr. Taylor explains that he has found me fighting.

Mr. Brown continues to tap on his keyboard throughout the story of my fight and then for a while more. He seems to be reading what is on his screen. Then he takes a deep breath, turns to Mr. Taylor, and thanks him for his vigilance.

Mr. Brown takes another deep breath and looks at me for the first time. He gives me instructions about acceptable behavior, instructions about my detention, and instructions to go back to my class. He's obviously done this before and rattles through the whole procedure in less than five minutes.

I have to go back to class. Computer Technology will still be going on.

"No." The word comes out of my mouth before I even think it.

Mr. Brown says, "What?"

"No. I'm not going back to that class."

"Mr. Taylor will escort you back." Mr. Brown says this with finality, and turns back to his computer.

Mr. Taylor starts to grunt as he rises from the chair.

I shove him back down.

"No."

I turn and snatch Mr. Brown's keyboard from under his hands, which are left poised above the bare desk. I smash the keyboard into the side of the computer and push the whole lot of it onto the floor.

"I said, 'No.'"

Mr. Taylor is still sitting down, but he grabs hold of my wrist again and pulls me to him. I don't resist but use his momentum to turn and slam into him, and we topple backward. Mr. Taylor flaps his arms in an attempt to fly us back upright. It isn't going to happen. But I am now free and, unlike Mr. Taylor, I have a soft landing.

I get to my feet and walk out of the office.

I'm not sure that I've done quite enough for expulsion, so I grab the secretary's chair and throw it through the window then head to the front exit, setting the fire alarm off on my way out. Just to make sure, I smash the windshield of the headmaster's car with the secretary's chair that has handily landed nearby.

The police are waiting for me when I get home.

I have to go back to the school, but only once, when I have to formally apologize to Mr. Brown and Mr. Taylor. For some reason, I don't have to apologize to Connor. Gran complains about paperwork and the visits from the Community Liaison Officer. I have to do fifty hours of community service.

There are four of us doing community service, cleaning the sports center. I think the days might pass more quickly if we do something—even clean—but Liam, the oldest and most experienced in terms of repaying the community, won't have any of that. We spend the first hour pretending to look for mops and brushes; at least I pretend but Liam just wanders around. Then we go outside for a break and a smoke. I have never smoked before, but Joe is an expert and can blow rings, and rings through rings. He teaches me all he knows.

Occasionally the muscular young man who works on

reception at the sports center comes out and tells us to go back inside and clean. We ignore him and he goes away.

I spend most of the time sitting out the back, smoking and listening to the others talk.

Liam has been caught stealing many times. He takes anything, valuable or valueless, useful or useless. Stealing is the point, not the thing being stolen. Joe has been caught shoplifting, and Bryan crashed while joyriding and still has his neck in a brace.

When we aren't sitting smoking, we wander the sports center. I sometimes carry a mop. Saturday mornings are the busiest. Joe and I like to watch the karate class. It's for children, from beginners up to black belts. Afterward we go out back to practice our smoking.

One Saturday, after karate finishes, we see that Bryan has an expensive-looking pair of Nikes on. He says, "I might get fit now. Now I've got the neck brace off."

Liam says, "Too right, mate. Just do it, that's my motto."

Joe and I lie on our backs on top of the low wall and get out our Marlboros. I am working on a series of three rings with a small one going through the center of them all. I have nearly got this to work when someone comes out of the emergency exit and shouts, "Which one of you shits has taken my trainers?"

I finish blowing smoke and look over at the boy. He is one of the black-belt kids, but he is in jeans now, though still barefoot.

Liam and Bryan have disappeared.

"I want them back. Now!" Black Belt Boy advances on me and Joe.

I don't get up but lift my feet in my scruffy boots, saying, "I haven't got them."

Joe sits up and bangs the heels of his old gray trainers on the wall, but doesn't say anything. He blows a smoke ring and then a beautiful cigar-shaped missile of smoke that sails through the middle of the ring into the boy's face.

I sit up and say, "We saw you practicing kung fu."

"Karate."

"Right . . . karate. You're a black belt, yeah?"

"Yes."

"If you can knock me down I'll get you your shoes back."

Joe laughs. "Oh yeah, a challenge."

"But if I knock you down you let whoever's got them keep them."

Black Belt Boy doesn't need to think about this for more than a second. He is a head taller than me and at least ten kilos heavier, and I guess he's fairly sure I am no black belt. He gets straight into his fighting stance and says, "Come on then."

I take the cigarette out of my mouth and reach across as if to pass it to Joe, but at the same time I raise my legs to put my feet on the edge of the wall and launch myself at the boy, jumping on to his shoulders with my knees. He is on the floor in a second and I manage to land on my feet.

I keep clear of him. He looks pretty mad.

I realize I have dropped my cigarette and move to pick it up but then, like in some kung fu movie, out of nowhere the karate teacher appears. This guy is short, probably in his fifties and not to be messed with. Unlike the kids in his class, he looks like he's hit more than a few things that have hit him back.

However, he says to Black Belt Boy, "A deal's a deal, Tom. He won. And you should have been faster."

Joe sniggers.

Mr. Karate pulls Black Belt Boy to his feet and steers him away.

Casually as I can, I pick up my cigarette and drag on it.

Mr. Karate calls back to me, "Those things'll kill you."

Joe blows out a huge smoke ring, but it's a strange shape because he can hardly stop grinning.

When the karate pair have disappeared, Joe asks, "You planning on living long enough to die of lung cancer?"

The Fifth Notification

•‥•‥•‥•

About a week after my expulsion Gran says that she is going to homeschool me. It sounds great. No school. No "conforming," no "fitting in."

She says, "It is school, but it's at home."

She gets Arran's old books and pens and papers and we sit at the kitchen table. We work through some exercises, very slowly. I struggle to read the questions and Gran paces around the kitchen while I write out the alphabet for her. After she's looked at what I've written, she puts all Arran's books away.

In the afternoon we go for a walk in the woods, and we talk about the trees and plants and have a look at some lichen with a magnifying glass.

When Arran gets home Gran asks him to sit with me while I read. Arran is always patient, and I'm never ashamed when I'm with him, but it's slow and exhausting. Gran stands and watches. Later she says, "Books will never work for you, Nathan. And I certainly haven't the patience or ability to teach you to read. If you want to learn, Arran will have to try."

"I'm not bothered." Though I know Arran will insist I don't give up.

"Fine by me. But you've got lots of other things to learn about."

The next day Gran and I go on our first field trip to Wales. It is a two-hour journey by train. It's cold and windy, though not actually raining. We walk in the hills, and I love seeing where the wild plants and animals live, how they grow, where they are at home.

On the first warm day in April we stay overnight, sleeping outside. I never want to sleep inside again. Gran teaches me about the stars and tells me how the moon's cycle affects the plants that she collects.

Back at home, Gran teaches me about potions, but compared to her I'm clumsy and don't have her intuition about how the plants will work together or counteract each other. Still, I learn the basics about how she makes her potions, how her touch and even her breath add magic to them. And I learn to make simple healing lotions for cuts, a paste that draws out poison, and a sleeping draught, but I know that I won't ever make anything magical.

I have maps of Wales, and I get to know them well. I can read maps easily; they are pictures, and I can see the land in my head. I learn where all the rivers, valleys, and mountains are in relation to each other, the ways across them, the places I can find shelter or water, where I can swim, fish, and trap.

Soon I travel to Wales on my own, often spending two or three days away from home, sleeping outside and living off the land.

The first time I'm away by myself I lie on the ground. Lying on a Welsh mountain is special. I try to work it out: I am happy when I'm with Arran, just being with him, watching his slow and peaceful nature. That's a special thing. And I'm happy with Annalise, really happy, looking at how beautiful she is and forgetting who I am for the time she's with me. That's pretty special too. But lying on a Welsh mountain is different. Better. That's the real me. The real me and the real mountain, alive and breathing as one.

My twelfth birthday and another assessment comes round. I hate them, but I control myself, make myself put up with one day of the Council, the Councilors, the weighing and measuring, so that I can be free again. At the end of this assessment they question Gran about my education, though it is fairly obvious that they know I have been expelled from school. Gran tells them little and doesn't mention the field trips. The assessment seems to go okay. My Designation Code is still *Not ascertained*.

A week later another notification arrives. We are sitting round the kitchen table and Gran reads it out.

"*Notification of the Resolution of the Council of White Witches of England, Scotland, and Wales.*

"**In order to ensure the safety of all White Witches it was agreed that any and all movements of Half Codes (W 0.5/B 0.5) away from their recorded place of residence must be approved by the Council before journeys are undertaken. Any Half**

Code found in a place that has not been approved will have all movements restricted."

"This is too much. He's going to end up under house arrest," Deborah says.

"Do you think they know that Nathan is going to Wales?" Arran looks worried.

"I don't know. But, yes, we have to assume that they do. I thought they allowed it because . . ." Gran's voice tails off to silence.

I know the rest of her thoughts. The Council may be using me to lure Marcus in, to tempt him to see me, and if he does appear they will swoop in and kill him . . . kill us. But now they seem to want to restrict me.

Deborah has obviously been thinking of Marcus too. She says, "It might be something to do with the family that Marcus attacked up in the northeast."

We all look at her.

"You haven't heard? They were all killed."

"How do you know this?" Gran asks.

"I've been keeping my ear to the ground. We all have to, don't we? For Nathan's sake . . . and our own, for that matter."

"How exactly have you kept your ear to the ground?" Arran asks.

Deborah hesitates but then holds her chin up and says, "I've made friends with Niall."

Arran shakes his head.

"I just hang on his every word and tell him how handsome and clever he is and . . . he tells me things."

Arran leans toward Deborah to warn her, I think, but before he can say anything she insists, "I've done nothing wrong. I talk to him and listen to him. What's wrong with that?"

"And when he says bad things about Nathan? What do you say then?"

Deborah looks at me. "I never agree."

"Do you disagree?" Arran is as close to sneering as he can get.

"Arran! I think it's a great idea," I interrupt. "The Council uses spies all the time, Gran says. It's okay to use their own tactics against them. Besides, Deborah's right, she's not doing anything wrong."

"She's not doing anything right."

I go to Deborah, kiss her shoulder, and say, "Thank you, Deborah."

She hugs me.

"So, Deborah, what did you find out?" Gran asks.

Deborah takes a breath. "Niall said that Marcus killed a family last week, a man, woman, and their teenage son. Niall's father had been called to an emergency Council meeting about it."

"I can't believe he told you all this." Arran is shaking his head again.

"Niall loves bragging about his family. He must have told me ten times that Kieran is training to be a Hunter and coming out on top all the time in the trials they have—unless Jessica is beating him, of course. Apparently Kieran is desperate to be sent on this investigation as his first assignment."

"Who were the family?" Gran asks.

"Niall said they were called Grey. She was a Hunter and he did something for the Council. Do you know them?"

Gran says, "I've heard the name."

"Niall said that the Greys were custodians of something called the Fairborn, and the Fairborn was what Marcus was after. I don't know what the Fairborn is; I'm not even sure Niall knows. When I asked him, I think he realized that he'd said too much, and he's hardly said a word to me since."

I don't say anything. For whatever reason, my father has just killed three more people, including a boy only a few years older than me. Was this a misunderstanding? He was trying to explain to them that he wasn't really evil, he didn't want to hurt them . . . He just wanted the Fairborn. Maybe he needed the Fairborn, whatever it is, but they wouldn't give it to him, they wouldn't listen . . . They attacked him and he was defending himself and . . .

Gran says, "I'll write to the Council and request permission for you to travel to Wales."

"What?" I'd not really been paying attention.

"The notification says you'll need approval to travel. I'll write to the Council and get permission."

"No. I don't want them to know where I go. I don't want their permission."

"You intend to go without me informing them?"

"Please, Gran. Just ask for permission for me to go to the local woods and the shops and stuff like that. Stuff that I don't really care about."

"But Nathan, it says"—Gran looks at the parchment—"'Any Half Code found in a place that has not been approved will have all movements restricted.'"

"I know what it says. And I know what I want to do."

"You're twelve, Nathan. You don't understand that they—"

"Gran, I understand. I understand it all."

Later that night, when I am getting undressed, Arran has a go at talking to me. I guess Gran has asked him to try. He says I should "rethink," "perhaps ask permission to go to one place in Wales," and some other stuff like that. Adult stuff. Gran's stuff.

I just say, "Can I have permission to go to the bathroom, please?"

He doesn't say anything, so I throw my jeans on the floor, get on my knees, and say, "Can I have permission to go to the bathroom? Please?"

He doesn't say anything but drops to his knees with me and hugs me. We stay like that. Him hugging me and me still stiff with anger at him, wanting to hurt him too.

After a long time I hug him back, just a little.

My First Kiss

•∵•∵•

The Council grants me permission to go to places within a few miles of our home, including not much more than some local shops and our woods. A year goes by and then another. My thirteenth and fourteenth birthdays are the only blots on the landscape, but I get through the assessments and still have the *Not ascertained* Designation Code. Gran continues to teach me about potions and plants. And I continue to go to Wales on my own. I learn how to survive outdoors in the winter, how to read the weather, and how to cope with the rain. I never stay away from home for more than three days, and I am always careful to move around discreetly. I leave and return by different routes, always on the lookout for potential spies sent to watch me.

My thoughts are often of my father, but my plans to join him remain vague. My thoughts are also more and more of Annalise. I have never stopped thinking of her, her hair, her skin, and her smile, but after my fourteenth birthday these thoughts become more persistent. I want to look at her again for real, and my plans to see her rapidly become less vague.

I'm not stupid enough to go near her house or school,

but between them is Edge Hill, the place where we had said we would meet one day.

I go there.

The hill is shaped like an upturned bowl, flat on top with steep sides and a path round the base. On its south side is an outcrop, from the top of which is a view out across the plain, a green expanse of farmland broken up by a network of hedge-lined country roads and spotted with a few houses. The hill is wooded, and the trees are straight and tall and widely spaced. The outcrop is coarse sandstone cut by deep horizontal and vertical clefts. At the cliff's base is a flat patch of bare earth. It is brick-red and sandy and dusts my shoes as I walk across it.

Climbing the outcrop is simple, as the handholds and footholds are large and open. When I sit at the top on a flat slab of the sandstone I can't see the path at the bottom for the slope of the hill but I can hear the voices of occasional dog-walkers and the shouts and calls of a few children making their slow way home after school. If anyone other than Annalise were to approach the outcrop, I'd have plenty of time to disappear up and over the hill.

I wait every school day on the outcrop. I once think that I hear her voice talking to one of her brothers, so I climb over the hill and make my way home.

It's late autumn when the shine of Annalise's blonde hair appears over the curve of the slope.

I concentrate on making my legs swing casually over the edge of the outcrop.

Annalise doesn't look up until she is over the steepest part of the hill. She slows when she sees me and looks around but carries on walking until she is almost directly below me. She looks up, smiles, and blushes.

I have waited so long to see her and I know what I want to say, but everything that I have thought of opening with seems wrong. I realize my legs have stopped swinging, and I concentrate on them again. My breathing has gone funny too.

Annalise climbs up the rock face. She does even this elegantly and in a few seconds is sitting next to me, swinging her legs in unison with mine.

After a minute I manage to speak. "You'll have to inform the Council that you've had contact with me."

Her legs stop swinging.

I remind her, "According to the Resolution of the Council of White Witches any contact between Half Codes and White Whets is to be reported to the Council by all concerned."

Annalise's legs start to swing again. "I haven't had contact."

I can now feel each thud of my heart; each beat seems like it is going to break open my chest.

"Besides I have a terrible memory. My mum's always on at me about forgetting things. I'll try to remember to tell her about seeing you but I've got a feeling it'll slip my mind."

"I'm glad I'm forgettable," I mumble as I watch her school shoes, covered in red dust, swing into and out of view.

"I've never forgotten you. I remember all the drawings

you did, all the times you looked at me across the class-room."

I almost fall off the escarpment. *All the times?*

"How many times did I look across the classroom then?"

"Twice on the first day."

"Twice?" I know it was once. I can feel her eyes on me, but I continue to watch her shoes.

"You looked so . . . miserable."

Great.

"And sort of in pain."

I blurt out a laugh. "Yeah well, that's probably fairly accurate." It all seems like a long time ago.

"Ten times on the second day," she says.

It was once, and now I know she is teasing me.

"But only twice on the third day, which was the day I sat next to you in art and even then you didn't look at me but kept on looking at that sparrow."

"It was a blackbird, and I was drawing it."

"After that I thought we'd got over your shyness, but you still haven't looked at me now." She stops swinging her feet and holds them up, knocks her shoes together and lets them fall.

"I'm not shy, and I have looked at you."

"This bit of me, I mean."

I can tell she is pointing at her face, but I am still staring at the space where her feet have been swinging. I turn and swallow. She is as beautiful as ever. White chocolate hair and clear honey skin, slightly tanned and slightly flushed. She isn't smiling, though.

"Do you know how amazing your eyes are?" she asks.

No.

She nudges me with her shoulder. "Don't be so glum when I'm saying nice things to you."

She leans closer, peering into my eyes and I look into hers, watching the silver glints tumble in the blue, some moving fast, some slow, some looking as if they're moving toward me.

Annalise blinks and leans back, saying, "Maybe not so shy." She pushes off the escarpment and lands softly on the ground below. It's a long drop.

I follow her down, and as I land she runs off like a gazelle and we chase around the hillside for too short a time before she says she has to go.

Alone, I lie back on the slab of sandstone and relive it all. And I try to work out what to say to her the next time. A compliment, like she has given me about my eyes: "Your eyes are like the sky in the morning," "Your skin looks like velvet," "I love the sunshine on your hair." They all sound so pathetic, and I know that I could never say them.

We meet a week later, and it's Annalise's turn to look glum and stare at her shoes.

I guess the problem. "Do they say lots of bad things about me?"

She doesn't answer straightaway, possibly counting all the things.

"They say you're a Black Witch."

"I'd be killed if that was true."

"Well, they say that you are more like your father than your mother."

And that's when it hits me how dangerous this is. "You should go. You shouldn't see me."

She catches me out, turning to look me straight in the eyes, saying, "I don't care what they say. I don't even care about your father. I care about you."

I don't know what to say. What can you say to that? But I do what I have wanted to do forever, and take her hand and kiss it.

From then on we meet every week and sit on the outcrop and talk. I tell her about my life, but only in part, the bits about Gran, Arran, and Deborah. I never tell her about Wales and the trips I make there, even though I want to. But I'm afraid. And I hate that. Hate that I can't be honest because of my sick, horrible fear that the less she knows, the safer it will be for her.

She tells me about her life. Her father and brothers sound like male versions of Jessica, while her mother is an unusually powerless White Witch. Annalise's life sounds miserable, and it makes my home life seem free and relaxed. She has never heard of assessments and doesn't believe me until I describe the blond Council member who sits on the left of the Council leader. Annalise says that sounds like Soul O'Brien, her uncle.

I ask her one question that has always intrigued me. How many Half Codes are there? She doesn't know but will try to find out from her father, who works for the Council.

The following week she says his answer was, "Just the one."

Another time she asks, "Has Deborah found her Gift yet?"

"No. She's struggling. She's too logical."

"Niall is frustrated too. He's desperate to be able to become invisible, like Kieran and my uncle, but I don't think it's him at all. He didn't want Mum to perform the Giving ceremony; he said he'd have more chance of getting invisibility from Dad. But I don't think it would make any difference. Kieran drank Mum's blood, not Dad's. I think the Gift relates to the person: it's in you from birth and the magic of the Giving allows it to come out. Niall's just too open to have invisibility."

"Yes, I think it works like that too. Jessica can disguise herself. She's always been a natural at lying. Her Gift suits her down to the ground. But she drank Gran's blood and there's no one on Gran's side of the family with that Gift."

"I think I'll have potions."

"My Gran has potions. She's clever but instinctive as well. I think that's why she's good with them. You're like her. She has a strong Gift."

"I don't think my Gift will be very strong. I think I'll be like my mum."

Annalise is not often wrong, but she's way off the mark with this. I pick her hand up and kiss it. "No, you'll have a strong Gift."

Annalise blushes a little. "I wonder about you. Sometimes you seem wild and mad and I think you'll have the same Gift as your father. But then other times you're so gentle and I'm not so sure . . . maybe you'll be like your mother. It won't be potions, though."

We continue to meet once a week during the school term through winter, spring, and early summer. We are careful to meet only for a short time, and we vary the days. We don't meet in the holidays.

I'm stroking Annalise's hair, watching how it falls from my fingers. And she studies the palm of my hand and smoothes her fingertips across my skin. She says she can tell my fortune by reading the lines.

She says, "You will be a powerful witch."

"Yeah? How powerful?"

"Exceptional." She smoothes my hand again. "Yes, it's quite clear. I can see it in this line here. You will have an unusual Gift. Few have it. You will be able to turn into animals."

"Sounds good." And I'm holding her hair back and watching it fall.

"Only insects, though."

"Insects?" I let go of her hair.

"You will only be able to become insects. You will make an especially good dung beetle."

I snicker.

She carries on smoothing out my palm. "You will fall deeply in love with someone."

"Human or dung beetle?"

"Human. And that person will love you forever, even when you're a dung beetle."

"And what's this person like?"

"That I can't see . . . there's a patch of mud on that bit."

And I stroke her cheek with the back of my fingers. She stays still, letting me touch her. My fingers move over her cheeks and round her mouth, over her chin and down her neck and then back up again to her cheek up to her forehead, slowly down the center of her nose over the tip and down to her lips, where my finger stays. And she kisses it once. And she kisses it again. And I reach forward and only dare take my finger away when my lips replace it.

And we are pressed together, my lips, my arms, chest, hips, my body desperate to get closer to her.

I can't bear to take my mouth from her skin.

It feels like just a few minutes but it is getting late, getting dark, when we finally manage to part.

As we say good-bye she takes my hand and kisses the side of my index finger, her lips and tongue and teeth on my skin.

We have arranged to meet in a week's time. The next day seems to take forever to pass. The day after that is worse. I don't know what to do with myself; all I can do is wait. I am physically aching to see her. My guts are in turmoil.

Finally, the day of our meeting crawls into the light and then takes a year to drag itself to the afternoon.

I wait on the sandstone slab, lying on my back, looking at the sky and listening for Annalise's footsteps. I am straining at each sound, and when I hear her scrambling up the slope I roll on to my side and sit up. Her blonde head appears over the curve of the hill and I spring down from the outcrop, landing in a crouch with bent legs, the fingertips of my left hand on the ground and my right hand out to the side, showing off a little. I straighten up and step forward.

But something is badly wrong.

Annalise's face is distorted . . . terrified.

I hesitate. Do I go to her? Do I run? What?

I look around.

It has to be her brothers, but I can't see them or hear them. It can't be the Council . . . can it?

I step forward. And then the figure of a man appears, standing next to Annalise. He has been there all the time, his hand on Annalise's shoulder, steering her up the slope and holding her still. But he had been invisible.

Kieran.

Annalise's eldest brother is tall like the rest of the family, but he has huge shoulders, and rather than white hair his is red-blond, thinner and cut close to his scalp. His eyes don't leave me as he bends forward slightly and says something I can't hear in Annalise's ear.

Annalise's body is rigid. She nods her head jerkily in response to Kieran. Her eyes are staring ahead, not looking at me, looking at nothing. Kieran takes his hand off her shoulder and she runs off, stumbling down the slope.

BW

•·•·•·

Kieran has the lower routes of escape covered. And now, approaching high to my left, is Connor; to the right is Niall. I could get up some good speed running down the slope but Annalise has told me that Kieran is fast. I could swerve down to the left or right but he is quite a bit below me and if he is fast he'll . . .

Kieran grins and beckons me forward.

No, forward doesn't feel like a good option.

I turn and run up the sandstone escarpment. I have made the climb numerous times before and know each handhold and each ledge. I can do it blindfolded. There is no way that Kieran can catch me from his position farther down the slope. But the few seconds' delay have given Niall and Connor the advantage, and by the time I clear the top Connor is running toward me, not stopping until he stretches out his arms and plants his hands on my chest to shove me back over the edge.

I fall backward, turning in the air to land in a crouch on the bare ground below, back in the position I had been in a minute earlier. It's a good landing, and now my only option is to barrel down the hill. I have only lifted my hand, though, when a boot wallops into me from the side and my stomach lifts into the air and then I am flat on the ground, winded, face-down.

I start to crawl. Another kick thumps into the side of my ribs. And another. The boots scuff around, kicking up dust and sand into my eyes, and one stomps on the back of my head, pushing my face into the ground.

"Sit on his legs," Kieran instructs Connor. "Get his arms, Niall."

Niall gets my arms and holds them down with his hands and feet while sitting on my head. I'm struggling to breathe underneath his sweaty trousers. There's nothing I can do. I can't see a thing except gray wool but I can hear Niall panting and Connor's gasping, nervous giggle. I can't move.

Kieran says, "You know what this is, Connor?"

Connor has to think about it, but eventually says, "A hunting knife."

Now I squirm and grunt and curse them.

"Hold him still, Niall. To be exact, it's a French hunting knife. They make great knives, the French. Look at that blade. It folds away beautifully into the handle. Great design. The Swiss go for all the fancy gadgets in their knives, but all you need is a good blade."

I hear the rip of my T-shirt and feel the cool air on my back. I buck and shout curses again.

"Hold him still and shut him up with this."

Niall's legs move and my T-shirt is pushed into my mouth and I'm trying to bite him but then the blade brushes over my back and I try to shrink from it but it follows me and the point stops in the middle of my left shoulder blade.

"I'll start here, I think. This half is the Black half, I'd say."

Then the point goes in. And slowly the pain cuts down my back and I scream and swear into my T-shirt, the sounds muffled.

Kieran hisses in my ear. "Niall told you to stay away from our sister, you Black piece of shit."

He puts the point back into my left shoulder blade and I clench my jaw and scream while he makes another cut.

He stops again and says, "You should have listened to him."

He makes another slow cut.

And I am going mad screaming and praying for someone to make him stop.

But he makes another cut and then another and all I can do is scream and pray.

"Time for a break."

No one makes a noise. But it's not silent in my head. My head is full of the noise of prayer. Praying and praying to please, please not let him do any more.

Kieran says, "Nice here, isn't it, Connor? Good view."

I stop praying to listen.

Connor doesn't answer.

Niall says, "Kieran, he's bleeding a lot." He sounds worried.

"I almost forgot. Thanks for reminding me, Niall. I got

some powder from camp." His voice is closer to me. "They use it in Retributions."

And I'm praying again, praying louder than ever to please not let him do it, please.

"It stops the bleeding. Can't have Black Witches bleeding to death. I have heard that it hurts a bit. We'll find out, won't we?"

And then I start begging. Just in my head, but I am begging. *Please don't, please don't, don't, don't, don't—*

"Hey. Wake up."

I can breathe better. Niall is off my head. The T-shirt is out of my mouth.

"Wake up."

A black boot, polished but flecked with sand and a few drops of blood is all I can see. I close my eyes again.

Kieran's voice is in my ear, close enough for me to feel his breath.

"How you feeling? Okay?"

I'm feeling frightened.

The pain in my back has faded. But I don't want any more. I would do anything to stop him doing more. I would beg and plead, and in my head I'm saying, *Please don't do any more. Please.* I can't speak the words, no words come out, but in my head I'm begging, *Please, don't do any more.*

"You're crying. Hey, Niall! Connor! He's crying."

Silence.

"Do you think he's sorry, Connor? Sorry that he beat you up?"

Connor mumbles something.

"Maybe. But I'm not sure. What do you think, Niall?"

"Yes." I can just hear Niall. He sounds angry.

"Okay . . . Well, that's good." And Kieran's mouth is close to my ear as he says, "So are you sorry you beat up my pathetic brothers?"

And I want to say yes. I do want to say it. In my head I'm saying sorry. But nothing will come out of my mouth.

"And are you sorry you met my sister?"

And I know as soon as he says that, the way he says it, that he hasn't finished. It isn't over. He has no intention of stopping there. And nothing I can say will make any difference. All I can do is hate him.

"I said, are you sorry you've been seeing my sister?"

And I hate him with all my tears and screams and begging.

"What else have you been doing with her?"

And I want him to know what we did, but there's no way I'm going to tell him anything.

"I don't think you're sorry at all . . . are you?"

And I'm not. I'm not sorry about any of it. I'm too full of hate to be sorry about anything.

"Let's try again, shall we? On this side. This must be the White half."

The T-shirt is stuffed back in my mouth and I feel the blade across the right side of my back, close to my spine. All the cuts he has made so far are on my left side and I know what is coming. That was the whole point of his talking; it was just so that I would know what to expect.

The cuts are bad, but all the time I think about the powder. That's what I fear. Kieran is in no rush, though . . .

"Wakey, wakey." A slap on my cheek. "Nearly finished. We still have my favorite bit left. Leave the best till last, that's what they say, isn't it?"

I've given up thinking; given up praying a long time ago. I look at the sand. The small grains: orange, brick orange, red, some tiny black ones.

"Do you want to put the powder on him, Niall?"

"No."

"No? So it's up to you, Connor."

"Kieran." Connor sounds really quiet. "I . . ."

"Shut up, Connor! You're doing it."

Kieran kneels close to my face and says, "Make sure there isn't a next time, you Half Code heap of shit, because if there is I'll cut your balls off before I rip your innards out."

And I hate him and curse him and scream at him into the T-shirt.

It's dark. The ground beneath me is cold. And I am cold inside, but my back's on fire. I can hardly move but I have to put the fire out. I roll on the ground. Someone, somewhere far off, screams.

*   *   *

Shouting . . .

Arran's voice . . .

The trees are like sentries, but they're moving past me.

Blackness.

"Nathan?" Arran's voice is soft in my ear.

I open my eyes and his face is close to me. I think we're in the kitchen.

I'm on the table. Like a chicken served for dinner. Gran has her back to me; she is making gravy. Deborah is carrying a bowl that steams. Maybe it has potatoes in it.

"You'll be okay. You'll be okay," Arran says. But he says it in a strange way.

Deborah puts the bowl beside me and I know it doesn't have potatoes in it, and I'm afraid, so afraid. She is going to touch my back. And I beg Arran not to let them touch me.

"They have to clean the cuts. You'll be okay. You'll be okay."

And I beg him not to let them touch me. But I don't think the words come out.

He holds my hand tighter.

I wake again. Still a chicken on the table. Arran's hand locked on mine. My back is hot inside but cool on the outside.

Arran asks quietly, "Nathan?"

"Stay with me, Arran."

* * *

The sun is warm on my face. My back is tight and throbs fast with my pulse. I don't dare move anything except my fingers. Arran is still holding my hand.

"Nathan?"

"Water."

"Move your head really slowly. I'll put the straw in your mouth."

I blink my eyes open. I am lying at an angle on my bed with my head on the edge of the mattress. Below me is a glass of water with a long straw.

After I drink I doze for a few minutes then I wake as my stomach churns. I throw up into a bowl that has replaced the glass of water, terrified because each lurch of my stomach sends tight spasms across my back.

When I next wake up Arran is still by my side. He says, "Gran's made a drink for you. She says you have to take small sips."

The drink is disgusting. It must have a sleeping potion in it as I remember nothing else until I wake again in the evening.

I move my fingers, but Arran isn't beside me. It's dark in the room, but I can see the shape of him in his bed, asleep. The house is quiet, but then I hear subdued voices and I move my head a little to see through the crack in the door. Gran is on the landing with Deborah. They are talking and I strain to hear what they are saying and then I realize that they aren't talking; they are crying.

The next morning I wake up thirsty once again. There is a glass of water beneath me; at least I don't have to have more of the potion. I suck hard, making a slurping noise as I empty the glass.

"You're only supposed to sip."

I tilt my head up to see Arran sitting sideways on his bed, leaning on the wall. He is pale and has dark circles beneath his eyes.

"How you feeling?"

I think about it and move my head. The tightness in my back is bad. "Better. And you?"

He rubs his face and says, "A bit tired."

"At least you're not crying," I say. "I've never seen Gran cry before."

I suck at the straw again, even though there is no drink left, and then I look at him as I ask, "Is it that bad?"

He meets my look. "Yes."

We are silent for a while.

"Did you come looking for me?"

"When it got late, I went looking in the woods; that was about ten o'clock. You weren't there so I checked all the back streets. Debs rang me at midnight. Someone had phoned here telling us where you were. Debs thinks it was Niall."

I tell Arran what happened and about my meetings with Annalise.

He doesn't say anything, so I ask, "Do you think I'm stupid for seeing her?"

"No."

"Really?"

"You like each other. She's nice to you and she's . . . you know . . . beautiful."

We are silent again.

"Promise me you won't see her again."

I stare at the floor, thinking of Annalise and her smile, her eyes, and the look on her face when I last saw her.

"Nathan. Promise me."

"I'm not that stupid."

"Promise me."

"I promise that I'm not that stupid." I still stare at the floor.

Arran slides across the floor to sit by me. He strokes my hair back from my face and kisses my forehead, whispering, "Please, Nathan. I couldn't stand it."

I heal quickly, even for a whet, but it's still five days before I have the bandages off. I stand in the bathroom with my back to the large mirror and a small mirror of Gran's in my hands. Arran asked me on the second day if Kieran had said what he'd done. I knew then that it was more than just cuts.

The scars stretch from my shoulder blades to my lower back: a "B" on the left and a "W" on the right.

Post-Trauma

•⋅•⋅•⋅•⋅•

I know I have to stay away from Annalise. I'm not stupid; I won't try to see her again, at least not at the moment, but I want to know if she's all right.

Since Deborah finished school she has had no contact with Niall, apart from the phone call telling her where I was. But even if they were in touch I wouldn't trust what Niall said about Annalise anyway. I ask Arran if he can get a message to her. He tells me that Niall has warned him off: "You will get what your brother got if you go near her." I suspect Niall didn't say "your brother" but the message is clear, and I tell Arran to forget it.

Arran says, "Don't blame yourself."

I don't. Kieran and his dumb brothers are to blame.

And I know that Annalise would think the same way, and she will know that I never meant to cause her problems . . . but I screwed up. I was naive. I knew there would be serious trouble for both of us if we got caught, and I ignored that. But so did she.

Gran sits at my bedside and cleans her creams off my back. She runs her fingers over my scars, and I reach around to touch them too. They are uneven, shallow grooves.

Gran says, "They've healed well. They look like they've been there for years."

I arch my back, bend forward, and then roll my shoulders. There's no pain there now; the tightness has gone.

"The creams have done some of the work but so have you. Your healing abilities have begun."

All witches can self-heal faster than fains. Some a lot faster. Some instantly. And I know Gran is right. I feel so good. Buzzy, on a mini high . . .

But the healing has finished now. The first night after the creams are off I curl up in bed, at last able to lie in any position I like. It feels good, but not for long. I start to sweat, and the headache I have been ignoring grows until my skull feels like it is going to break open. I go to the kitchen for a drink of water, but that makes me feel sick, so I sit on the back doorstep, and the relief is instant. I stay there in the open doorway, leaning against the wall. The sky is clear, and the full moon seems heavy and huge. It's quiet and still, and I don't feel tired. I look around and see that my shadow lies long and dark across the kitchen floor. I get a small knife from the drawer, taking my time, feeling the nausea build again while I'm in the kitchen, but as soon as I return to my spot on the back step it disappears.

I balance the knife in my hand, wondering where to try first.

I make a small cut with the point of the knife in the pad of my index finger. I suck the blood and then look at the cut, pulling the skin apart. More blood, another suck, and then I stare at the cut and try to heal it.

I think, *Heal!*

More blood appears.

I relax, look at the moon, feel the cut, the throb of my finger. Feel it. Keep my awareness on it and on the moon. It takes I don't know how long. A while. But I know something is happening because I'm smiling, can't stop it. The buzz is there. This is fun. I push the point of the knife into my fingertip again.

The next night I try to sleep in my bed but am sweating and nauseated soon after it goes dark, so I go outside and instantly feel better. I sleep in the garden and go back to the bedroom before Arran wakes up.

I do the same the third night, this time only going back inside when Arran is getting dressed.

"Where did you go last night?"

I shrug.

"You're not seeing Annalise?"

"No."

"If you are . . ."

"I'm not."

"I know you like her, but—"

"I'm not! I just had a bit of trouble sleeping. It was too hot. I slept outside."

Arran doesn't look convinced. I walk out and Deborah is there on the landing, brushing her hair, pretending not to have been listening in.

When we are in the kitchen having breakfast Deborah leans toward me, saying, "It wasn't hot last night. I think you should tell Gran about not being able to sleep."

I shake my head.

So Deborah announces to us all, "I've been reading up on post-traumatic stress disorder."

Arran rolls his eyes. I stab my cereal with my spoon.

"The reaction to shock can be delayed. Nightmares and flashbacks are typical. Anger, frustration . . ."

I glare at her as I put a huge mound of cereal in my mouth.

Gran asks, "What are you talking about, Deborah?"

"Nathan has suffered a terrible trauma. He isn't sleeping. He's sweating."

"Oh, I see," Gran says. "Are you having nightmares, Nathan?"

"No," I insist through the cereal.

"If he is having nightmares, and certainly if he is suffering from stress, then bringing it up at the breakfast table is not very thoughtful," Arran says.

"Gran can probably give him a sleeping potion, is all I'm thinking."

"Do you need a sleeping potion, Nathan?" Arran asks.

"No, thanks," I say, stuffing more food in my mouth.

"Did you sleep well last night, Nathan?" Arran puts on a tone of extreme mock concern.

"Yes, thanks." I speak through the cereal.

"Yes, but why didn't you sleep in your own bed, Nathan?" Deborah looks from me to Arran as she asks.

I stab at the mush in my bowl. Arran glares at Deborah.

"You're not sneaking off to see Annalise?" Gran asks.

"No!" Bits of cereal spray on to the table.

Gran stares at me.

Why does no one believe me?

"You still haven't said why you didn't sleep in your own bed last night," Deborah says.

Arran says, "We all know he likes to sleep outside, Deborah."

I bang my spoon hard on the table. "I didn't sleep in my own bed 'cause I felt sick, okay! That's all."

"But that—" Deborah starts.

"Please be quiet. All of you," Gran interrupts. She massages her forehead with her fingers. "I need to tell you something." Gran stretches her hand out to hold my arm and says, "There are many different rumors about Black Witches and their affinity with the night."

I stare at her, and her eyes are concerned and old and serious, and locked on mine. *Black Witches and their affinity?* Is she trying to tell me that I'm some kind of Black Witch because I've slept outside for a couple of nights?

I pull my arm out of her grasp and get up.

Arran says, "But Nathan isn't a Black—"

"There are stories about weakness too," Gran says. "Some Black Witches can't stand to be indoors at night. They are stories. But that doesn't mean they aren't true."

Gran massages her forehead again. "Being indoors at night drives them mad."

Arran looks at me and shakes his head. "This isn't happening to you."

Gran continues, "I should tell you one of the stories. It's important for Nathan."

By this time I'm backed into the corner of the kitchen. Deborah comes to stand with me. She puts her arm round me and leans on my shoulder whispering, "I'm sorry, Nathan. I didn't know. I didn't know."

The Story of the Death of Saba

•··•·•·

Saba was a Black Witch. She had killed a Hunter and was on the run. Virginia, the leader of the Hunters, and a group of her elite were on Saba's trail. They had tracked her across England, through countryside, cities, and towns, and they were closing in.

Saba was exhausted, and in desperation she hid in the cellar of a large house on the edge of a village. She must have been desperate or she wouldn't have tried to hide. It doesn't work, hiding from Hunters. She must have known that they would track her there. And they did. The Hunters found the house and quickly surrounded it. There would be no escape for Saba. Some of the Hunters wanted to charge into the cellar, but Virginia didn't want to lose anyone else. There was only one way into the cellar, through a trapdoor, and Virginia ordered that the entrance be blocked up for a month, by which time Saba would be either dead or so weak that she could be captured with no losses on the Hunters' side.

Virginia knew that most of her Hunters weren't happy about this. They wanted revenge, glory, and a quick end to Saba and this hunt. Virginia set a guard on the entrance to the cellar to stop Saba escaping but also to ensure none of the Hunters disobeyed her orders.

Night fell, and the Hunters found places in the house and

its gardens to sleep. But no one slept, because soon after dark, terrible screams came from the cellar.

The Hunters ran to the trapdoor, thinking that one of their number had disobeyed Virginia's orders, had entered the cellar, and was being tortured by Saba. But, no, the guard still stood at the blocked-up entrance. The screams came from the cellar and carried on until dawn. The Hunters tried to sleep and covered their ears or plugged them with bits of material from their clothes but nothing would stop the sounds from piercing their heads. It felt as if each one of them was screaming too.

The next morning the Hunters were exhausted. These were all tough men and women, the toughest, but they had been hunting Saba for weeks, and now they were drained.

The second night the screaming returned and again no one slept.

This carried on every night, so that by the end of the first week the Hunters were arguing and fighting among themselves. One Hunter had stabbed another, and one had deserted. Even Virginia was desperate: she had not slept, and she could see that her elite group was descending into anarchy. On the eighth night, when the screaming started again, she ran to the cellar in a rage and began to strip back the barricade from over the trapdoor. The Hunters gathered around her but they were unsure what to think. They all wanted to go in and end the torture, but seeing their leader, normally the epitome of control, tearing at the trapdoor made them wonder if she had lost her mind.

One Hunter stepped up and dared to remind Virginia that she had ordered that Saba should be shut up for a month, and *it had been only one week. Virginia pushed the Hunter back, saying that she was willing to risk her life and theirs to end the torment.*

Virginia opened the trapdoor and descended into the cellar with her Hunters crowding behind her.

The cellar was dark. Virginia used her torch to throw light on to the floor and pick her way between crates, boxes, an old chair, bottles of wine, and a sack of potatoes. There was a doorway to another room. The screaming was coming from there. Virginia made her way to the door and the Hunters followed.

The second room appeared to be empty. But in the farthest corner, barely discernible, was a low pile of rags.

Virginia strode up, lifted the rags back and there was the body of Saba. She was half dead, totally mad, and still screaming. She had clawed at her face, which was a mass of scars. She couldn't speak, as she had bitten off her own tongue. But still she screamed.

Virginia could have killed her there, but she said Saba should be taken to the Council for interrogation. Saba was barely alive, but she was a powerful Black Witch, so Virginia ordered her to be tied up before she was carried out.

It was now the middle of the night, but outside, the light from the moon made it seem almost like day. As the Hunters bore her body out of the house, Saba began to hum and then she began to writhe. Too late, Virginia realized that Saba's strength was returning now she was outside in the night air. Saba sent flames from her mouth, setting on fire the two Hunters carrying her. She fell to the ground and used her flames to burn through her bonds. Virginia drew her gun and shot Saba in the chest, but Saba had enough life in her to grab hold of Virginia and set fire to her too. They were both in flames when Virginia's son, Clay, shot Saba in the neck. She fell, silent at last, on the lawn of the house.

Virginia died from her burns, and Clay became the next leader of the Hunters. He's still their leader today.

Gran rubs her face with her hands and says, "A Hunter told me that story a long time ago. We were at the wake of her partner, another Hunter. She was upset and very drunk. I took her outside and gave her a potion to calm her. We sat on the grass and talked.

"She told me that her partner was the Hunter who had deserted. Clay had tracked her down and had her executed. This girl, the drunk one, had been made to pull the trigger on her partner."

Debs is shaking her head, "They're all monsters. The Hunters are as bad as—"

"Deborah! Don't! Don't ever say that," Arran cuts in.

I ask, "Who was Saba?"

Gran takes a breath and says, "She was Marcus's mother."

Somehow I'm not surprised. I push myself away from Deborah and go to sit on the back step.

Arran comes and sits next to me. Leaning close he says, "It doesn't mean anything."

"Saba was my grandmother."

"None of this means that you are like that."

I shake my head. "It's happening to me, Arran. I feel it. I'm a Black Witch."

"No, you're not. That's your body, not you. The real you is nothing to do with being a Black Witch. You have some of Marcus's genes in you, and some of Saba's. But that's physical. And the physical stuff, the genes, your Gift, they are not what makes a Black Witch. You have to believe that. It's how you think and how you behave that shows who you are. You aren't evil, Nathan. Nothing about you is evil. You will have a powerful Gift—we can all see that— but it's how you use it that will show you to be good or bad."

I almost believe him. I don't feel evil, but I'm afraid. My body is doing things that I don't understand, and I don't know what else it will do. It feels like it has a will of its own and it's leading me down a path I have to follow. The night tremors are taking me outside, forcing me to move away from my old life. The noises in my head also seem to be driving me away from people.

Whenever Jessica used to say I was half Black, Gran would say, "Half White too." And I had always thought of my mother's genes and my father's mixing in my body, but now it occurs to me that my body is my father's and my spirit is my mother's. Perhaps Arran is right, my spirit is not evil, but I have to put up with a body that does weird things.

I leave for Wales that morning, intending to stay away for a day or two. It feels good sleeping outside and living off the land, and after my talk with Arran I'm feeling more positive, more like I know who and what I am. It's a different way of looking at things, nothing more than that, but it allows me to watch my body and learn what it's capable of. I observe it in a more detached way, testing its healing capabilities and working out how the night affects me.

I stay in Wales one more day, and then one more, and then one more. I find an unused barn and try sleeping in it, and discover that the moon has an effect on how I feel. A full moon is worst for being indoors at night, and I can't help but shake and vomit. A new moon and being in the barn is bearable with nothing worse than slight nausea. At the full moon my healing ability is enhanced. I test this by cutting my arm. A cut in the day during a new moon takes twice as long to heal as a similar cut at night under a full moon.

The days go by and I learn a lot, but I know that I can't share what I've learned, not even with Arran. Everything that is Black has to be kept secret, and I know my body is that of a Black Witch.

Mary

I spend over a month in Wales. I feel good learning about my body, but I'm also self-conscious. I have this idea that somehow my father is watching me. He sees everything I do. He nods his head wisely at the discoveries I make about my body, smiles approvingly when I catch a rabbit, skin and cook it, but he shakes his head at the bad decisions I make, when I end up cold in a poor shelter or cross a stream in a bad place. Everything I do is with an awareness of him judging me, and every day I think that maybe he will appear.

Of course my father never comes. I sometimes wonder if it's because I'm half White, not Black enough. But then I tell myself that these aren't real tests; the true test will be that I can find my way to him, and I'm ready to do that now.

My fifteenth birthday is three weeks away; I don't want to risk going to another assessment. I am sure that the Council will see what is happening to my body, that I'm changing, and my Designation Code won't be *Not ascertained* any more. Nobody has told me what will happen if I am designated as a Black Witch, but as all Black Witches in Britain are captured or killed on sight, I've got a good idea.

I have to leave. But first I have to see Arran. It's his seventeenth birthday in a week's time, and I want to be with him for his Giving. After that I will go in search of my father.

On my first morning at home Deborah passes me an envelope that arrived a couple of weeks earlier. It's addressed to me. I have never received anything through the post before. Notifications are always sent to Gran. I expect some new Council decree, but inside is a thick, white card on which is beautifully scripted writing.

I pass it to Arran.

"Who's Mary Walker?" he asks.

I shrug.

"It's her ninetieth birthday. You're invited to her birthday party."

"Never heard of her," I say.

"Do you know her, Gran?" Arran asks.

Gran is frowning but she nods cautiously.

"And?"

"She's an old witch."

"Well, I think we worked that out for ourselves," Arran says.

"She's . . . I . . . I haven't seen or heard from her in years."

"Since?"

"Since I was young. She used to work for the Council but she went a bit . . . odd."

"Odd?"

"Unusual."

"She's mad, you mean."

"Well . . . she went a bit strange, making accusations left and right. Only dangerous to herself at first, but then it was clear she was mad. Apparently she would dance around in meetings or sing love songs to the Council Leader. She left the Council in disgrace. There wasn't much sympathy for her."

"Why would she invite Nathan to her birthday party?"

Gran doesn't answer. She reads the invitation and then busies herself making more tea.

"You going to go, then?" Arran asks.

Gran holds the teapot, ready to fill it. I say, "She's a mad old witch. No one else in the family has been invited. I don't know her, and I'm not supposed to go anywhere without the Council's permission." I grin for Arran's benefit. "So of course I'm going."

Gran puts the teapot down and doesn't fill it.

The birthday party is four days away. In those four days I learn nothing more about Mary from Gran, whose only concern when I bring up the subject is that I memorize the directions to Mary's home that are written on the reverse of the invitation. There is a tiny map with instructions that give times when I should be at certain points. Gran says that I have to follow the map and the timings precisely.

I set off early on the morning of the party, heading for the railway station in town. I catch a train, followed by another train, then a bus, followed by another bus. The journey is slow—in fact I could catch two earlier buses—

but the instructions are clear, and I stick to them.

Then I have a long walk. I make my way to the points in the woods that are shown on the map and wait for the allotted times to pass before moving on to the next place. The woods are more forest than woods and the farther I go the quieter it becomes. As I wait for the final leg of the journey I realize that there are no noises in my head, and all around me it is beautifully silent. I almost miss the time to leave as I'm trying to work out what noises aren't there any more. But I keep to the schedule and eventually come to a ramshackle cottage in a small clearing.

There's a vegetable patch to the left side of the cottage, a brook to its right, and some hens pecking around in front of it. I skirt around to the right and scoop up some water to drink. It's sweet and clear. I don't have to change my stride to step over the clear running water. I make a circuit of the cottage, which is so rundown that it is actually falling down at the back and I can see into a bedroom where a chicken is pecking around. I carry on around to the small, green front door and knock lightly in case the rotten wood gives way.

"It'd be a waste to be indoors on a day like this."

I turn.

The strong, loud voice doesn't seem to fit the stooped old witch with a floppy, big-brimmed hat, baggy, holey wool jumper, baggy, holey jeans, and baggy, muddy wellington boots.

"Mary?" I'm not sure; the person in front of me, with a wispy white mustache, could be a man.

"No need to ask who you are." The voice is definitely female.

"Umm. Happy birthday." I hold the basket of presents out toward her but she makes no move to take them.

"Presents. For you."

She still says nothing.

I lower the basket.

She makes a noise that is a cackle or maybe a cough, sending saliva dribbling down her chin, which she wipes away with her sleeve.

"You never met an old witch before?"

"Not many . . . well, not . . ."

My mumbling tails off as she peers closer at me.

She is bent almost double and has to lean back and turn sideways to look up at me. "Maybe you're not so much like your father as I first thought. You certainly look like him, though."

"You know him . . . I mean . . . you've met him?"

She ignores my question and now takes the basket from me, saying, "For me? Presents?"

It's as if her hearing isn't too good, but I think she can hear fine.

She walks to the brook and sits on a patch of thin grass. I sit beside her as she pulls a jam jar out of the basket. "Is it plum?"

"Apple and bramble. From our garden. My gran made it."

"That old bitch."

My jaw drops.

"And this?" She holds up a large earthenware tub, sealed with wax and tied with ribbon.

"Umm . . . a potion to soothe aching joints."

"Huh!" She sets the tub on the grass, saying, "She was always good at potions, though. I take it she still has a strong Gift?"

"Yes."

"Nice basket too. You can never have too many baskets, I've found." She studies the basket, turning it round. "If you learn nothing else today, at least remember that."

I nod stupidly and again stumble out my question: "Have you met Marcus?"

She ignores me and pulls out the final present, a rolled-up piece of paper tied with a thin strip of leather, which she slides off and puts into the basket, saying, "And a leather shoelace too. I am doing well, aren't I? Not had a birthday like this for . . . for oh so long."

Mary unrolls the paper, a pen drawing that I made of trees and squirrels. She studies it for some time before saying, "I believe your father likes to draw. He has a talent for it, as have you."

Has he? How does she know this?

"It's polite to say thank you when someone pays you a compliment."

I mumble, "Thank you."

Mary smiles. "Good boy. Now, let's get tea and some cake . . . ninety candles will be interesting."

*   *   *

Much later we are sitting on the grass in silence with a picnic of tea and cake. The candles, ninety of them, counted out slowly by Mary, were placed on a small cherry cake by me, although I don't know how they all fitted on. The candles were lit with a muttered spell at the snap of Mary's fingers. Her spittle-laden blow wasn't powerful enough to put out the candles so I smothered the flames in a tea towel. During all that I learned nothing from Mary apart from the ingredients of the cake, where she kept her candles, and how she wished someone would come up with a spell that kept slugs off her vegetable garden.

Now I ask her why she has invited me to her birthday party.

She says, "Well, I didn't want to spend it on my own, did I?"

"So why didn't you invite my gran?"

Mary slurps some cold tea from her teacup and lets out a resonating belch.

"I invited you because I wanted to talk to you, and I didn't invite your gran because I didn't want to talk to her." She belches again. "Oh, that cake was good."

"What do you want to talk about?"

"The Council and your father. Though I don't know much about your father. But I do know about the Council. I used to work for them."

"Gran told me."

Silence.

"What do you know about the Council, Nathan?"

I shrug. "I have to go for assessments and follow their notifications."

"Tell me about those."

I stick to the facts.

Mary doesn't ask any questions while I speak, but she nods and dribbles occasionally.

"I think they'll kill me if I go to the next assessment."

"Maybe . . . but I think not. There's a reason they haven't so far. And it's not because they're feeling kind and generous, you can be sure of that."

"Do you know the reason?"

"I have an idea what it may be." She wipes her mouth with her sleeve and then pats my arm, saying, "You will have to leave soon."

The sun was behind the trees now. "Yes. It's late."

She grabs my arm in a tight clawlike grip. "No, not leave here. You must leave your home soon. Find Mercury. She will help you. She will give you three gifts."

"But my father . . ."

"You mustn't try to find your father. Mercury will help you. She helps many witches who are in trouble. Of course she will expect some payment in return. But she will help you."

"Who is Mercury?"

"A Black Witch. An old Black Witch. Ha! You think *I'm* old. *She* is old. Her Gift is strong, though, very strong. She can control the weather."

"But how can she give me blood? She's not my parent or grandparent."

"No, but she is a very astute businesswoman. Ironically, the Council is the source of Mercury's success. You see, they decided years ago to keep a bank of blood of all White Witches, so that if a child should be orphaned the Council would be able to step in and arrange the Giving ceremony."

"And it worked?"

"Yes, perfectly. The spell is modified, I believe, but the blood is of the parent or grandparent and three gifts are given."

"Let me guess . . . Mercury stole some of the blood." And so she must have some of my mother's.

"Well, it isn't hard to guess that. Any fool could have told the Council that this was bound to happen, and many did. And while they were warning the Council, and the Council was assuring everyone that the blood was secure, Mercury was stealing parts of the store. Never whole bottles, just enough to ensure that if any whet fell into bad books with their parents or the Council they could run to Mercury for help.

"There are many potions requiring witches' blood. White Witches go to Mercury when they can't get help within their own community. Black Witches go to her when they need White Witch blood for a potion. Mercury does not help people for free, but she doesn't get paid in cash; she gets paid in kind. She exchanges the blood for potions, spells, rare ingredients, magical items . . . You get the idea. She has learned how to make potions and cast spells even though that is not her Gift. She has access to strong magic, and she has grown into a very powerful witch."

"And how do I find her?"

"Oh, I don't know where she is. Not many people do. But there are a few White Witches who don't agree with the Council's methods or for some reason or other have fallen out with them. Mercury uses such people. And one of them I do know."

"And I can trust this person?"

"Yes, you can trust Bob. He has his own reasons for despising the Council. He's a good friend."

We're silent. I think I can trust Mary, but Mercury doesn't sound like a good solution to my problems. And I want to see my father.

I say, "But I think my father—"

Mary interrupts, "Yes, let's talk about your father. Of course, I don't know him at all well, and your gran knows him better than I do."

I'm not sure that I heard that right.

"I take it from that look on your face that she's never mentioned that."

"No! How does Gran know Marcus?"

"We'll come to that shortly. First tell me what you know about your father."

My head is spinning. *Gran knows Marcus*. That means . . .

Mary prods me on the arm. "Tell me what you know about Marcus. We'll get back to your gran soon enough."

I hesitate. Gran said never to talk about Marcus, and

she never talked about him. But all the time she's kept this secret from me. . . .

I say it loud and clear. "Marcus is my father. One of the few Black Witches left in England."

I was always afraid to talk about him because the Council might be listening, but now it feels like *he* is listening.

And then I'm angry at him, and angry at Gran, and I say, "He's powerful and ruthless. He kills White Witches and takes their Gifts. He mainly kills members of the Council, and Hunters too, and their families. His Gift, the one he didn't steal from other witches, is that he can turn—transform—into animals. This means he can eat the hearts of witches whose Gifts he wants. He becomes a lion, or something like that, eats their beating hearts and steals their Gifts."

I'm breathing heavily.

"His mother was Saba; she was killed by Clay. Saba killed Clay's mother, Virginia. Saba struggled with being indoors at night. So do I. And I guess Marcus is the same.

"I'm good at drawing, and Marcus is too. I'm rubbish at reading, and I guess that's one of the few things Marcus is bad at. I have weird noises in my head, and I bet that runs in the family as well.

"Marcus hates White Witches. I'm not fond of most of them either. But I don't go around killing them!" I shout that last bit at the treetops.

"He leaves no survivors. He kills women, children, everyone, except he didn't kill my mother. He would probably have killed Jessica, Deborah, and Arran, but they were with my gran the night he attacked my mother. He killed their father."

Silence.

I look at Mary and speak quietly now. "He didn't kill my mother. He didn't kill Gran either, though you say they've met. You say Gran knew him better than you did, so I guess they met more than once . . ."

Mary nods.

"So Marcus knew my mother. And Mother didn't hate him . . . or fear him, or despise him?"

"I don't believe so."

I hesitate. "But they couldn't be . . . friends . . . or lovers . . . That would be . . ."

"Unacceptable," Mary says.

"If they were, they would have to keep it secret. . . . Though my Gran found out?"

"Or knew from the start."

"But either way it wouldn't make any difference; Gran couldn't do anything except try to keep it secret too."

"That was the best way, the only way, in which she could protect your mother. I admit she did well, considering. I believe your mother and father met once a year."

"So, Marcus and my mother . . . they wanted to see each other . . . they arranged to meet, sent the kids to Gran's . . . but the husband turned up unexpectedly . . . and Marcus killed him."

Mary is nodding to each one of my statements.

"But my mother killed herself because of the guilt. . . ." I sense Mary is shaking her head.

"Because she couldn't be with Marcus?"

Mary is still shaking her head.

I hold my gaze away from her, eventually saying what I have always known. "Because of me?"

Mary's hand is on my arm and I turn to look at her pale eyes, watery with age. "Not in the way you think."

"How many ways can there be?"

"I suspect she hoped that you would look like her, like her other children. You didn't. It was clear once you were born that your father was Marcus."

So it was because of me.

Mary pushes me on. "What would the Council want your mother to do?"

I remember Jessica's story and the card she said had been sent to Mother. I say, "Kill me."

"No. I don't think the Council has ever wanted that. But your mother was a White Witch; she loved a Black Witch and had his child. And, because of her relationship, her husband—a White Witch, a member of the Council—was killed."

The truth leaves me hollow. They would want her to kill herself. They made her do it.

Two Weapons

•·:·•·˙

The next morning Mary makes porridge. She sucks hers up slowly, making disgusting noises. I haven't slept, and the slurping sets me on edge.

Between spoonfuls she says, "Your gran has done the best she can with you."

I scowl at her. "My gran has lied to me."

"When?"

"When she didn't tell me that she had met Marcus, that she knew Marcus. When she didn't deny that my mother was attacked by him. When she didn't tell me that the Council was responsible for my mother's death."

Mary pokes me with her spoon. "If the Council ever found out where I was and what I'd helped you discover, what do you think they'd do to me?"

I look away.

"Well?"

"Are you trying to tell me that they would have killed Gran?"

"And will do."

I know she's right, of course, but that doesn't make me feel any better.

Mary gives me a string of chores to "help me get out of my morning grouchiness."

As she supervises my scraping out of the chicken house, I say, "Gran told me that you left the Council in disgrace."

"Well, I suppose that's one way of describing it."

"How would you describe it?"

"A lucky escape. Finish that and close it all back up. Then make some tea and I'll tell you."

I boil water on the stove in the cottage and Mary sits outside in the sun. When I bring the tea she pats the grass beside her. We lean back against the wall of the cottage.

"Remember, Nathan, the Council is dangerous. They will not allow anyone to show the slightest weakness toward Black Witches. I was foolish enough to once voice a concern I had. I worked as a secretary for the Council. My job was to keep the records. They have many files and I kept them well, but one day when I was tidying up I had a few minutes of free time and I decided to read one. It described the Retribution delivered to a Black Witch. It was horrific.

"I stupidly told one of the Council members that the Retribution was terrible. This was not a problem. Retribution is terrible, it's supposed to be, and if I had stopped there nothing would have happened. But I didn't. It bothered me greatly. I couldn't sleep. I had always known about Retribution but somehow I hadn't realized how much suffering was inflicted. A month of torture before they let the witch die. I worked for the Council because I believed White Witches were good, superior, and I was now faced with the fact that they were as bad as Black Witches, as bad as fains, as bad as them all.

"There was a Black Witch in the cells and I knew what they would be doing to him.

"It was stupid to even try to help him. He would never be able to escape. But I was full of righteous anger. And so I did what I could.

"I pretended that I was mad with hate at the Black Witch. He had killed the family of one of the Council Members so it wasn't hard, though in truth they were a stuck-up snotty bunch who always treated me like muck."

She slurps her tea.

"I made an excuse to get into the cells. I didn't really have a plan, I had no weapon, but by the door was a table and on that were knives and . . . other things. Instruments of torture, I suppose you'd call them. I picked up a knife and started screaming and shouting and pretending to attack the prisoner. It was pointless as an attack. There was no possibility that I could have killed him. But in the struggle with the guard I made sure that the knife landed within the reach of the witch who was chained in the cell. He stabbed himself in the heart within a second of picking it up."

Mary put her teacup down.

"I pretended that I was mad. I got off. But there were doubts. Some thought I was faking it. So now I try to . . . Oh, what's that phrase? Stay off-grid."

"Wow."

"Yes, I'm often surprised at what I did. But I don't regret it. I saved that man from weeks of torture."

"Who was he?"

"Ah, a good question at last."

She puts her hand gently on my arm.

"He was Massimo. He was Marcus's grandfather."

Later that morning Mary makes me memorize the instructions for my departure. They are similar to the ones for my arrival.

"Is this a spell to ensure that I'm not followed?"

"One of my specialties and, though I say so myself, quite tricky to accomplish well. Most witches don't have the patience for it. You have to take time over each step. And, if you do, even Hunters can't track you."

"Hunters would follow me here, I suppose."

"Hunters follow you everywhere, Nathan, and always have. Apart from your journey here. And your journey away from here, *if* you follow the instructions."

"They always follow me?"

"They're Hunters, Nathan. The clue is in the name. And they're very good."

I nod. "Yeah, I know."

"No, I don't think you do. Never underestimate the enemy, Nathan. Never. Hunters follow you everywhere and could kill you at any time. They want to, Nathan. But they work for the Council and the Council manages to keep them in check, just."

"So I should be grateful to them?"

Mary shakes her head. "The Council is more dangerous than the Hunters, remember that too. They use the Hunters. They use everything they can."

I'm not sure what she means by "everything." I say, "Gran has told me they use spies."

"Yes, spying is one of their favorite methods. Trust no one, Nathan. Not friends, not even family. If they're White then the Council will use them as spies if they can. And they usually can.

"The Council and Hunters are united in one aim: they want Marcus dead. And all his bloodline too."

"Yesterday you said that you thought the Council has never wanted to kill me."

"Not yet. At the moment they think that you are more use to them alive."

"So they want to use me to trap Marcus?"

"I'm sure they have considered it, probably tried it. But there's more than that. Don't go to any more assessments. Find Mercury. She will hide you until your Giving. Go as soon as you can."

I nod again, but I can tell she is building up to tell me one last thing. But she goes quiet again.

I say, "There's something else I've remembered about Marcus. A few years ago there was an attack on a family of White Witches, the Greys. Marcus killed them. But I think he was trying to get something that they had. Something called the Fairborn. Do you know what that is?"

Mary nods. "Yes, I do. It's a knife."

"Why would Marcus want it?"

"It's a special knife. A vicious thing. Fairborn is the name of the man who made it, over a hundred years ago, I believe. He engraved his name on the blade. I came to know the knife very well during the investigation that the Council made into my attack in the cells: it's the same knife that I threw to Massimo. It was Massimo's knife."

"I see why Marcus would want it back."

"No. I don't think you do, Nathan."

Mary rubs her forehead with the back of her hand and sighs.

"Marcus visited me a few weeks ago. He came to ask me a favor. He sees glimpses of the future . . . possible futures. I think it's a burden more than a Gift. He told me one of his visions, one that he first had many years ago and still sees today. He wanted me to tell you about it. He thought if you knew, you might understand him better."

"He has a message for me! And you've waited till I'm leaving to tell me?"

"If it was up to me I wouldn't tell you at all. You must understand, Nathan, this is a vision. A *possible* future. It is only that. But the more store you set in visions the more they have a habit of coming true."

"Do you have any idea how much I want to hear from him?" I walk away from her and then back again, leaning close to her face. "Tell me."

"Nathan, there are many White Witches who see visions of the future. If Marcus has seen this vision, you can be sure that the Council will know of it too. Marcus wants you to understand him but also understand the Council."

"Are you going to tell me?"

"There are two weapons that together will kill your father. Both are protected by the Council, until they are ready to be used."

"What are they?"

"The first is the Fairborn."

"And?"

"The other weapon is—"

But then I don't want to hear it. I know what she is going to say, and there is a sound in my head like thunder and animal growling and I want it to stay, grow louder, because this message is not the message I have been waiting for. It has to be wrong. Mary is saying it, but maybe I haven't heard it right with this noise in my skull. And if the noise carries on I won't have—

"Nathan! Are you listening?"

I shake my head. "I won't kill him."

"That is why you must leave. If you stay any longer with White Witches, the Council will make you do it. You are the second weapon."

The Sixth Notification

It's just one possible future.

That's the mantra I repeat to myself. There are millions, billions, of possible futures.

And I won't kill him. I know that. He's my father.

I won't kill him.

And I want to see him. I want to tell him. But he believes the vision. He won't want to see me. Ever.

And if I try to see him he'll think I want to kill him. He'll kill me.

Mary has given me the address of Bob, her friend who will help me find Mercury. She says that I should leave immediately and I tell her that I will, though I'm just saying words. I don't know what I will do.

I head home.

I want to talk to Gran. I need to ask her about Marcus. She has to tell me something. And Arran's Giving is now only a day away. I want to be with him for that and then I'll leave.

I arrive in the evening. It's still light. Gran is in the kitchen making a cake for after the Giving ceremony. She doesn't ask about Mary's party.

I don't say "hello" or "missed you" or "how's the cake coming on?" I say, "How many times have you met Marcus?"

She stops what she's doing and glances at the kitchen door saying, "Jessica's come home for Arran's Giving."

I move close to Gran and say quietly, "He's my father. I want to know about him."

Gran shakes her head. She tries to persuade me that she'll tell me tomorrow but I threaten to shout for Jessica to come and hear the story too. Even though Gran must know I'd never do that, she slumps down in the chair and, in a voice that's only a murmur, she tells me all she knows about Marcus and my mother.

In our bedroom I open the window. It's dark now and a thin sliver of moon is rising. Arran gets out of bed and hugs me. I hug him back for a long time. Then we sit on the floor by the window.

Arran asks, "How was the birthday party?"

"I don't know what you're talking about."

"Can you tell me anything?"

"You tell me about tomorrow. How are you feeling?"

"Fine. A bit nervous. I hope I don't mess it up."

"You won't."

"Jessica's come back for the ceremony."

"Gran told me."

"Will you come?"

I can't even shake my head.

He says, "It's okay."

"I wanted to."

"I'd rather you were here now. This is better."

Arran and I talk for a bit, reminiscing about the films that we watched together, and eventually talking more about his Giving. I say I think his Gift will be healing, like our mother's. She had a strong Gift, and she was exceptionally kind and gentle; Gran has told me that. I think Arran will be like her. He thinks it will be a weak Gift, whatever it is, but he doesn't mind, and I know he's being honest.

Much later he goes to bed and I draw a picture for him. It's of him and me playing in the woods.

I sit on the floor through most of the night, my head by the open window, watching Arran sleep. I know that I can't stay for the Giving, not if Jessica will be there. And I can't tell Arran where I'm going. I can't even tell him good-bye.

I'm still trying to make sense of my mother and father's relationship, and why Gran hid it from me, but in the end it's easier not to think about it at all.

It's still dark when I leave. Arran is sprawled across his bed, one foot over the side. I kiss my fingertips and touch them to his forehead, put the picture on his pillow, and scoop up my rucksack.

In the hall I switch on the table lamp and pick up the photo of my mother. She looks different to me now. Perhaps her husband loved her—he looks happy enough—but she looks sad, trying to smile but squinting instead.

I put the photo down and walk quickly through the kitchen.

As soon as I'm outside I feel the relief of fresh air. I take a step, two at most, before I hear the hiss of mobile phones rushing at me. Two black figures appear and their hands are on my arms and shoulders, turning me and slamming me into the house wall. I struggle and am pulled away from the wall and slammed into it again. My wrists are cuffed behind my back and I am pulled away from the wall and slammed into it again.

I'm back in the assessment room. My restraints had been removed after the journey down, which was in the back of a car with a Hunter either side of me. I gathered from their conversation that Gran was in another car that was following behind.

I think about Arran's Giving ceremony. Gran will not be there, and I realize Jessica came back not to attend the ceremony but to conduct it. The Council will have given her the blood. Arran will hate it. And that's all part of it too. They love to twist the knife.

I stand before the three Council members. The Council Leader speaks first. "You have been brought here today to answer some serious questions."

I make an effort to look wide-eyed and innocent.

The woman to the right of the Council Leader gets up from her chair and slowly walks around the table to stand in front of me. She's shorter than I expected. She's not in the white robe that Council members normally wear for my assessments; she's wearing a gray pinstriped suit with a white blouse underneath. Her high heels click sharply on the stone floor.

"Pull up your sleeve."

I'm wearing a shirt over a T-shirt, and the cuffs are undone as the buttons have been lost long ago. I raise the arm of my left sleeve.

"And the other one," the woman says. Now that she is close to me I can see that her eyes are dark brown, as dark as her skin, but they contain silver shards that spiral slowly, almost fading and then reappearing brightly.

"Let me see your arm," she insists.

I do as she says. The inside of my arm is marked by a series of faint thin scars, twenty-eight of them, one for each day that I had tested my healing ability.

The woman takes my wrist between her forefinger and thumb, gripping hard and raising my arm so that it's directly in front of her eyes. She holds it there and I can feel her breath on my skin, then she lets me go and walks back to her seat. She says, "Show your arm to the other Council members."

I step forward and hold my arm out over the table.

Annalise's uncle, Soul O'Brien, hardly gives it a glance. His hair is slicked back in a yellow-white sheen. He bends to the Council Leader's ear and whispers.

I wonder if they know about the scars on my back. Probably. Kieran would have bragged about what he'd done.

"Step back from the table now," Soul says.

I do as I'm told.

"Can you heal cuts?" he asks.

Denial seems ridiculous but I never want to admit to anything here.

He repeats his question and I stand silently.

"You must answer our questions."

"Why?"

"Because we are the Council of White Witches."

I stare at him.

"Can you heal cuts?"

I carry on with the staring.

"Where have you been for the last two days?"

I don't take my eyes off him but I answer this one. "I was in the woods near our house. I camped out for the night."

"It is a serious offence to lie to the Council."

"I'm not lying."

"You were not in the woods. You were not in any area that the Council has given you approval to be."

I try to look innocently surprised.

"In fact, we could not find you anywhere at all."

"You're mistaken. I was in the local woods."

"No. I am not mistaken. And, as I said before, it is a serious offence to lie to the Council."

I'm still holding his gaze, and I repeat, "I was in the woods."

"No." Soul doesn't sound angry, more bored and unimpressed.

The Council Leader holds her hand up. "Enough."

Soul looks from me to his fingernails and reclines in his chair.

The Council Leader calls to the guard at the back of the room, "Bring Mrs. Ashworth in."

The latch rattles and Gran's footsteps approach slowly. I turn to look at her when she is standing beside me, and I'm shocked to see a small and frightened old woman.

The Council Leader speaks. "Mrs. Ashworth. We have asked you here so that you can answer the accusations leveled against you. Serious accusations. You have failed to comply with notifications of the Council. The notifications clearly state that the Council must be informed if there is any contact between Half Codes and White Witches and White Whets. You failed to do this. You also failed to prevent the Half Code from moving to unauthorized areas of the country."

The Council Leader looks down at her papers and then up again at Gran. "Have you anything to say?"

Gran is silent.

"Mrs. Ashworth. You are the Half Code's guardian and it is your responsibility to ensure that the notifications are followed. You have failed to ensure that the Half Code remained in certified areas and you have failed to inform the Council of meetings between the Half Code and the White Witches Kieran, Niall, Connor, and Annalise O'Brien."

"My grandmother doesn't know about anything. And

I had no intention of meeting Kieran, Niall, and Connor. They attacked me."

"Our understanding is that you attacked them," the Council Leader replies.

"One attacking three. Yeah, right."

"And Annalise? Did you intend to meet her?"

I go back to staring.

"Did you intend to meet Annalise? Or attack her? Or something else?"

I want to kill her with my stare.

The Council Leader turns back to Gran. "Mrs. Ashworth, why did you ignore the notifications?"

"I didn't ignore them. I followed them." Gran's voice is shaky and small.

"No. You did not follow them. You have failed to control the Half Code. Or perhaps you knew of his trips to unauthorized places and decided not to inform the Council of these infringements?"

"I followed the notifications," Gran repeats quietly.

The Council Leader sighs and nods to Annalise's uncle, who pulls out a piece of parchment from under the desk. He reads out times and dates of when I left home, where I went, and when I returned. Every trip to Wales.

I feel sick. I was so sure that I had not been followed. But there is no mention of the trip to see Mary. Her instructions worked, but clearly my disappearance aroused suspicion.

"Do you deny that you made these trips outside authorized areas?" the Council Leader asks.

I don't want to admit anything still, but denying it seems pointless now. "My gran didn't know what I was doing. I told her I was going to the woods, where I am authorized to be."

The woman says, "So you admit you failed to comply with the notifications. You lied to the Council. You deceived your own grandmother, a pure White Witch."

Annalise's uncle says, "Yes, it is clear that he has tried to deceive us all. But it is Mrs. Ashworth's responsibility to ensure compliance with the notifications. And"—he pauses now to look at the Council Leader who inclines her head slightly—"as Mrs. Ashworth has clearly failed to do that, we will have to appoint someone who can."

At that moment a huge woman steps forward from the far corner of the room. I had noticed her before but I thought she was a guard. She comes to stand to the left of the table. Despite her size she moves with grace, and though she stands straight, almost to attention, she has a poise that is strange, as if she's a cross between a dancer and a soldier.

The Council Leader produces another parchment from beneath the table saying, "We agreed to a new resolution yesterday." She reads slowly:

"Notification of the Resolution of the Council of White Witches of England, Scotland, and Wales.

"All Half Codes (W 0.5/B 0.5) are to be educated and supervised at all times only by those White Witches who have the approval of the Council."

"He is educated under my supervision. I am a White Witch. I am teaching him well." Gran's voice is timid. It is almost as if she is talking to herself.

The Council Leader says, "Mrs. Ashworth, it is clear that you have failed to comply with at least two of the notifications of the Council. Punishments have been considered."

Considered? What does that mean? What would they do to her?

"But the Council agrees that we are not here to punish White Witches. We are here to assist and protect them."

The Council Leader starts reading from the parchment she holds. Annalise's uncle is looking bored and studying his fingernails; the woman in the gray suit is looking at the Council Leader.

I can't dodge past the guards behind me, but there is a door in the far wall through which the Council members enter the room.

The Council Leader reads on, but my attention is not on her. ". . . and we realize that the task . . . too onerous. The new notification . . . relieve you of the burden . . . the education and development of a Half Code . . . not to be taken lightly . . . monitored and controlled."

I run for the far door, leaping onto the table between

the Council Leader and the woman in gray. I jump from the table to shouts from the guards and the Council Leader reaches a hand out too late to grab my leg. It is five or six strides to the door and I'm clear of them all. Then the noise hits me.

A high-pitched whirring sound fills my head so suddenly that I'm unable to do anything but clamp my hands over my ears and scream. The pain is excruciating. I am on my knees, staring at the door, unable to move. I scream for the noise to stop, but it carries on to blackness.

Silence.

I'm on the floor, snot running out of my nose, my fingers still in my ears. I must have been unconscious less than a minute. The big guard/dancer woman's black army boots are near my face.

"Get up." Her voice is quiet, soft.

I wipe my nose on the back of my hand and shakily get to my feet.

The woman is wearing green canvas trousers and a heavy army-style camouflage jacket. Her face is so plain that she can only be called ugly. Her skin is pockmarked and lightly tanned. She has a wide mouth and fat lips. Her eyes are blue, with a few small silver glints. She has short, white eyelashes. Her blonde hair is short, spiky, and thin, barely covering her scalp. She is, I guess, about forty years old.

"I'm your new teacher and guardian," she says.

Before I can react she turns from me and nods to the guards, who lift me up by my arms and carry me out of the room. I fight as best I can but my feet don't even touch the ground. Between my struggles and the thick arm and chest of a guard I catch a glimpse of Gran. Tears are in her eyes and her cardigan is off one shoulder as if someone pulled her or held her back. Now she is just standing alone, looking lost.

I'm carried off down the corridors and outside into a paved courtyard where a white van is parked, its rear doors open. I'm thrown inside. Before I can scramble to my feet a knee is in my back pinning me down and my wrists are being handcuffed behind me. Then I'm dragged farther into the van and thick fingers, her fingers, put a collar round my neck. I spit and curse and receive a hard slap on the back of my skull. My head swims. The collar is chained closely to a ring in the van's floor.

Still I struggle and kick and swear and scream.

But the noise hits me again.

This time I can't protect my ears. I scream in panic and kick and fight my way into black silence.

When I come to, the van is moving and I'm being bounced around on its rusting metal floor. The journey goes on and on. I can see the back of the big woman's head. She is driving the van, but there don't seem to be any guards or Hunters with us.

I shout that I need to pee. I think there may be a chance of escape with her alone.

She ignores me.

I shout at her again. "I need to pee." And I really do.

She half turns her head and shouts back, "Then shut up and have one. You'll be cleaning the van tomorrow."

Still she keeps driving. When it gets dark my guts are in turmoil from being inside as well as from the motion of the van. I fight not to throw up but don't manage to hold it off for more than a few minutes.

Because of the collar and chain, my head is resting in my own vomit. She doesn't stop until we arrive at our destination many hours later and by then I'm lying in a brew of my own sick and piss.

PART
THREE

THE SECOND WEAPON

The Choker

You've got to give her credit: she's an ugly witch from Hell, but she's a worker. She's been up all night and most of the day perfecting a new band of acid.

She puts it on. Tight.

"You'll get used to it."

You can squeeze one finger between the band and your neck.

"I'll loosen it if you want."

You blank her.

"You only have to ask."

You can't even gob up, it's so tight.

You're in the kitchen again, sitting at the table. No morning exercises, no breakfast, but you won't be able to eat with this thing on anyway. She can't seriously mean to leave it like this. You can hardly swallow, hardly breathe.

The buzz from healing has gone, like it's been used up. Your hand is swollen and has healed only slightly. It's throbbing. You can feel your pulse in your arm and your neck.

"You're looking tired, Nathan."

You are tired.

"I'm going to clean your hand."

She dips a cloth into a bowl of water and wrings it out.

You pull your hand away but she takes it and strokes the cloth over your wrist. It's cool. It feels good. Taking away some of the burning even for a second is good. She slides the cloth down the back of your hand and then gently turns your hand and cleans the palm. The dirt won't come out but the water feels fresh. She's very gentle.

"Can you move your fingers?"

Your fingers can move a little but your thumb is numb and won't move at all because of the swelling. You don't move anything for her.

She rinses the cloth in the bowl of water, wrings it out, and holds it up.

"I'm going to clean your ear. There's a lot of blood."

She reaches over and wipes round it; again she does it slowly and gently.

You can't hear with your left ear but it's probably just dried blood blocking it up. Your left nostril is blocked too.

She puts the cloth back in the bowl, blood mixing with the water. She wrings the cloth out and reaches out to your face. You lean back.

"I know the choker's tight." She smoothes the cloth across your forehead. "And I know you can stand it." She's dabbing the cloth tenderly over your cheek. "You're tough, Nathan."

You turn away slightly.

She puts the cloth in the bowl again, mud and blood and water mixing together. She wrings the cloth out and hangs it on the side of the bowl.

"I'll loosen it if you ask." She reaches over and brushes your cheek with the back of her fingers. "I want to loosen it. But you have to ask," she says again so quietly and gently.

You pull back and the choker cuts in.

"You're tired, aren't you, Nathan?"

And you're so tired of it all. So tired you could cry. But there's no way you're going to let that happen.

No way.

You just want it to stop.

"All you have to do is ask me to loosen it and I will."

You don't want to cry and you don't want to ask for anything. But you want it to stop.

"Ask me, Nathan."

And the choker is so tight. And you're so tired.

"Ask me."

You've hardly spoken for months. Your voice is croaky, strange. And she wipes away your tears with her fingertips.

The New Trick

•··•·•·

The routine is the same as ever. And so is the cage. And so are the shackles. The choker is still on, loose but there. If I try to leave, I'll die, no doubt about it. I'm not at the point of wanting that just at the moment.

The morning routine is the same. I can do the outer circuit in under thirty minutes now. That's down to practice and the diet, which means I'm a lean, mean running machine. But mainly it's down to the new trick.

The new trick is no easier than the old trick.

The new trick is to stay in the present . . . Get lost in the detail of it . . . Enjoy it!

Enjoy the fine tuning of where I put my fingers when I'm doing push-ups, I mean really finding the finest tuning of where my fingers are in relation to each other, how straight or how bent, and how they feel on the ground, how the sensation changes as I move up and down. I can spend hours thinking about the feeling in my fingers as I do push-ups.

There's so much to enjoy, too much really. Like when I'm running the circuit, I can concentrate on the deepness of my breathing but also the exact dampness of the air and the wind direction, how it changes over the hills and is slowed or speeded up as it's funneled through the narrow valley. My legs carry me effortlessly downhill—that's the bit I love best, where all I've got to do is spot the place to put my foot: on a small patch of grass between the gray stones, or on a flat rock, or on the stream bed. I do the spotting, looking ahead all the time, and move my leg to the right position, but gravity does the hard work. Only it's not just me and gravity; it's the hill as well. It feels as if the earth itself is making sure I don't put a foot wrong. Then the uphill section and my legs are really burning and I've got to find the best foothold and handhold if it's steep, and push and push. I'm doing the hard work and gravity is saying "payback time" and the hillside is saying, "Ignore him, just run." Gravity is heartless. But the hill is my friend.

When I'm in my cage I can memorize the color of the sky, the cloud shapes, their speed and how they change, and I can get up there, be in the clouds in the shapes and colors. I can even get into the mottled colors of the bars of the cage, climb into the cracks beneath the flakes of rust. Roam around in my own bar.

My body's changed. I've grown. I remember my first day in the cage and I could only just reach the bars across the top, had to do a little jump to grab them. Now when I stretch up, my hands and wrists reach freedom. I have to bend my legs to do pull-ups. I'm still not as tall as Celia, but she's a giant.

Celia. I admit she's hard to enjoy, but sometimes I manage it. We talk. She's different from what I expected. I don't think I'm what she expected either.

The Routine

.•.•.•.

Don't get me wrong. This is no holiday camp, but Celia would say it's no gulag either. This is the routine:

GET UP AND GET OUT OF THE CAGE—same as ever, at dawn Celia chucks the keys to me. I asked her once what would happen to me if she died peacefully in her sleep. She said, "I think you'd last a week without water. If it rains you could collect water on the tarpaulin. You'd probably starve rather than die of thirst, given the rain here. I'd say you'd last two months."

I keep a nail hidden in the soil. I can reach it from the cage and I can unlock the shackles with it. I've not managed to undo the padlock to the cage yet but I'd have plenty of time to work on it. But then I'd have to get the collar off. I reckon I'd last a year with the collar on.

MORNING EXERCISES—run, circuit training, gymnastics. Sometimes two runs. This is the best bit of the day. Usually I run barefoot. The mud is part of my feet now.

CLEANING ME, MY CLOTHES, AND MY CAGE—empty my bucket, fill my bucket with water from the stream, wash in stream, wash my shirt or my jeans if it looks like they will dry quickly (I only have one set of clothes), sweep out my cage, oil and clean the cage, locks, and shackles, though most nights she doesn't make me put them on.

BREAKFAST—I make it and I clean up after it. Porridge in winter, porridge in summer. I might be allowed honey or dried fruit.

MORNING CHORES—collect the eggs, clean out the chicken coop, put out chicken feed and water, feed the pigs, clean the kitchen range, chop wood. The ax is chained to a log and Celia always watches while I chop. (One of my first, admittedly not well thought out escape attempts was when I tried to chop away the log holding the chain.)

LUNCH—make lunch, clean up after lunch. I bake bread every other day.

AFTERNOON EXERCISE—self-defense, running, circuit training. I am improving at self-defense but Celia is seriously fast and strong. Basically it's an excuse for her to beat the shit out of me.

AFTERNOON STUDY—reading. Celia reads to me, which sounds sweet but isn't. She asks questions about the things she reads. If my answers aren't good enough I get slapped, and those slaps sting. But at least I don't have to read. Celia tried to teach me, but we came to an agreement to stop that; it was too painful for both of us. She even said, "Sometimes you have to admit defeat," and then slapped me for smirking.

Last week I picked up a book and started to spell out some of the words, but she snatched it out of my hands, saying she might have to kill me if I carried on. Celia has a few books. There are three witch books: one on potions, one about White Witches from the past, and one about Black Witches. She reads them to me and to herself, I guess. The fain books make a bigger pile: a dictionary, an encyclopedia, a few books on bush craft, mountaineering, survival, that sort of thing, and some novels, mostly by Russian writers. I prefer the witch books, but Celia says she is providing a "rounded education," which seems a blatant lie. Sometimes when she's reading these other books Celia doesn't seem like a White Witch; she seems . . . almost human. She is currently reading us a book called *One Day in the Life of Ivan Denisovich*. She loves all these books about the gulags. She says that it shows that even fains can survive in much tougher conditions than I have to cope with. The way she says it makes me wonder if she is planning something harsher.

TEA—make tea, eat, clean up.

INDOOR EVENING WORK—thankfully this is short in winter, as it's soon dark and I have to be outside. But for the time we are together we talk about the day, things I've learned, stuff like that. Celia says she doesn't teach, she talks, and I have to learn by listening and talking back "using my intelligence." After that, if it's still light, I may be allowed to draw.

OUTDOOR EVENING EXERCISE—in winter when it gets dark early this takes most of the late afternoon as well as the evening. I can run fine in the dark. I can't see, but something guides me and I let it and just run. This is the one thing that I don't need a trick to enjoy.

As well as running, we practice combat in the dark. I'm stronger and faster at full moon. If it's full moon Celia can't beat me, as long as I keep out of her reach. A number of times now she has said, "Good work. That'll do for now." I think she might have been struggling a bit.

BEDTIME (CAGETIME)—shackle myself up if she's in a bad mood.

NIGHT—sleep most nights, bad dreams most nights. It's good if I just look at the stars, but it's often cloudy, and I'm usually too knackered.

Lessons about My Father

·•·•·•·

Celia is an ex-Hunter. She won't tell me when she retired or why. All she says is that she's employed by the Council to be my guardian and teacher.

She guards against me escaping and she teaches me about fighting and surviving. We have now moved from unarmed to armed combat, though we are only armed with wooden knives. I asked if we could practice with guns and she said, "Let's see if you can master the knife," like she's some ninja expert, which of course she turns out to be. The pretend knives are all the same unusually long and slender shape. I'm guessing that the Fairborn is like this.

Celia also teaches me about Marcus.

So it all seems to be heading in a certain direction. At first I said nothing, played dumb, but I can't play along any more. I have to make some effort to fight back, and so the other day I tackled it head on.

"I won't kill my dad. You know that, don't you?"

She blanked me.

But I know blank looks and I shook my head. "I won't kill him."

She said, "I've been instructed to tell you these things. I tell you them. I don't question why."

"You teach me to query everything."

"Yes, but some queries won't get answered."

"I won't kill him."

"Let's suppose Marcus has threatened to kill a member of your family: Arran, say. The only way you can save Arran is by killing Marcus."

"Let's suppose something more realistic. The Council threatens a member of my family: Arran, say. The only way I can stop them killing Arran is by killing Marcus."

"And?"

"I won't kill my father."

"All your family. Your grandmother, Deborah, and Arran are being tortured."

"I know the Council would kill them all. They are murderers. I'm not."

Celia raised her eyebrows at that one. "You would kill me to escape here."

I gave her a big smile.

She shook her head. "And if they threatened you? Tortured you?"

"They threaten me constantly. Torture me constantly."

We were silent.

I shrugged. "Besides, I'm not good enough to do it."

"No, you're not."

"Do you think I'll be good enough, one day?"

"Perhaps."

"I'll need my Gift."

"Probably."

"Will the Council give me three gifts?"

Silence. And the blankest of looks. I'd tried that question before and not got anywhere.

"What happens to Black Witches if they don't get three gifts? Do they die?"

"There was one girl I know of, a Black Whet, captured when she was sixteen. She was kept prisoner by the Council, not mistreated. Of course, she wasn't given three gifts. She became ill with a disease of her lungs and also of her mind. She died just before her eighteenth birthday."

Would I be another experiment to see what happens? And what would happen to me?

The lessons about Marcus cover his attacks and his Gifts. There is a huge list of the witches he has killed, where, and when. By *where* I mean what country, town, or city, but also whether it was inside, outside, near water, mountains, streams, cities . . . By *when* I mean dates, but also times of day or night and phases of the moon, weather conditions . . . There are one hundred and ninety-three White Witches on the list and also twenty-seven Black Witches, though the list is probably incomplete for them. Marcus is forty-five years old now, and so in the twenty-eight years since he received his Gift that averages between seven and eight killings a year.

The numbers are dropping off, though; he peaked when he was twenty-eight with thirty-two murders in that year. Perhaps he's getting old, perhaps he's mellowing, or perhaps he's killed most of the ones he wants to.

The Gifts for all these witches are on Celia's list. He hasn't eaten all their hearts, just the ones with Gifts that he wants.

Marcus's Gift, his own original one, is that he can transform into animals. He favors turning into cats, big cats. Most of the evidence is from tracks, a few distant sightings, and the bodies. There aren't a lot of survivor accounts. In fact, there are just two: a young child who hid behind a bookshelf, and my mother. The child didn't see anything but described hearing growling and screaming. My mother said she hid too, said she never saw Marcus, so that's a lie, though the lie only became obvious after I was born, but she never said what really happened, not even to Gran.

The majority of witches Marcus has killed didn't have great Gifts, potion-making mostly, so he wasn't killing those witches for their Gifts. Mostly they were Hunters who were trying to capture him, but there are others, Council members and other White Witches. I guess he had his reasons, but Celia doesn't tell me what they are, even if she knows.

As well as potion-making the Gifts he has stolen are:

+ Breathing fire and sending fire from hands (Arran's father, Council member)

+ Invisibility (Kieran's grandfather, Hunter)

+ Moving objects by thought (Janice Jones, an esteemed

old White Witch who sounds more like a crook to me)

+ Seeing the future (Emerald, a Black Witch. I wonder if she saw that coming?)

+ Disguising himself as any human being, male or female (Josie Bach, Hunter)

+ Flying (Malcolm, a Black Witch from New York— this ability is questionable, though it seems he can make very big leaps)

+ Making plants grow or die (Sara Adams, Council member—does he like gardening?)

+ Sending electricity from his body (Felicity Lamb, Hunter)

+ Healing others (Dorothy Moss, Secretary to the Council Leader)

+ Bending and contorting metal objects (Suzanne Porter, Hunter)

And weirdest of all:

+ Slowing time (Kurt Kurtain, Black Witch)

I ask about Marcus and his ancestors. Celia has told me the names of the male line. It's an illustrious list of powerful

Black Witches. They all had the same Gift, the turning-into-animals one. Still, I wonder about my Gift. Will being half White change things?

And although Marcus is no longer a taboo subject that doesn't mean I'm allowed to know everything about him. Most of my questions are answered by a simple "That's not relevant."

I have asked about:

The female line of Marcus's ancestors. Not relevant.

Where Marcus was born and brought up. Not relevant.

How Marcus knew my mother. Slap.

I know how Marcus knew my mother, though, and more, since after I returned from Mary's, Gran told me what happened. And I wonder if Celia actually does know anything of the truth of that or any of my other questions.

One day Celia asks, "How do you think I control my Gift?"

I'm not in the mood. I've had to kill, pluck, and gut a chicken today. I shrug.

Next thing I'm on the kitchen floor clutching at my ears. She doesn't often use her Gift on me; usually it's just slaps.

The noise stops abruptly and I get to my feet, using the range to pull myself up. I've got blood running out of my nose.

"How do I control my Gift?"

I wipe my nose on the back of my hand and say, "You think about it and—"

And I'm on the floor again.

The noise shuts off and I'm looking at the floorboards. The floorboards and I are old friends. I look to them for the answer. They are never much good at stuff like that, though.

I get to my knees.

"Well?"

I shrug again. "You just do it."

"Yes." She slaps me across the top of my head. "Like hitting. I know I want to do it, where and to whom, and it's almost a reflex. I just do it. I don't have to think about raising my arm and moving my hand." She gives me another slap.

I get to my feet, moving a step away as I do.

"How does Marcus control all his Gifts? The ones he stole?" she asks.

"Can he control them all?"

Celia gives me a nod for that. "There is some evidence that he uses the lightning and moves objects, leaps . . ."

"Some people can play lots of musical instruments. They just pick up the instrument and play. I guess they have to practice to become expert, though."

Celia says, "But there is always one that they favor?"

"I don't even have my Gift, how would—"

Those slaps really sting.

Celia is also teaching me about the history of witches. I don't know how much to believe—I often wonder how much I should believe of *anything* she tells me. Anyway, according to Celia, hundreds and thousands of years ago, when the world was not split into countries but was inhabited by different tribes, each tribe had a healer: a shaman. Few of the healers had real power, but one called Geeta was special: powerful, good, and kind. She healed the sick and wounded in her tribe but also people from other tribes.

This didn't go down well with the tribe leader, Aster, who ruled that no one outside the tribe was to see Geeta without his permission. He kept her a virtual prisoner in the village. Geeta wanted to help everyone, so she escaped with the assistance of one of her patients, Callor, a wounded warrior from her tribe.

Callor and Geeta lived in a remote cave. Geeta healed those who came to her. Callor hunted and protected Geeta. They were in love and had children: twins, two identical girls, Dawn and Eve. Geeta trained them both in witchcraft, gave them both three gifts and her blood on their seventeenth birthday. They would become great witches.

The old leader from Geeta's tribe, Aster, was ill and he sent a message requesting Geeta to return and heal him. Although Geeta wanted to help, as she helped everyone, Callor didn't trust Aster and he persuaded Geeta to send their daughter Eve, the younger of the twins, rather than go herself. But instead of healing Aster, Eve, the hateful vicious twin, put a curse on him and fled. Aster died after a month of agony. Aster's son, Ash, took revenge by killing Callor and capturing Geeta and Dawn.

The story goes that Dawn, the compassionate twin, fell in love with Ash and they had a daughter. This daughter was the first of the White Witches.

Eve roamed from tribe to tribe. She also had a daughter, who became the first of the Black Witches.

I asked Celia, "Do you believe that story?"

"It's our history."

"History according to White Witches."

Today Blacks mock White Witches for living closely within fain communities, for pretending to be fains. They see White Witches as becoming weaker, more fainlike, needing guns to kill, using phones to communicate.

And Whites hate Black Witches for their anarchy and lunacy. They don't integrate within fain communities but don't have a community of their own. Their marriages never last, often ending in abrupt violence. They usually live alone, hate fains and fain technology. Their Gifts are strong.

Celia won't talk about the female line of my Black ancestors but she has told me the names of the male line. It's an illustrious and yet depressing list. Each one was a powerful Black Witch and none of them died quietly in his sleep at a ripe old age. My great-grandfather Massimo committed suicide, so you could argue that he wasn't killed by White Witches, but there is a clear trend in that direction:

- Axel Edge (Marcus's father)—died in the cells of the Council under Retribution

- Massimo Edge (Axel's father)—committed suicide in the cells of the Council

- Maximilian Edge (Massimo's father)—died in the cells of the Council under Retribution

- Castor Edge (Maximilian's father)—died in the cells of the Council under Retribution

- Leo Edge (Castor's father)—died in the cells of the Council under Retribution

- Darius Edge (Leo's father)—died in the cells of the Council under Retribution

Celia says that the name of Darius's father is less clear, as this was around the time the Council of White Witches became a formal organization, and records before this time are poor. But from stories a few more generations can be added with reasonable certainty, which are:

- Gaunt Edge (Darius's father)—killed by Hunters in Wales

- Titus Edge (Gaunt's father)—killed by Hunters in woodland somewhere in Britain

- Harrow Edge (Titus's father)—killed by Hunters somewhere in Europe

I asked Celia, "Did any of my ancestors live a long and happy life?"

"Some of them lived to their fifties. I don't know how happy they were."

So it's no wonder my father is a little cautious. And I think of my ancestors and all their pain and suffering, and I still don't understand why. I just don't understand. I am kept in a cage, and none of it makes sense. I don't want to live in a cage and I don't want to die in a cell and I don't want to be tortured and I don't want to kill my father. I don't want any of it, but it just goes on and on and on.

I wonder, if I ever have a son what the future will hold for him. Maybe I'd do what Marcus has done, just leave him and hope that somehow he will have a better future without me. And yet here I am shackled up in a cage and I know it's hopeless and hopeless and hopeless.

But even with all that suffering and pain and cruelty I think that maybe my ancestors did find happiness, even for a brief time. I think I'm capable of that, and they must have been too. I hope so. I hope so. I hope so. 'Cause if I'm going to die in a cell I want to have something first. And I think of Arran and Annalise and being in Wales and running and every breath, every breath has to be precious and worth it and something important.

Fantasies about My Father

·•·•·•

The routine keeps me busy and tired, but there are still times when I'm in the cage and I'm not in the mood for going into clouds or doing more pull-ups, so I just think.

I still like to imagine my dad coming to rescue me on my seventeenth birthday. I'm lying here in the cage all shackled up and there's this silence, and then a distant sound—not wind, not thunder but his anger and rage. He appears over the hills to the west and he's flying, not on a broomstick or a horse but standing as if on a surfboard, though there's no surfboard or it's invisible, and he's flying toward me, dressed in black. And the noise gets bigger, the cage just explodes apart, and my shackles fall off. He zooms around and slows down, and I jump onto my own invisible surf-board and I'm flying off with him. It's the best feeling in the world to be with my dad and flying and leaving the broken cage behind forever.

We go to the mountains where he lives and it's lush and green, almost tropical. There, among the old trees and moss-covered stones, beside the clear stream, we sit and I am there with my father and he gives me three gifts—a knife, a ring, and a drawing—and I drink his blood warm from his hand and he whispers the secret words in my ear and we stay together forever, hunting and fishing and living in the woods.

That one's my main fantasy, I guess: the one I always go back to.

I have other fantasies as well. Annalise features in most of them, and there's lots of skin and sweat and kissing and tongues. Mostly I imagine I'm with her on the sandstone slab; she's in her school uniform, Kieran has never found us, and I kiss her and undress her, sort of slow but nice, unbutton her blouse and her skirt and kiss her skin all over.

My other fantasy is pretty similar: Annalise and I are on the sandstone slab and she undresses me, pulls my T-shirt off, unbuttons my jeans, and kisses my chest, my stomach, my skin all over.

Then there are variations: she is undressing me on a hillside in Wales; she is undressing me on a beach; she is undressing me in the sunshine, in moonlight, in a rain shower, in mud and puddles.

In those fantasies I don't have any scars.

The most recent variation is that I am in my cage and I blast it apart just by thinking about it, then Annalise appears and we kiss and I undress her and kiss her all over and she undresses me and kisses my chest and my stomach and my back. I have all my scars but she doesn't mind and we make love on my sheepskins surrounded by the broken bits of cage.

That's a good one. I like it that she doesn't mind my

scars. I don't think she'd like them really, but maybe she wouldn't mind them too much.

And then there's the fantasy that I don't like to use too often, but I sometimes can't help myself. In it I'm living in a cottage in a beautiful valley by a shallow, fast-flowing river that's so clean and clear it sparkles even at night. The hills are covered with green trees that are almost humming with life, the forest is full of birds and animals. And my mum and dad are alive and living in the cottage and I live with them. Mostly I spend time with my dad, and we don't sleep there in the cottage, we sleep in the forest and hunt and fish together. But we also spend time with Mum; she keeps chickens and grows vegetables. And summers are hot and sunny, and winters are cold and snowy, and we live together forever. My mum and dad grow old and are happy, and I stay with them and every day is beautiful forever.

Thoughts about My Mother

•··•·•·

When I got back from Mary's, Gran told me that Marcus and my mother were in love. But my mother knew it was wrong to love a Black Witch. She felt guilty about it. She married Dean and had his children and tried to be happy, but basically from the moment she met Marcus she was in love with him.

I wonder if she still loved Marcus after he killed her husband, the father of her children.

I guess when Dean found Marcus and my mother together there would have been a bit of a fight. Dean's Gift was the ability to send flames from his hands and mouth, though it didn't do him much good in the end, as Marcus must have fancied having that ability and he took Dean's Gift.

When did the flames stop? Did they curl out with his last breath?

And where was my mother while all this was going on? Was she there? Watching my father eat the living heart of her husband?

And was it easy to kill herself, knowing that she'd loved someone who could do that? She loved someone who killed men, women, and children, who killed the father of her children. She loved someone who ate people. And when she looked at me, her child—Marcus's child—and saw I looked like him, did she wonder what I'd be capable of?

Assessments

· · • · ·

I have a monthly assessment now. Celia carries it out.

She starts off by weighing me, measuring my height, and photographing me. I don't get to see the measurements or the photographs.

Then come the physical tests: running, circuit training. All the results are noted down. None of the results are shown to me.

After that I have to do some memory tests, general intelligence tests, and some maths. I'm all right at those. Then it's reading and writing, which Celia says we have to do, even though we both know what the results are going to be.

That's it.

The next day I'm left in the cage, shackled up. She drives off in the morning and gets back late in the afternoon. I don't know if she meets someone. I ask sometimes, and my questions are ignored.

The other change, which Celia has just been told about, is that I don't have to go down to the Council building for my annual assessment. For my sixteenth birthday the Council is coming to me. Apparently I have to look my best.

Punk

·•.•··•·

"What are you trying to achieve?"

"Eh?"

"With that." Celia indicates my head with a slight movement of hers.

I grin.

Once a month, before the assessment, I'm allowed into the cottage bathroom for a proper bath. There is hot water, which is a peaty brown color, and soap. I shave the hairs that are sprouting above my lip and on my chin. The razor is a really crummy throwaway one, and as weapons go I have decided a pencil is more lethal. Celia cuts my hair once a month, keeping it short, but today I've shaved off the sides to give myself a Mohican.

"You should shave it all off. You'd look like a monk."

"A look that says pure and holy and searching for the Truth?"

"A look that says meek and mild. A look that says novice."

"That's not really me."

"It would be best not to antagonize them."

Celia wants me to do well. It will reflect well on her, I guess.

I sit at the table. "Now what?"

"Now I wait here while you go back in there and shave that mess off."

"You've no sense of humor."

"You do look absurdly funny, I'll give you that, but it would help things along if you shaved it all off voluntarily."

I go back into the bathroom. The reflection of me is strange. The hair is okay, a tufty Mohican. But I don't recognize myself. I guess I'm not used to looking at myself in a mirror. I watch myself stroking my hair, see my scarred right hand brush it back, but the face doesn't look like me. I know it is me 'cause of the scar on my cheekbone that Jessica gave me, and there's the scar near my ear, white against the black specks of my shaved scalp, where Niall got me. But my face looks different from the way I thought it looked. Older. Way older. My eyes are large and black, and even when I smile there's no hint of a smile in them. They look hollowed out, the black triangles rotating slowly. I lean into the mirror and try to see where my pupils end and my irises begin and my forehead hits the glass. I step back to the far end of the bathroom, turn away, and turn back quickly, trying to catch something, a light perhaps. I don't catch anything.

"What's taking so long?" Celia shouts.

I pick up the razor and then put it down.

A minute later I walk out.

She laughs and then stops herself and says, "Now you're being ridiculous. Take them out."

I grin at her and feel my eyebrow. I've pierced it with three small metal rings, put a metal ring in my right nostril and a bigger one in the left corner of my bottom lip.

"It's all part of the punk look." I run my fingers across the choker. "It would be better with safety pins."

"Where did you get that thing in your lip?"

"They're all from the plug chain."

"Why don't you attach the plug as well? You might as well look totally mad."

"You're just too old to understand."

"Can we go back to my original point? *What are you trying to achieve?*"

I look out of the window to the hills and sky, pale gray high clouds leaching the color from everything.

"Well?"

"Freedom from persecution." I say it flatly.

Silence.

"Do you think I'll ever get that?"

Nothing moves outside; the heather on the hills is undisturbed by wind, the clouds are motionless.

Later on in the evening I do a drawing. I use pencil, as we've run out of ink and I've gone off charcoal. Pencil is okay. I've drawn the animals and plants I see around here. Celia has put a few aside to show the Councilors. I am tempted to ask, "What are you trying to achieve with that?" but I don't bother, as I'll just get a blank.

Tonight I'm drawing Celia. She hates me drawing her,

which is all part of the fun. Warts and all is my approach. Take no prisoners. She'll burn it afterward. She always burns the portraits of her. I don't take this as an artistic insult; it's the original that's the problem.

I do self-portraits, but just of my right hand. The melted skin is like runs of thick oil paint ending in a rounded, not quite solidified blob. The skin on the back of my hand between the smooth runs is cracked and lifting like an old painting too. My hand is art.

I did a drawing of my hand holding a long, slender dagger a few weeks ago. I thought Celia was going to faint, she was holding her breath so long. I scrunched the paper up, saying it was "rubbish" and threw it on the fire before she could stop me. I've not done it again; it wasn't that funny.

My landscapes really are rubbish. I can't get them right at all, and my buildings are boringly bad. I've drawn the cage, though. I captured that. I caught its sucked-out blackness, a holding-something-down-ness. I know that cage so well. It was my best piece. I told Celia we should show it to the Council. She didn't say anything and I've not seen the picture since. I guess she burned it.

"They'll be here late morning," she says as I draw. "I'll weigh you, photograph you before they get here."

"Nervous?"

She doesn't reply, and I lean away, anticipating a slap, but she doesn't take the bait.

"I won't mess up. Don't worry. I'll be a good boy and

answer all their questions nicely. And I won't spit at them until the end."

Celia sighs.

We're quiet again, me trying to draw her hair. I think it's thinning; perhaps it's worry.

"Will you be in the room when they do the assessment?"

"What do you think?"

"Probably not . . . Definitely not."

"Then why ask?"

"Just making conversation."

"Then make it better."

I draw her mouth at that point. She has a great sneer that somehow makes her big lips seem less ugly and more interesting. I'd like to draw her standing to attention outside my cage, holding the key, with the look she sometimes has on her face, the look that's almost pity. The reason she does this job, I think.

"Well?" she asks.

"Well what?"

"I know you want to ask something."

How can she tell that?

"Umm. Well. I was wondering . . . How come you got the job of being my jailer?"

"Teacher and guardian."

"There weren't many applicants, I guess." I'm finishing off her mouth now, but the downward curve of the original has softened.

She turns to me, disturbing the position she's been holding.

"I believe I was their first choice for the post."

"Their only choice, you mean."

I wait, but she's giving nothing away.

"And your life is so empty that sitting in the middle of nowhere acting as jailer for an innocent child must seem pretty rewarding."

She's actually beginning to smile at this.

"And I bet the pay isn't that great."

She nods a little.

"Imprisoning, beating, physically and mentally scarring a boy who isn't yet sixteen years old . . . a boy who has never done anything wrong . . . they're all the plus points of the job."

"Yes," she says. "They are all plus points."

The smile has gone, but the sneer hasn't returned. She resumes her previous pose and doesn't look at me as she says, "Marcus killed my sister."

Her sister must be on the list. I don't know Celia's surname. I've asked before but apparently it's not relevant.

"What Gift did she have?"

"Potion-making."

I nod. "Can Marcus do your thing . . . your Gift . . . with the noise?"

"Is it on the list?"

"You should watch out. I'd bet he'd like it to be."

We are silent again.

I had sort of guessed that Celia had an issue with me, or rather with me being the son of you-know-who. It wasn't a wild guess. Let's face it, she was bound to know or be related to someone on the list.

I say, "I'm not Marcus."

"I know."

"I didn't kill your sister."

"It's unfair, isn't it? But I think that there is a chance, admittedly a small one, that he does care about you and that it irks him that his son is here."

"Does he know I'm here?"

"No, I don't mean here. This place is well hidden, even from his abilities." She stretches her neck and arms. "I mean that he will know that we have you. And will assume you aren't in any state of luxury. I'd hate to disappoint on that level."

"Why not leave me in the cage all day, then? You can't seriously think I'd ever be able to kill him? This training is stupid."

She gets up and walks around the room. This is usually a sign that she doesn't want to answer the question.

"Perhaps, but leaving you in a cage all day would be cruel."

I'm so amazed that I don't start laughing for a second or two. When I've managed to calm myself I say, "You beat me. I wear a choker that can kill me. You shackle me up at night in a cage."

"You're well fed. You're sitting here drawing."

"And I'm supposed to be grateful?"

"No. You're supposed to sit there with a full stomach and draw."

"I've finished it," I say and push it across to her.

She picks the paper up and turns it round to study it. After a minute she rolls it up and puts it onto the fire.

I pick up the pencil again and begin another. This time I draw myself, my face as I saw it in the mirror but even older, how I imagine Marcus looks. I can tell Celia is watching closely. She is hardly breathing. I've never done this before. I do the depths of his eyes like mine, exactly like mine. I can't imagine them blacker.

When I'm finished I'm not that pleased. He looks too handsome, too nice. "Burn it," I say. "It's not right."

Celia reaches over to take it and studies it longer than she studied her own portrait. Then she takes it out of the room.

"It doesn't mean he looks like that," I call after her.

She doesn't reply.

I pack up the pencils, eraser, and sharpener in the old tin. The lid pushes on and that's that. Celia comes back to sit opposite me again.

"Has anyone ever come close to catching him?" I ask.

"Who knows how close they get? No one succeeds. He's very good. Very careful."

"Do you think they will get him one day?"

"He'll make a mistake—it only takes one—and he'll get caught or killed."

"Are they using me as bait to get him?"

She sounds pleased as she says, "I should imagine they are."

"But you don't know how? In what way, I mean?"

"My job is to act as your guardian and teacher. That's all."

"Until when?"

"Until they tell me to stop."

"What will happen to me if they catch him?"

She sticks her lower lip out. It's huge and flat. Slowly she draws it back in, but she doesn't say anything.

"Will they kill me?"

The lip goes out again but comes in quickly this time and she says, "Maybe."

"Even though I've done nothing wrong."

She shrugs.

"Better safe than sorry, hey?"

She doesn't respond.

"What would you do if they told you to kill me? If they said, 'Put a bullet in the Half Code's brain.'" I mime a gun, pointing a finger to the side of my head, and make a shooting sound.

She gets up and walks around behind me, pushes a finger hard against the back of my skull, and makes the same sound.

I don't sleep well. It's not cold. There's no wind, not a breath. The clouds are still. There's no rain.

I'm nervous about seeing the Council. My hands are shaky. Nerves, just nerves.

I can still feel Celia's finger on the back of my skull. I know they can kill me at any time. Who would do it and how is irrelevant; the end result is the same. But still the thought of it being Celia has got to me. I know she'd do it. She'd have to, or someone would do it to her.

The trick is to enjoy it. How do you enjoy that?

You have to find a way.

Celia has told me that Annalise is unharmed, as are Deborah, Arran, and Gran, but the implication is that that may change at any time. When I'm dead they will be safe.

That's the upside.

I can enjoy thinking they are all alive and well and safe.

Annalise is in the woods, running around, smiling, laughing, climbing the sandstone cliff. I want to see her and touch her skin again; I want her to kiss my fingers, my face, my body. And I know it will never happen, and instead she will be with some shithead White Witch who has his paws all over her. Enjoy that!

Deborah will marry a nice guy, have kids, and be happy. I can imagine that. That's true. She'll have three or four kids and she'll be a great mum and they'll all be happy. Gran will live peacefully in her house drinking tea and feeding the chickens.

They are good thoughts. And then I remember Gran and Deborah crying on the landing. But their tears dried then and they'd dry again—maybe they already have. Maybe they think I'm dead already.

I don't think Arran will believe I'm dead. I remember him sweeping my hair back and saying, "I couldn't stand it." His foot is sticking out of the bed and my fingertips are kissing his forehead, and I am crying.

A Hunter

•·•·•

It's my sixteenth birthday. I've been weighed and measured by Celia. She's shaved my head and removed my piercings.

It's midmorning and I'm back in the cage, shackled up. I guess Celia thinks it makes her look conscientious.

A jeep appears on the track. In the stillness, it seems grotesquely loud. And it just keeps getting louder. Eventually it stops and they get out.

The Council Leader hasn't bothered to come, and neither has the other woman. But Annalise's uncle, Soul O'Brien, is here, and with him are two other men. A dark-haired youngish man, dressed in new walking boots, jeans, and a pristine, waxed jacket. He's so pale he looks like he's not been outside for years. In contrast the other man looks like he's spent his life outdoors. His blond hair is mixed with gray. He is tall, muscular, and dressed in black, which gives me a clue to what he is. But it's easy to tell them. They have a way of looking down at everyone else, even the Councilors.

Celia goes to meet them. I wonder if she will salute or shake hands. Neither.

They come over to look at me. Caged up. The Hunter

has pale blue eyes that are hardly blue at all they have so much silver in them.

They all look at me, then they all turn their backs on me and look at the scenery, and then they all go inside.

It's the usual routine for assessments after that. I'm left to wait.

Eventually Celia comes to get me. She doesn't say anything, just unlocks the cage and leads the way to the cottage. She stops by the front door. As I walk past her and go inside I wonder if she'll say good luck, but she's not that nervous.

The three visitors are sitting at the kitchen table. I'm standing, of course. Outside, Celia passes the window, pacing.

Annalise's uncle asks all the questions and makes notes. The same sort of questions that Celia has asked me every month. He squirms when I try to read, but mostly his expression is one of boredom. He never hurries, and we eventually work through all the mental tests.

He says, "That's all my questions."

He's not talking to me but to the Hunter. The Hunter's not spoken yet. Not to me, nor to them.

The Hunter gets up and walks around me, eyeing me. He's taller than me, but not by much, and he's solid. His chest is twice as thick as mine and his neck is huge.

He stands behind me and speaks quietly, close to my ear so that I can feel his breath. "Take your shirt off."

I do as he says. Slowly, but I do it.

The third man, the dark-haired one, gets up and walks around to look at my back. He takes hold of my arm, and it's all I can do not to pull away. His fingers are clammy, weak. He turns my hand over, looking at the scars on my wrists. "You can heal well. And quickly?"

I'm not sure what to say.

"Let's go outside and see," the Hunter says. Again I feel his breath on my neck.

The Hunter speaks to Celia. She nods and walks over to the area where we practice self-defense.

"Show me what he can do," the Hunter says.

Celia and I do a bit of sparring.

The Hunter says to stop and calls Celia over to him for a quiet word in her ear.

Celia comes back to me and I can see she's serious. We fight. She beats me; I let her get too close. I've got a bloody nose and a swollen eye.

Now I am summoned over. The dark-haired man wants to see me heal. I do it, slowly.

I think that's going to be it, but the Hunter speaks with Celia and then turns to me and says, "Do the outer circuit."

I do a fair pace. No point in killing myself.

When I get back the Hunter makes Celia and me fight again. But Celia is armed with a knife this time. She wins again. I have a cut on my arm. I have to heal that for the dark-haired man.

"Do the outer circuit again." The dark-haired man says it this time.

I do as I'm told. I don't push too hard, because I'm fairly sure I'll be beaten up again at the end of it.

Correct. And Celia wins again. She's obviously been told not to hold back. I get stabbed in the thigh. Deep. I'm pissed off now. I heal and . . .

"Do the outer circuit again."

I do it but I'm not thinking about the run, just thinking about that little dark-haired man standing there, smiling.

This time when I get back the Hunter is smiling too.

I have a bad feeling.

I have to fight Celia again. I've just done the circuit three times and been beaten up three times already today. I do my best to keep out of Celia's reach, and I even land a kick, but when I'm backed up near the Hunter he pushes me into Celia and it's all over. I'm on the ground. The Hunter comes over and kicks me hard in the ribs. And again. His boots are like breeze blocks.

"Get up. Do the outer circuit."

I know that a few ribs are broken. He does too, I suppose.

I heal them and get up slowly.

Then he hits me and knocks me to the ground again. More kicks. More broken ribs. I stay down.

"I said, get up and do the outer circuit."

I can heal but it's not as strong. My ability is being used up. I get to my feet slowly. Then I set off, slowly again.

I tell myself to relax on the run. Forget about them. Pretend they don't exist. I do the circuit, but my ribs are only just healed by the time I get back.

The dark-haired man comes over and looks at my chest. The bruising has gone.

Then the Hunter comes over, carrying a sort of truncheon. I look at Celia, but she is looking down.

When he's finished I'm just left there on the ground. The truncheon was strange. I don't think anything's broken, but I'm feeling odd.

The dark-haired man stands over me. "Can you heal?" he asks me. "Can you get up?"

Yeah, I can get up. I get to my knees but then everything swirls around and it's nice to lie down.

When I open my eyes again Celia is crouched beside me. I ask her, "Have they gone?"

"Yes."

"I'll just rest here."

"Yes."

Early evening and I'm fully healed. I'm having extra helpings of stew and bread. Celia is quiet, watching me eat.

I say, "Typical White Witches, that lot. Kind, gentle, healing natures."

Celia doesn't reply.

"I wouldn't have minded, but I didn't even spit at them."

Celia still doesn't reply so I try a different approach. "I can't be that important; the Council Leader didn't bother to come."

"Do you know who the blond man is?"

I shrug.

"He's Soul O'Brien. He's recently been appointed as the deputy Council Leader."

I nod. Interesting, Annalise's uncle is moving up in the world. "Who was the Hunter?"

Celia gives a short laugh. And I stop eating to look up at her.

"I thought you knew. That was Clay."

"Oh!" The leader of the Hunters came to check me out. "And the dark-haired guy? Who's he?"

"He said his name was Mr. Wallend. I've never seen him before."

I finish my stew and wipe the bowl out with the last of the bread. Then I push my bowl away, saying, "I thought I'd let you win all the fights, so you didn't look too bad in front of them."

"Very considerate."

"They can't have been too impressed, though. With me, I mean. If I can't even beat you I'm not going to match up to Marcus."

"Perhaps."

"And I didn't even try to hit Clay."

"A wise decision."

I think so too, but still if I'd known it was him . . .

"What?" Celia asks.

I don't know . . . I don't know how I feel about Clay except to say, "He killed Saba—Marcus's mother, my grandmother."

Celia nods. "Yes, and Saba killed Clay's mother."

I nod.

"Your mother . . ." Celia says this and hesitates. I don't look at her, can't risk breaking whatever tightrope of confession she is balanced on. "Your mother saved Clay's life once. He was badly hurt by a Black Witch, his shoulder was being eaten by poison. Your mother was the only person able to heal him. He would have died without her help."

I still don't look at Celia. There's nothing to say to that.

"Your mother had an exceptional Gift for healing. Truly exceptional."

"My gran told me." Though she never told me that story.

"They are interested in your ability to heal yourself."

"And?" I look at Celia now.

"I think you're healed enough to do the washing up now."

Gran

•·.•·•

The months after my assessment pass; the routine is the same as ever. Autumn comes, the nights get longer and it's good. Winter. Snow. Winds. I'm stronger than ever. I don't mind the rain. The frost is beautiful. My feet are tough as hide.

The snow melts, though a few pockets remain in a few hollows. The sun has some warmth in it, but I have to really stay still to soak it into my skin.

My seventeenth birthday is months away, not years.

Celia never talks about my birthday. I ask her often, but she doesn't tell me anything.

I'm inside one day, making bread. Celia is writing at the kitchen table.

I try again, with a well-worn question. "On my birthday, will I be given three gifts?"

Celia doesn't answer.

"If you want me to kill Marcus I'll need my Gift."

She carries on writing.

"Will my gran give me three gifts?"

I know they wouldn't let me near her, not in a million years.

Celia looks up, opens her mouth as if to answer but closes it again.

"What?"

She puts the pen down. "Your gran."

"What?"

"She died a month ago."

What? A month ago! "And you forgot to mention it until now?"

They can tell me nothing or anything, and how do I know if any of it is true?

I throw the dough on the floor.

"I'm not supposed to mention it at all."

So Celia's being considerate, and for all I know that is another lie. And Gran is dead. That's true for sure. They will have killed her or made her commit suicide, and everyone else can be killed as well if they want.

"And Arran?"

She blanks me.

I kick the chair over, pick it up, and slam it down.

And they'll do just what they want and kill everyone and I hate them, hate them, hate them. And I'm slamming the chair down again.

"I'm going to have to put you in the cage if you carry on like that."

I throw the chair and leap at Celia, shouting.

I wake in the cage, shackles on.

Visitors

A few weeks after Celia tells me about Gran, I'm collecting eggs. I'm thinking about Gran and her hens and how they tried to get into the house, and Gran with her beekeeper's hat on, lifting the honeycombs . . .

I put the egg basket on the ground and listen.

Listen hard.

A faint, not-quite-there sound; distant, but somewhere in the hills.

And a clatter from the kitchen.

I run on to the wall and from there leap onto the cage to look toward the southwest, where Marcus will come from in my fantasy.

The hills sit there quietly, giving nothing away. I swivel around, looking and listening, holding my breath.

That is not the wind.

It's a growling, a distant growling.

Celia is at the kitchen window staring at me. She hasn't heard it but knows something is up 'cause I'm on the cage. She disappears then reappears at the front door. And now it's there, the unmistakable sound.

Not my father. A vehicle.

"Get in the cottage!" Celia shouts at me.

A 4x4 appears as a distant black cube moving along the track.

"Get off the cage!"

But if these are people, real people—fains, walkers, holidaymakers—then I must be able to do something. I'll tell them I've been kept in the cage. The choker—they might be able to get it off. Maybe I should wait until she gets rid of them and . . . club her with something . . .

But then she changes. Her body slumps a fraction. She says, "Get in the cage, Nathan." Her voice is flat now. She knows who it is.

I watch the jeep for a couple of seconds more before jumping down and going into the cage.

"Padlock it."

She walks toward the track.

I pull the door shut but don't lock it. I go to the back of the cage and find my nail in the soil. I put it in my mouth, digging it into my cheek and healing it over.

The jeep revs and churns louder. It stops at the far side of the cottage. Celia walks over to it.

She's talking through the driver's window. Waving her hands around, in frustration it looks like. Unusually dramatic for her.

I can't see the driver.

The jeep doors open and Celia is holding her arms wide as if she can stop them. They are almost as big as her. All in black, of course. I don't see the driver's face until Celia moves to the side, but I know who it is.

Have they come to kill me? What other reason? To give Celia instructions to do it? Do I padlock the cage now? It seems pretty pointless.

Clay is walking toward me.

Celia is a step behind him, and behind her are two female Hunters.

Celia says, "But I've not been informed about this."

"You're being informed now. Get him out of the cage."

Celia doesn't hesitate for more than a second before she swings the door open.

They can only be here to kill me. Maybe they'll walk me to the end of the field and do it there, or not even go to the trouble of that, just do it by the cage. I'll be buried with the potatoes. And this must mean that they've killed Marcus. They don't need me any more. My father is dead.

"Come out." Clay's voice is casual.

I back up and shake my head. They'll have to kill me here. And I can't believe my father is dead.

Then I hear a buzzing in my head—not Celia, a phone. And it's not coming from the Hunters behind Celia; it's closer. I feel something grab my right arm and go around my wrist, and the fourth Hunter materializes beside me. He's as big and as ugly as I remembered. Kieran is holding my arm, the handcuff now visible. I try to strike his face with my free hand but he drops down, pulling me by the handcuff, and another of the Hunters has run into the cage and grabbed my left arm. I get a kick in to a female Hunter, but then I'm slammed into the bars, my arms are cuffed tightly behind me, and I'm slammed into the bars twice more.

"Move again and I'll rip your arms out," Kieran growls in my ear.

The great thing about hate is that it takes away everything else so that nothing else matters. So then the old trick is easy. I don't mind about having my arms ripped off, about pain, about anything. I whip my head back and catch Kieran in the face, a cushioned scrunch of his nose on the back of my skull.

He squeals but doesn't loosen his grip.

My arms get pulled up so I can't move, but they don't get ripped off, so I've got to wonder how serious Kieran really is.

Kieran drags me out of the cage and pushes me to the ground, but I roll and kick up so my boot makes contact with the side of his face. Roll again and get to my feet, but the two female Hunters are on me then and the punch to my kidneys is explosive.

I'm on my knees, my face on the path.

Celia is shouting at Clay, "This is unacceptable! I'm his guardian."

Clay's voice is calm. He says, "The orders are for us to take him."

There's a boot on my head keeping my face crushed against the ground.

Celia complains, argues, says she has to come, says she's going to come, but Clay is good. He just says no.

In the end Celia says she has to take the choker off me. She asks permission.

As she unlocks it her hands are gentle and she says, "I'm going to follow you down."

Clay says, "No. We're going to have to borrow your van. He's too dangerous to risk putting in the jeep."

"Then I'll drive your jeep."

"No, Megan'll drive it. If you insist on coming I suppose you could ride with her."

There's a threat in his voice; Celia must hear it. Megan couldn't hurt Celia, but she'll go the wrong way, get lost, run out of petrol. Celia won't risk falling out with the Hunters; she'll stay here. She'll do what they want.

"Oh yes, I was supposed to give you this." Clay's voice is casual again now.

"A notification! When did this happen?"

He doesn't reply.

"Two days ago? I should have been told. He's my responsibility."

Clay still doesn't reply.

"It says that all Half Codes are to be 'codified.' What does that mean?" And I know Celia is saying all this for my benefit.

"I'm just providing the transport, Celia."

"I'll come down—"

But Clay cuts in. "I've told you the situation, Celia. He's ours."

"And when are you bringing him back?"

"I haven't got instructions about that."

Codified

•˙•●•˙•

I'm in Celia's van, face down on the metal floor. It's nearly two years since I was last here, and yet the rusting paint seems familiar.

Kieran has begun to heal his broken nose but it's well mashed. He is holding a chain that is attached to my hand-cuffs and wrapped round my ankles, and he jerks on it to pass the time.

Clay is sitting in the passenger seat at the front, Tamsin is driving, Megan is following in the 4x4, and I guess Celia is still at the cottage.

The only thing to do is rest, but as soon as I doze Kieran yanks at my ankles or lashes my buttocks with the chain. When he's fed up with that he shouts to the front of the van, "Hey, Tamsin, I've got another."

"Yeah?" she shouts back.

"What's the difference between a Half Code and a trampoline?"

She doesn't answer and I get a heavy stomp on my back as Kieran says, "You take your shoes off to jump on a trampoline."

His next joke he says quietly, just sharing it with me. "What's the difference between a Half Code and an onion?"

He lifts my shirt up. I feel his fingers scratch over the lower part of my scars, his scars, as he says, "Cutting up an onion makes you cry."

After four or five hours the van stops. From the few voices I hear it has to be a motorway service station. They fill up with petrol and then sit around eating burgers and chips and slurping drinks. The smell would be tempting, but I'm desperate for a piss and don't want to think about food and drink.

It probably isn't going to be worth it, but I say it anyway. "I need to pee."

The chain whips across the top of my thighs. I have to clench my teeth and breathe through my nose.

When the pain eases I say, "I still need to pee."

The chain hits my thighs again.

The van sets off. Clay is giving mumbled instructions to the driver but I can't hear them.

Twenty minutes later the van stops. I'm dragged backward by the ankles and out of the back of the van, which is backed up into some bushes. There is little traffic noise. They've found a quiet spot.

"Any trouble. Anything. And you're dead." Kieran says it so close to my ear I can feel the spray of spit.

I don't acknowledge him.

He undoes my handcuffs and frees my right hand.

I piss. A long, long wonderful piss.

I've hardly zipped up and I'm back in the cuffs and

shoved into the van again. I'm smiling inside at the relief, and because I'm thinking of Celia. She is tougher than these idiots.

The journey just keeps joggling along. Kieran must be sleeping 'cause he's not bothering me. The nail is still in my mouth, but there's no chance of escape with three Hunters round me.

The rust of the van's floor scratches across my cheek as I'm pulled out of the back end of the van once more.

"On your knees."

I'm in the courtyard of the Council building, the place where I was taken from just before my fifteenth birthday.

I'm pushed down. "Your knees!" Kieran shouts.

Clay has gone. Tamsin and Megan are by the cab of the van. Kieran is standing to the side of me and I squint up at him. His nose is swollen and he has one black eye.

"Your healing's a bit slow, Kieran."

His boot flies at my face, but I roll out of its way and up to my feet.

Tamsin laughs. "He's fast, Kieran."

Kieran feigns disinterest and says, "He's their problem now."

I look around as the two guards reach me, grab my arms, and drag me off without a word.

They take me into the Council building through a wooden door, along a corridor, then right and left and past an internal courtyard, through another door to the left.

Then I am in the corridor I recognize and sitting on the bench outside the room where they do the assessments.

I heal the various scrapes and bruises.

It's almost like old times. I have to wait, of course. My hands are still cuffed behind me. I stare at my knees and at the stone floor.

A long time passes and I'm still waiting. The door at the far end of the corridor opens; there're footsteps but I don't look up. And then the footsteps stop and a man's voice says, "Go back the other way."

I look up and then I stand up.

Annalise's voice is quiet. "Nathan?"

The man she's with must be her father, and he's pushing her back through the door. The door shuts and that's it.

The guard stands in my way, blocking the view. I know he wants me to sit, and I hesitate but I do it, and the corridor is the same as it always is.

But Annalise was here. She looked different: older, paler, taller. She was wearing jeans and a light blue shirt and brown boots. And I replay it over in my head: the footsteps, "Go back the other way," seeing her, our eyes meeting and her eyes are pleased, and she says my name softly, "Nathan?" and the way she says it she isn't sure, like she can't believe it, and then her father pushes her back, she resists, he pushes and blocks the way, she looks around his arm, our eyes meet again, then the door shuts. The door blocks all noise out; footsteps and voices on the other side can't be heard.

I replay it all again, and again. I think it was real. I think it happened.

They take the handcuffs off to weigh, measure, and photograph me. It's the same as before an assessment, but it's not my birthday for months so I'm not sure if I'm going to be assessed or what. I ask the man in the lab coat, but the guard who stands watching it all tells me to shut up, and the man doesn't answer me. The guard puts the cuffs back on, and I am back in the corridor, and there is more waiting.

When I'm taken in it's Soul O'Brien sitting in the center seat this time. I'm not surprised. The woman Councilor is back on the right, and Mr. Wallend is sitting on the left. At least Clay isn't here.

They start asking me questions like the ones in my assessment. I'm uncooperative, in a silent sort of way. Soul is his usual bored self, but I'm more convinced than ever that it's an act. Everything about him is an act. He asks each question twice and doesn't comment on my lack of response, but they soon give up and don't even seem that bothered. After his last question, Soul whispers to the woman and then to Mr. Wallend.

Then he speaks to me.

"Nathan."

Nathan! That's a first.

"It is less than three months until your seventeenth birthday. An important day in your life." He looks at his nails and then up at me again. "And an important day in mine. I'm hoping that I will be able to give you three gifts on that day."

What?

"Yes, that may seem a little surprising, but it's something I've been considering for many years, something I would be . . . interested in doing. However, before I can give you three gifts I must—we all must—be sure that you are truly on the side of White Witches. I have the power to choose your Designation Code, Nathan. I suggest that it is in your interest that you are designated as a White Witch."

And I used to want that, used to think it was the solution, but now I know for sure that I don't.

"Nathan, you are half White Witch by birth. Your mother was from a strong and honorable family of White Witches. We at the Council respect her family. Some of her ancestors were Hunters and your half-sister is now a Hunter too. You have a proud and respectable heritage on your mother's side. And there is much of your mother in you, Nathan. Much. Your healing ability is a sign of that."

And I'm not sure if he's talking a load of bollocks, because I'm convinced my father is pretty good at healing too.

"Do you know the difference between Black Witches and White Witches, Nathan?"

I don't reply. Waiting for the usual good-versus-evil argument.

"It's an interesting question, isn't it? Something I've often pondered." Soul O'Brien looks at his nails and then at me. "White Witches use their Gifts for good. And that is how you can show us that you are White, Nathan. Use your Gift for good. Work with the Council, the Hunters, White Witches the world over. Help us and . . ." He leans back in his chair. "Life will be a lot easier for you." His eyes seem to glow silver as he says, "And longer too."

"I've been kept in a cage for nearly two years. I've been beaten and tortured and kept from my family, my family of White Witches. Tell me which bit of that is 'good.'"

"We *are* concerned for the good of White Witches. If you are designated White—"

"Then you'll give me a nice bed to sleep in? Oh, yes, of course, as long as I kill my father."

"We all have to make compromises, Nathan."

"I won't kill my father."

He admires his nails again and says, "Well, I'd be disappointed if you agreed readily, Nathan. I've watched you with interest every year since we first met, and you rarely disappoint me."

I swear at him.

"And in a way I'm glad you haven't done so now. However, one way or another you will do as we require. Mr. Wallend will ensure that."

I'm not given a chance to reply, because Soul nods at the guards and they come up to me and take an arm each.

As I'm hauled out of the room and along the corridors I try to keep track of the directions—the lefts, the rights, the benches, windows, and doors—but it's too complex and

I'm soon in a part of the building where the corridors are less straight, and this one is descending until it becomes so narrow that one guard is in front of me and one behind. Stone steps take us farther down. It's cold. There's a row of metal doors on the left.

The guard ahead stops by the third door, which is painted blue, though the paint is scratched off in places to show gray beneath. It's not a door to fill anyone with hope. He slides it open and the guard behind me pushes me through.

I'm standing in a cell. The only light is from the corridor. The cell is empty except for a chain attached to the wall, which the guard is now shackling to my ankle. Then he's out of the door, turning the lock and slamming a bolt.

Complete blackness.

I'm still handcuffed. I step forward and make my way around the room, feeling the uneven stone walls with my toes, my body, and my cheek. Three paces to the left of where the chain is attached is the corner and then two paces farther I run out of chain. It's the same on the right. The short chain stops me from getting near the door.

The floor is cold and hard but dry. I sit with my back against the wall. Four stone walls, one door, a length of chain and me.

But soon nausea and fear join us.

The moon is halfway through its cycle, so things are bad but not really bad. I've not been inside at night for a long time, though. I jiggle my feet. Then I jiggle my body. This helps the panicky feeling but not the nausea. I roll on to my side but keep jiggling and crawl into the corner and push my head into it. Some of the time I jiggle, some of the time I don't.

I bring up watery vomit, but there's not much of it. I haven't eaten since breakfast, but my stomach retches repeatedly. There's nothing to come out, but it clenches and turns, and I'm coughing up nothing, but still my stomach wants to get rid of something.

Then the noises start. I hear hissing and banging, but I'm not sure if I'm imagining them or if they're real noises. The hissing is horrible, persistent; the bangs make me jump, they're so loud. I try to anticipate them but I can't. All I can do to help is to shout. Shouting drowns out the noises, but I can't keep it up all night. I'm sick again, and I lie with my head pressed into the corner, and I hum and jiggle and shout back at the noises from time to time when they make me jump.

It's dawn. The cell is still dark, but the nausea and noises leave as quickly as they arrived.

No one comes.

I should make a plan but I'm too exhausted to think of one.

Still no one comes.

I try to rest. I'm hungry. My mouth tastes disgusting. Will they bring food and water? Or will they forget about me and leave me here to die?

*   *   *

They have remembered me. They have brought water but not remembered that I need to eat as well. They have forgotten my name too.

I can't seem to remember it either.

"I'll ask you once more to state your name." The young witch has stopped saying please.

I'm going with my usual plan, the one where I say nothing. It's not the most sophisticated plan; it's bound to cause irritation, and it's not likely to have a profound effect on anything that will ultimately happen. But at least it's a plan.

I stare back at her, taking in her appearance from the top of her neatly brushed, mousy hair, past her small, pale blue eyes, perfectly applied mascara, smooth, thin coating of foundation, and precisely painted, pink lipstick. Her narrow frame is well dressed in a beige suit, tights, black patent shoes. She looks like she's made an effort, and she looks like she's had a decent night's sleep. She is even wearing perfume, which is floral.

And the more I look, the more overcome I am by her appearance, her prettiness, and her basic, cruel stupidity. She is dressed for some business meeting, and I've been kept in a cell.

And I now have a new plan. I slouch on one hip and leaning forward slightly toward her I say, "My name is Ivan. Ivan Shukhov."

The woman looks a little confused and irritated. She's probably trying to work out if it's some sort of rhyming slang.

"No, you are Nathan Byrn. Son of Cora Byrn and Marcus Edge."

I lean back and try to sound casual. "Nah, I'm Ivan. You must be after the guy in the next cell."

"There isn't anyone in the next cell."

"You mean he's escaped?"

She pulls her lipsticked lips into a smile, perhaps to show she has a sense of humor.

"We just need to ensure that you are aware of what is happening."

"Course I'm aware of what is happening." That wasn't at all casual, and I have to recover my tone. "I've been treated like a king by the wonderful Council of White Witches. Fed the best food, given the best bed and"—I lean forward again—"been introduced to the most charming, fresh-smelling White Witches." The guard pulls me back by one arm. "My name is Ivan Shukhov, and I am aware of what is happening. Are you?"

"You are not Ivan Something-or-other. You are Nathan Byrn and you are going to be codified."

"I've no idea what that means."

Her eyes are cold, fixed on me, pale blue shimmers glacially in pale blue.

"It doesn't sound too good," I say. "I kind of feel sorry for this Nathan guy."

"*You* are Nathan."

"What does codified mean? I'd like to tell Nathan if I see him."

"It's a sophisticated tattoo."

"I can't imagine you think any tattoos are sophisticated."

She smiles. "This one is. Mr. Wallend has been working on the potion for some time."

"What is the tattoo?"

"It's your code, of course."

I lean forward and the guards grab my arms and hold them back. "A brand, you mean."

She opens the pink lips on her beautifully made-up face to speak again and I spit at them. The gob lands perfectly.

She screams and splutters, rubbing at her mouth. The guards hold me back.

The woman has backed away a pace; her makeup is not so immaculate as she wipes it with her handkerchief. She holds the handkerchief to her mouth as she says, "You are Nathan Byrn. You have a mother who was a White Witch and a father who is a Black Witch. You are a Half Code and as such you are to be codified."

This time my spit lands on the hem of her skirt. She staggers back as if I've hit her. The guards still keep hold of me.

"Take him to Room 2C."

The guards shuffle through the cell door, dragging me out, and in the narrow corridor they have to go sideways, which is better for me as I can climb the walls with my legs, even though one guard has me by the neck. They get me in front of a green metal door with 2C painted on it. It slides open and I stop struggling for a second.

Room 2C contains what looks like an operating table with lots of black plastic straps. Again I start struggling and shouting.

In the end they have to knock me out with a punch to the side of my head.

I wake and begin to gag and choke. There's something in my mouth. I can't spit it out. It's rubber and metal.

The woman is standing beside me, looking down at me. She smiles and says, "Ah, awake at last."

I squirm and squeal, but it's pathetic so I stop. Room 2C has painted white walls and the ceiling is bare except for a light and what looks like a camera nestled in the far corner. That's all I know about Room 2C because I can't move to see anything else. I'm lying down, my body strapped to a table. My hands are no longer handcuffed, but they are secured, and I can feel with my fingertips that the table has a thin layer of padding under a sheet. My head is strapped by my forehead and rests in a sort of hollow in the table. It feels like there are straps over my body, arms, legs, and ankles.

I'm trying not to think of Retribution. I don't want to think of the powder Kieran put on my back. But I have a clamp in my mouth. Is *codified* another word for Retribution?

The door rattles and then I hear it slide open and there is the sound of something metal being dragged over the floor. A light is shone so bright that even with my eyes closed I see a red glare. There is the sound of more dragging and the clink of delicate metal objects.

"Nathan. Look at me."

It's Mr. Wallend. He has very dark blue eyes with white flecks in them. He's wearing a lab coat.

"You're here for codification. I'm going to carry out the procedure. It may be a little uncomfortable, but I'd like you to be as still as possible. Try to relax."

I start to squirm again.

"It's a bit like a tattoo, only a much quicker and easier process. We'll do the ones on your finger first. Give you the feel of it. You're left-handed, aren't you?"

He can't possibly make sense of my squirming and squealing.

He pushes a metal ring over the little finger of my right hand and tightens it.

"Okay. So this is simple. Just relax. It'll be over—"

I scream into the gag as a needle pierces into the bone of my finger.

It is drawn out.

Mr. Wallend loosens the ring and moves it up my finger. "Next one."

I scream and curse him and move my finger as much as I can but the ring tightens and the needle goes into me again.

As it comes out I'm sweating.

He moves on to the top of my finger, over the fingernail. The needle goes through again.

I bite on the gag and stare at him, tears streaming out of my eyes.

It stops.

My heart is thudding.

That was not a tattoo.

Mr. Wallend is undoing the ring and taking it off. He and the woman peer at my finger.

"Excellent. Excellent. There's hardly any swelling. Your body is exceptional, Nathan. Exceptional."

Mr. Wallend walks round the table to my left hand.

"Now for the bigger tattoos. These might feel a bit more intense."

I feel cold metal on the top of my left hand, along the line of my middle finger. I stare at him and curse into the gag.

Mr. Wallend ignores all that and gets on with his job so that all I can see of him is the top of his head. Dark brown wavy hair.

"Try to relax."

Yes, of course, easy. Something is scraping against the inside of my hand, on my bone.

Mr. Wallend's hair is wavy and still. I'm still too.

When the scraping stops I feel sick, dizzy.

Mr. Wallend looks up. "Not too bad, hey? Now, the thing to remember is that it won't come off. Ever. It's inside you now. If you try to remove it with scarring of the skin, say, it will reappear. So there really is no point in trying."

He looks at my hand again, smoothes it over with his

finger. It feels bruised and tender. "The code looks very good. Very good indeed."

He's moving down the bed.

"Now the ankle. Try to relax. It'll just be a few seconds."

I can't help but try to pull away, however feebly. It seems more than a few seconds that it's scraping into my bone and through into my marrow. The gag's in my mouth and I know I mustn't be sick.

"It takes longer on the bigger bones," he says. "Just the last one now."

He moves the machine round the table, disappearing from sight and reappearing on my right side.

He puts the machine on my neck.

Oh no . . . no . . . no . . .

"Try to calm yourself." He leans forward, his face close. "It may feel a bit strange here."

I am lying on a thin mattress, curled up. My right wrist is handcuffed to the metal bar of the bed. I can feel where I've been codified. My fingers and hand feel bruised. My ankle is the same. But my throat is more than that. There is a taste, a metallic taste.

I haven't opened my eyes yet. I woke up here some time ago.

I want to go back to my cage.

An image of Mr. Wallend comes into my head and he smiles at me. I open my eyes.

This cell is different from the stone cell. This one has a medical feel to it, like Room 2C. The room is lit by a weak, white glow emitted from a small light in the corner of the ceiling. In the other corner of the ceiling is a camera. The cell is empty except for the bed.

I raise my left hand to look at it.

B 0.5

It's a black tattoo. The one on my ankle is the same.

So much for being designated as a White Witch. To them I'll always be half Black.

I heal my hand and finger. The bruised feeling goes. The same works for my ankle and my neck. Slowly the taste fades and the buzz arrives. I curl up and look at the tattoos on my little finger. Three tiny black tattoos: B 0.5.

I need a plan.

The light is on so that they can watch me. I resist looking at the camera.

The nail is still in my mouth. I bite through my cheek and slide the nail out with my teeth and tongue, taking it with my left hand as if I'm wiping my lips. Picking the handcuff lock isn't difficult, though I have to do it while hiding what I'm doing. I leave the cuff on but open.

Now I have to get in role.

I start shaking and then fling my legs around, make choking sounds and grabbing at my throat. I only have to keep it up for twenty seconds before there is the sound of a bolt sliding back. I roll onto the floor, my right hand still looking like it is cuffed to the bed. My eyes are open but hidden under my arm.

The legs and bottom of the lab coat of Mr. Wallend rush toward me; he really must be worried. The black boots of a guard stop in the doorway.

Mr. Wallend bends over me, and I pull him down, punch his face, roll up to standing, and stamp on his balls.

The guard is in and grabbing at my arm. I kick his knee. There's a crack and the guard grunts and falls backward, but his arms are long and there's no room to get back from them. He's pulling me with him and I twist and roll to the side where I can kick his knee again. He's still got my arm, and his other arm swings over and catches my ear with a glancing blow. I slither around and kick him in the face. His grip loosens, and after another kick I pull away from him. He is quiet. Mr. Wallend is quiet too.

I get up and out, slide the door shut, and bolt it.

I'm holding the bolts in place and leaning against the door, in shock at how easy that was. My ear is throbbing fast, in time with my heart. I heal my ear.

If anyone else was watching the camera they'd be here by now.

I go left, passing Room 2C, and then turn right, away from the cell and up the stone steps. Along the corridor to the left, the way I was brought in, and still no one is coming. I slowly swing open the door at the end and peer through. Another corridor that's vaguely familiar, but they all look pretty much the same. I stride down it, past an internal courtyard, which I have definitely seen before, but I can't remember how it relates to anything else.

I keep going. It's not looking familiar now. I go left and left again. The door at the far end begins to open and I nip down another corridor to the right and dash as quietly as I can to the door at the end. It's bolted. I can hear footsteps down the far corridor.

The bolt is stiff, but I can jiggle it across. Faster . . . faster . . .

The footsteps are getting louder.

I slither through the door, closing it silently behind me.

I want to laugh at my luck, but I hold my breath and flatten myself against the door. I am in the courtyard where Celia's van picked me up and dropped me off. Her van is not here. There are no vehicles. There is a high brick wall with razor wire on the top. In the wall is a solid metal gate to allow vehicles in, and near the gate is an ordinary wooden door. It's probably locked, alarmed, protected by security spells of some kind, but maybe just a spell to stop people getting in, not getting out . . .

I keep close to the walls as I move quickly round the

edge of the courtyard. The wooden door is bolted top and bottom. These bolts slide easily.

The whole thing feels too easy.

And I'm now terrified of what's on the other side of the door—the disappointment of seeing a guard standing there.

I open the door slowly, silently.

No one's there.

I am shaking. I step through the door and close it quietly behind me.

It's an alley. Narrow, cobbled. And above is the sky; it's gray and overcast, early evening.

A person walks past the end of the street. An ordinary person talking on a mobile phone, just walking, looking ahead. Then a car goes past and a bus.

My knees feel weak. I don't know what to do.

PART
FOUR

FREEDOM

Three Teabags in the Life
of Nathan Marcusovich

I've been free for ten days. I'm okay. I'm in a house in the countryside, just having a cup of tea. I come in here most days but sleep in the woods a mile away. The woods are okay. They're warm and I can hear if anything approaches. Nothing human ever does. It's good not to be in the cage. I slept better in the cage, though. I'm having constant nightmares now. The nightmares don't sound that scary—I'm just running and running in the alley by the Council building.

Food was a problem before I found this place. It's a holiday home and hardly used. I managed to break in just by messing with the lock with a bit of wire. I shower in here most days, and sometimes I lie on one of the beds upstairs, like Goldilocks, only I never sleep. The beds are all really soft, and there's porridge too, which is sort of funny.

There's pasta and cereal in the cupboard, as well as the oats, so mainly I'm living off that. There's no milk, of course, so I make porridge with water. No lumps in my porridge, but I've used up all the honey, jam, and raisins so there's not much else in it either.

I try to have one meal a day, whatever time feels right. I don't eat much; there isn't much here to eat. Rice with salt is my favorite. There was a tin of tuna, but that went on day one and the can of beans on day two. I slip half a Weetabix into my pocket and suck on it slowly in the evening when I'm tucked up in the woods.

A family came and stayed here for two days. I guess it was the weekend. Mum, dad, two kids, and a dog, the perfect fain family. They didn't seem to notice that I'd been in the house and taken stuff. I always make sure everything is clean and tidy. When they left there was more pasta but no more oats. I was hoping for another can of tuna, but no luck.

I thought I heard something outside. Nothing there.

I've started biting my nails again. I used to do this when I was little, but I stopped because of Annalise. I've started again. I try not to think about Annalise too much.

It's raining. Drizzle.

I'd better check outside again.

I'm heading back to the woods. I think they are watching me. I can feel it sometimes. My skin crawls with it.

My escape was too easy. It's unbelievable that the Council took so much trouble to keep me under strict control all my life, all those assessments and notifications, keeping me prisoner with Celia, tattooing me—and yet they've allowed me to escape. It can only be some new plan of theirs.

They followed me before, when I was living with Gran and going to Wales. I didn't know it then but I know it now.

That family that stayed in the house looked like fains,

but I'm not sure. Maybe Hunters can disguise themselves as fains. And the first man I hitched with kept looking at me and asking me questions and stuff, though he was all right in the end 'cause he let me out, but I was shouting at him at that point and he looked scared.

These tattoos are some kind of tracking device. That can be the only explanation. I'm probably some blip on a screen. I saw that in a film once. *Blip . . . blip . . . blip.* And they're sitting in a van watching the screen and can see that I'm cutting down the side of the field and heading back to the woods.

My shelter's okay. It keeps the rain out and the ground dry. It's well hidden, half buried under the roots of a tree near a stream.

I sit here a lot.

And sometimes when I'm sitting here I think that I'm not being followed and I really have escaped and I say to myself, "I've escaped. I've escaped. I'm free."

But I don't feel free.

I cry sometimes. I don't know why, but it keeps happening. I'm just looking at the stream, say, which runs through the dark brown mud and yet is clear and bright and soundless, when I realize that I can taste tears. There are so many they run into my mouth.

I've had a nap and even with the blanket and some newspapers I brought from the holiday home I'm shivering. How does that work? It's April and it's not even cold. I've spent nearly two years living in a cage in the coldest, wettest bit of Scotland—which must be virtually the coldest, wettest bit of the planet; I've lived through snow, ice, and storms, and then I come down here to a nice warm place and I'm shivering all the time. A few sheepskins would be good here.

I think about Scotland quite a bit, about the cage, doing the outer circuit and cleaning the range, making porridge and digging the potatoes, killing and plucking the chickens. And I think about Celia and the book she was reading with me.

In the book the main character, Ivan Denisovich, is a prisoner. He's serving ten years, but even when he's served his time he won't be allowed home, because people like him are exiled when they are released. I thought that exile meant you had to leave your country and you could go anywhere—somewhere in the sun, a tropical island, say, or America. But exile doesn't mean that; it means you are banished to a specific place, and guess what, that place isn't in the sun and is no paradise, it's not even America. It's some cold, miserable place like Siberia, where you don't know anyone and you can barely survive. It's another prison.

And now I'm free. I don't want to be exiled.

And I want to see Arran so much.

So much.

I know if I go there, they'll catch me and maybe hurt Arran too. But I want to see him, and I keep thinking that if I sneak up to Gran's house in the night or leave a message for him somewhere and arrange to meet him it might work. But I know it won't. I know they'll catch me, and it'll be even worse than before, and I should never try to go back to Arran, never, but then I feel like a coward for not trying.

Ivan Denisovich's full name is Ivan Denisovich Shukhov, which is a killer name, though Denisovich means son of Denis, which spoils it a bit but shows he's just an ordinary guy, I suppose.

If you speak to a person in Russia, you wouldn't call them by their first name alone. You would use their first name and their patronym, so you would say, "Ivan Denisovich, pass the salt, please." And he would say, "You certainly like a lot of salt on your rice, Nathan Marcusovich."

I think of Marcus Axelovich quite a bit. I think he probably likes a lot of salt on his rice too. And then today I realized something amazing. I like thinking of my father, and I know I'd think of my son if I had one. I'd think of my son a lot. So I know Marcus is thinking of me.

The woods are a good place: quiet, no dog walkers, no people at all. It's interesting just sitting still and listening to what goes on. There are few sounds, the occasional bird not calling but sorting through the leaves, stuff like that, but this wood has deep pockets of nothing when there are no sounds at all, and I love sitting in those pockets.

My head is clear of noise here, like it was with Celia. No

hissing at all. No electrical equipment buzzing in my head.

And sitting in those pockets I begin to believe it . . . I have escaped.

I started running again today. Celia would be pleased with me, though I'm slow so she'd probably not be that pleased. And I'm doing push-ups. Can't even manage seventy, though. I don't know how I've got so out of condition in a few weeks. I wonder if it's the tattoos doing something to me, but maybe it's just that I need more food. My ribs are sticking out.

It's getting dark now. Another day nearly over.

When I was with Celia the days flew by, yet the years crawled. I was up at dawn, then exercising, doing chores— never enough time for the chores—and answering her damn questions, and more running and fighting and cooking and cleaning and learning witch names and Gifts and times and places and then back in the cage before I knew it. Now it's the opposite. The hours won't budge. And yet the time I've got before I'm seventeen seems to be slipping through my fingers, and I'm just sitting here watching it dribble away.

Another day dawns. I used to like dawns, but now they are just the start of another slow, shivery day. I've just remembered Ivan starts his day all shivery. I'd like to have that Ivan Denisovich book. I know I wouldn't be able to read it by myself or anything, but I'd like to hold it in my hands or put it inside my shirt against my chest.

I do have a book, though. It's an A to Z that I stole when I was leaving London.

What a great book! A book I can read. I look at maps and they make sense.

I stole it 'cause I knew I'd have to find the address of Bob, the man Mary told me about. The man who can help me find Mercury.

Muggy and rainy again. I'm watching telly and drinking tea. Well, not really watching telly, but it's on and I'm trying to analyze the sound in my head. There's a hissing in my skull, that's the nearest I can describe it as. It's not a sound in my ears, it's in my head, to the right upper side.

This is the same as the hiss from mobile phones, but much quieter. I never got any hissing with Celia. She didn't have a mobile. But when the Hunters came I could hear them hissing.

There is no hissing in the woodland here.

Just had a shower. There's a load of shampoo, soap, and stuff in the bathroom. And there's an electric razor, which is a nightmare and hacks bits off my chin, but I can heal quick enough so I use it.

I check the tattoo on my neck. It's just the same.

I check all my tattoos every day and they are all just the

same as the first day. I scraped the skin off the one on my ankle to see what would happen and Mr. Wallend was right: the tattoo reappeared. It even showed through on the scab as a fluorescent blue.

I look in the mirror at my eyes, my father's eyes. I wonder if he looks in the mirror and wonders about my eyes. I want to see my father for real one day, just once, just meet him once, talk to him. But maybe it's best for us both if we never meet. If he believes the vision he won't want to meet me. I wish I knew more about the vision. Was it of me stabbing him with the Fairborn? Stabbing him through the heart? I want to tell my father that I would never do that. I couldn't.

My eyes look so black now, the triangular hollows are hardly moving.

I'm back in the kitchen, the last teabag and me.

I've got to go. I've got to find the way to Mercury and get my three gifts. And I'm running out of time. It's just over two months to my birthday.

And that means I've got to go to Bob's place, the place in the A to Z. Only that leads me back to my problem. It leads me back to the alley.

When I stepped through the door from the courtyard of the Council building into the alleyway and I started running, I went at a good pace, a hard pace. I was still running three or four minutes later and I still wasn't at the end of the alley. It was like running on a conveyor belt that was going the wrong way, like they were drawing me back in. And I was panicking and almost screaming by the end of it but I kept at it and somehow I got to the end, where the alley turned. I held on to the corner of the wall, and a woman walked past and stared at me. Then I walked round the corner but I didn't let go of the wall, not for ages did I let go of that wall.

And now I have to go back there, past that corner and up the alley. The address of Bob, the man I need to see, is Cobalt Alley. *That* alley.

Nikita

•··•·•

The Council building is across the road on my left. I wasn't sure it was the right building at first. I was expecting it to be gothic with spires and leaded windows like it is inside, but it's different on the outside. It's a seventies office block, all big and square and concrete, dark gray and stained black in places. I know it's the right building because of the alleyway next to it. Also, I've walked round the block and found the entrance Gran and I used to use. It's at the back through a little gatehouse that's still there. That's the only old bit of building that can be seen from the outside.

I've been standing in a doorway for a while watching the building. It's sunny today, but this side of the road is in the shade and the shadows stretch across to halfway up the street frontage opposite. The Council building has rows and rows of regularly placed square windows, most of which reflect the sunlight in a blue-black shimmer, though tatty vertical blinds can be seen hanging unevenly at the lower ones in the shade, unwatered potted plants standing on the sills. It looks like an unloved, uncared-for office building. There's no movement inside. I've seen two people go in, two women. They might have been witches, but I couldn't see their eyes from here.

Nothing and no one has gone up or down the alley.

I told myself I would watch for an hour or two, but it feels like the office windows are watching me. I need to get this over with.

Feeling a bit shaky.

Couldn't do it. I got close but I couldn't go up there.

I will do it though. I've got to do it.

Just not yet.

Nothing happening at all. I was hoping to see the bloke, Bob, walk down the alley, but he hasn't appeared.

He has to come out at some stage though. The best idea is to keep well back and watch.

He might be having the day off or be away on holiday for all I know.

It's only one day gone. Only one day less.

Day two.

Okay. Day one was not a success. Nobody went up or down the alley (including me). A few people went in and out of the Council building.

But I'm here early now. Slept in a different doorway half a mile away.

And success already. A few people have gone into the Council building, but, more importantly, a van drove up the alley. It drove up, the gates to the courtyard opened, in the van went, and the gates shut. It all looked normal.

Nobody has walked up or down the alley yet. I'm waiting for my man to do that.

And waiting.

And waiting.

But everyone just walks on past the end of the alley, not even looking up there, like they don't even notice it. There's a dead-end sign and a brick wall at the far end, so no one's likely to go up there. But still it's like it's invisible to passersby.

And what if he never comes? Mary told me about him years ago. Maybe he's not here anymore. Maybe the Council has caught him.

Of course just when I'm not really paying attention, someone steps off the street and walks up the alley. A man. But is it Bob?

And now he has his back to me.

He's gray haired, thin, wearing beige trousers and a navy blue jacket, and carrying a holdall. He walks fast, not looking to the door on the left that I escaped out of, not looking at the gates that the van went through, and he carries on to the end where he turns to the door on his right and unlocks it. As he turns the handle and steps inside he looks toward me. Then he's gone.

So, if that is Bob, do I wait for him to come out again? He might stay in there for a few days. I've got to see him. Must stop being so pathetic. I'm crossing the road.

Now what?

A girl is walking up the alley ahead of me; she's moving fast and is already at the end and knocking on the man's door and going in.

What?

Do I do the same? Or wait?

A horn blasts. I'm in the middle of the road. I scuttle back to my side of the street and my doorway.

Was the girl watching too? Is she seeking help, or is she his assistant . . . daughter . . . friend?

She's coming out already. She's a kid, younger than me.

She's walking fast, jogging across the road through a gap in the traffic, turning to her right and glancing at me.

Beckoning me.

I look at the alley.

It will still be here later.

I swivel round in time to see the girl turn down another street and I jog to catch up.

She cuts down another side street and then another and out into a major road with people and shops. Busy, barging people and I can't see the girl. She could be in any of the shops. Clothes. Phones. Music. Books.

I turn round and she's standing right in front of me.

"Hi," she says and grabs my arm. "You look like you need a drink."

She's chosen a table at the back of the coffee shop. We're sitting opposite each other. She bought the hot chocolates and asked for extra mini-marshmallows, then told me to carry the tray, and now she has the cup to her lips and is staring at me over its pink and white mountain. Her eyes are definitely fain: green, pretty but lacking that witch thing . . . the sparks. Definitely fain. And yet they're weird; they have a liquid quality. There's another color in there, a turquoise that's sometimes there and sometimes not. Like a tropical ocean.

"You want to see Bob?" She flicks her long brown hair over her shoulder.

I nod and attempt to sip my drink but can't get at it for the pile of marshmallows. I eat all the marshmallows to get rid of them.

"I can help you." She picks at her marshmallows, waves a pink one in the air as she says, "What's your name?"

"Um, Ivan."

"Unusual name." She picks up another marshmallow and adds, "Well, not in Russia, I suppose."

She takes a sip of her hot chocolate. "I'm Nikita."

I don't think so.

"Do you work for Bob?" I ask.

She looks about fourteen, fifteen tops. She should be in school.

"Do the odd job for him. A bit of this. A bit of that. Run errands for him. You know."

Not really.

She finishes her hot chocolate, getting everything out with a spoon. After a lot of scraping she puts it down, and says, "Want a cookie?" She's up and gone before I can answer.

She comes back with two huge chocolate cookies and passes one over to me. I have to concentrate on not stuffing the whole thing in my mouth at once.

"You shouldn't hang around in front of the Council Building," she says.

"I was being careful."

"I spotted you."

I was being careful.

"You need to get some sunglasses to hide your eyes. And I've no idea what those are"—she points to my tattoos—"but I'd get some gloves."

I have a scarf round my neck that I took from the holiday home, but there weren't any gloves.

She leans over. "Cobalt Alley is protected."

"Yeah, how?"

She waves her hands around. "Magically, of course. Fains don't see the alleyway. Only witches see it."

So she is a witch. But her eyes are different.

"Once you're in the alley you won't get out of it unless you look at where you're going and think about where you're going. And I mean look hard and think hard. On the way in only look at Bob's door, think about the door and nothing else and you'll get to it. On your way out stare at the buildings on the street at the end. Don't look down. Never look down. If you look at the gates to the Council building, if you think about the Council building, that's where you'll end up."

"Right . . . Thanks."

"Your homeless disguise is good, by the way." And she gives me a smile, so I'm not sure if she's joking or not. Before I can reply, she gets up and walks out of the coffee shop.

My stomach gurgles, and I get that taste in my mouth and have to run for the toilet. I throw up into the bowl, a coffee-colored mix of little floating marshmallows and sludge.

I wait, and nothing more comes up, so I swing around to drink water from the tap. The face looking back in the mirror is pale with bloodshot eyes weighted down by black sacks. I do my best to heal, but decent food and water are the only solution. I look at the state of my old jeans, worn thin at the butt and knees. My shirt has holes on the arms and around some of the buttons. My T-shirt underneath is gray and frayed around the neck.

I head out of the shop but the woman behind the counter runs after me.

"Your friend just left you something," she says, handing me a large paper bag.

Inside the bag are two packs of sandwiches—ham and cheese and BLT—a bottle of water, a bottle of fresh orange juice, and a napkin with writing on it. It takes me five minutes to figure out what it says.

To Ivan
From Nikita

Cobalt Alley

I've eaten the BLT, drunk all the water, and I'm looking at Cobalt Alley. It can't be that hard. Can it? I've got to get on with it. Bob and Nikita kept to the narrow pavement on the righthand side. Bob's building stretches back from the corner to the wall at the dead end. It's a rundown low building, one story with a slate roof, and its one door and one window are way up the far end of the alley.

I keep a steady confident-looking but not rushed pace and have my head slightly angled away from the Council side. My eyes are staring at the entrance to Bob's place. I'm thinking, *Bob's place. Bob's place.*

I know I don't look casual, and I have to make myself slow down in case anyone from the Council building can see. But then I feel a pull toward the Council building and I think, *Shit! Bob's place. Bob's place.* And I keep my eyes locked on his door.

I get there. Thank you.

Bob's place.

I knock.

Bob's place. Bob's place.

I stare at the door. I'm muttering now, "Please hurry. Bob's place. Bob's place."

Nothing.

Bob's place. Bob's place.

I knock again. Louder. "Hurry up. Hurry up! Bob's place. Bob's place."

What do I do if guards come out of the Council building now? I'm trapped. The whole thing could be a Council trap. And I feel my body being pulled again toward the Council building.

BOB'S PLACE! BOB'S PLACE! I can't wait this long. *Bob's place. Bob's place.*

The door clicks and opens a fraction.

Nothing else happens.

I step into the room, turn and push the door firmly shut.

"Bloody hell! Bob's place."

"Yes, do come in. Glad you made it, but I'll have to kill you if you even glance at the painting." Far from being a threat, the words sound like a desperate plea for attention.

I turn to see a grubby room. Even the air tastes grubby. Against the far wall, which isn't that far, as the room is narrow, is a wooden table with a bowl of fruit on it. There are a few apples and pears scattered across the table. To my right there's a wooden chair and an easel and beyond them an open door through which the voice called. The position of the easel indicates the painting will be a still life of fruit. I go toward the next room, stopping to look at the work in progress on the way. It's good, traditional and detailed. Oil on canvas.

In the next room I see a man's hunched back. He's stirring something in a small, dented saucepan. There's a smell of tomato soup.

I wait in the doorway. The room has the chilly feel of a cave. It seems even smaller than the painting studio, but that's because against two walls are stacks of large canvas frames, all with their bare, pale backs to the room. The only light comes through two small skylights. There is a small black leatherette sofa, a low Formica coffee table with three legs, a wooden chair like the one in the first room, a row of kitchen cupboards with a stained worktop, on which stands a kettle and a single electric ring. On the drainer by the sink are a large number of mugs and an opened can of soup.

"I'm making lunch."

When I don't reply he stops stirring the soup and turns to look at me, straightening up as he smiles. He holds the wooden spoon in the air as he might hold a paintbrush and a reddish-orange blob drops onto the lino. "I'd like to paint you."

I don't think he'd get my eyes.

The man inclines his head. "Probably not. It would be a challenge."

I don't reply. Did I say that about my eyes aloud?

"You look like you could do with some." He holds the saucepan up and raises his eyebrows in a question.

"Thanks."

The man pours the soup into two of the mugs on the

drainer and puts the pan in the sink. Then he picks up the mugs and offers me one, saying, "I'm afraid I'm out of croutons."

He sits on the leatherette sofa, which is small and narrow.

"I've no idea what croutons are."

"What is the world coming to?"

I sit on the chair and hold the mug to warm my hands. The room is remarkably cold, and the soup only just warm.

The man sits with his legs crossed, revealing how incredibly thin his legs are beneath his baggy trousers, and also one red sock. He twirls his foot around and around and sips his soup.

I swallow most of mine in one gulp.

His foot stops. "It's the dampness that's the problem in here. Even on a summer's day it never gets any sun, and there's damp coming up from underneath. It must be the river." He sips his soup, pursing his lips after each taste, and then puts the mug on the table, saying, "And the electric ring's on the blink and not giving out much heat."

I savor the last mouthful of soup. It's not as good as the BLT, but it's good. And I realize I'm relaxed. I know it is him. He is definitely no Hunter. He is Bob.

"I'm serious, I'd love to paint you. Like that." He waves a hand at me. "Sitting on the simple wooden chair, half starved and young. So, so young. And with those eyes." He stops waving his hand and leans forward to stare into my face. "Those eyes." He leans back again. "One day maybe you'll let me paint you. However, that is not for to-day. Today is for business of a different nature."

I'm about to open my mouth to speak and he puts his finger to his lips. "No need for that."

I smile. I like this guy. I'm fairly sure his magic is mind-reading, which is incredibly rare and—

"I have a certain skill, but a bit like my painting it's competent and practiced—workmanlike you might say, rather than . . ." He stops and gazes at me. "I'm no Cézanne. For example, I have to concentrate hard to pull the key thoughts from the scrambled egg that is your mind. But still it is obvious why you are here." And now he taps the side of his nose.

I think loudly, *I have to find Mercury.*

"Now that I got clear as a bell."

Can you help me?

"I can put you in touch with the next person in the chain. Nothing more."

So it's not going to be straight to Mercury from here. But *I've got a deadline to work to. Two months away.*

"Time enough. But you must understand, and I'm sure you understand better than most, that caution is vital for all concerned."

Does he know who I am? *Why would I understand better than most?*

"I heard a rumor that a prisoner escaped from the Council. An important prisoner. The son of Marcus."

Oh.

"Hunters are out hunting him. And they are very good at that."

He stares at me.

I realize I have let a thought out of the bag.

"May I see them?"

I extend my hand toward him, but he gets up and goes into the far room. I hear a switch flick and the lightbulb above me dithers about coming to life. Bob returns and stands in front of me. He takes my hand in both of his. His hands are cool and thin and his bony fingers pull my skin so that the tattoo is distorted.

"They really are hateful, aren't they?"

I'm not sure if he means the tattoos or White Witches.

"Both, my darling, both."

He lets go of my hand. "May I see the others?"

I show him.

"Well, well, well . . ." Bob returns to his seat on the sofa and his foot starts to twirl round again. "We need to see if you are right, if these are some way of tracking you. If they are, well, my fate is sealed already."

He holds his hands up. "No, no. No apologies necessary . . . Indeed I think I may have to apologize to you, because we are going to have to get someone to look at those. I suspect it won't be a quick procedure, and I know it won't be pleasant. The man I'm thinking of is a philistine."

Bob gets up and takes the mugs to the sink.

"I don't think I'll bother clearing up. Time to move

on. You know, I've always thought I should paint in France, search for Cézanne's spirit in the hills. I can do better than this."

Yes.

"Should I take the paintings?"

I shrug.

"You're right, a clean start is best. You know, I feel better already."

He disappears again into the far room and comes back with a piece of paper and a pencil. Leaning on the kitchen worktop, he sketches. It's good to watch him. His sketch is better than his oil.

"You're very kind. I thought a picture would make more sense to you than some ugly words."

The sketch is of me reaching up to feel on top of a locker, in what looks to be a railway station. There is a sign, but I don't try to read it now. I'll spell it out later.

He hands the drawing to me, saying, "You know you are beautiful, don't you? Don't let them catch you."

I look at him and can't help but smile. He reminds me of Arran, his soft gray eyes filled with the same silvery light, though Bob's whole face looks gray and lined.

"No need to rub it in about my appearance. Oh, there's something else. You will need money."

I realize I haven't given Bob anything.

"You have given me the chance of a new life and a little inspiration. You are my muse and, alas, I will have to make do with this merest fleeting glimpse of you. But others are less interested in life's aesthetics and more in its grubbily begotten gains."

How much will they charge?

Now Bob spreads his arms and looks around the room, "As you can see I am not an expert with money myself. I've really no idea about it at all."

I now remember to ask about Nikita.

The girl who helped me—is she a witch?

"My dear boy, I hope you realize that if, twenty minutes after you leave here, I get a knock on the door from a man asking questions about you, it would be terribly rude of me to answer them. I would hate to talk about you behind your back and I would never dream of being that discourteous about anyone who comes here. Whether the knock comes in twenty minutes or twenty years, the same rules of conduct must always apply."

I nod.

Thank you for sending her to help me. And for the sandwiches.

"I didn't ask her to give you any food." He smiles. "She's a tough cookie with a bit of a soft center."

I grin at him and turn to leave.

He calls, "*Adieu, mon cher,*" as the door closes behind me.

I walk quickly down the alley, sticking close to the wall on my left, eyes fixed on the far buildings, thinking, *The end of the alley. The end of the alley.*

Money

•·•·•

Bob's warning about the Hunters has really got to me. I knew they'd be after me, but now my adrenaline spikes every time I see a person dressed in black. I find a park a few miles away and pace around. A dog walker helps me read the sign in the drawing, which says *Earls Court*. Also in the drawing is a man sitting on a bench reading *The Sunday Times*. The dog walker tells me that today is Wednesday, so I've got four days to get as much cash together as possible.

I've no idea where to begin but I know getting a job isn't going to be the answer. I remember Liam, whom I did community service with, giving advice about stealing. "Find someone stupid and rich—there's loads of 'em—and rob 'em."

I'm near St. Paul's Cathedral. It's all quiet. The few people I've seen have come out of a bar and got straight into a taxi. I'm waiting farther along the street.

It's late when a lone City gent appears, walking carefully and cursing the lack of cabs. He has really fancy clothes, shoes with no holes in them, and a waistline that indicates lack of food is not a problem for him. I'm not really sure how to do this, but I walk up to him from across the road.

He is pretending he hasn't seen me and speeds up. I move into his path and he stops. He must weigh over twice what I do, and he's not short, but he's weak and knows it.

"Look, mate," I say, "I really don't want to hurt you, but I need all your cash."

He's looking around and I realize he's going to start shouting.

I step up close and push him into the wall. He's heavy, but as he hits the bricks the air sort of flobbers out of him like a balloon deflating. "I really don't want to hurt you, but I need all your cash." I have my arm at his neck, pushing his head to the side. His eyes are staring at me, though.

He slides out a long, slim, black leather wallet from his jacket. His hand is shaking.

"Thank you," I say.

I take the notes, flip the wallet closed, hand it back to the man and then I'm off.

Later, when I'm curled up in a shop entrance, I think about the man. He's probably lying in a nice warm bed, and he definitely doesn't have a pack of Hunters after him, but he could have ended up in hospital with a heart attack. I don't want to kill people. I just need their money.

The next day I suss out Earls Court station. It takes me a while to find the platform and the place that matches Bob's picture, but the bench, the sign, and the locker are there. I've just got to come back in three days and get whatever is on top of it. I go and sweep my hand over it now but find only grime.

Now I need some rich, healthy young men to rob.

Liam should come down to London. He'd love it. The place is full of stupid rich people. A few struggle, and some try to hit me, but basically it's all over before it's started.

I've bought a suit and had my hair cut so that I blend in with the fains. But it's dead in Canary Wharf on Saturday, and I'm glad because stealing from these guys is pretty low and they are all pretty hopeless. I've got over three thousand pounds and a reasonably clear conscience, but it's no fun doing anything just for the money.

On Sunday I get the tube to Earls Court and walk around the station, checking for Hunters. No one is even looking at me; everyone is looking blankly ahead or at their phones. I walk to the end of the platform and back to the locker and reach up.

A piece of paper is there. I slide it to the edge with my fingertips, stuff it straight into my pocket, and carry on with hardly a break in my stride.

In a cafe I befriend a woman. She goes through the instructions. They are similar to the ones Mary gave me but not as precise. They are for Thursday.

Jim and Trev (Part One)

•··•·•·•

I've followed the instructions carefully. They have taken me to the outskirts of London, to a grotty house at the grottier end of the sprawl. I'm standing in someone's front room. It is dark in here. Jim is sitting on the stairs. Whereas Bob is a struggling artist, Jim appears to be a struggling criminal, a White Witch of the lowest ability. He's no Hunter, that's for sure.

The house is small, owned by fains who, Jim assures me, "don't know nuffin' 'bout nuffin'." The front door opens into a lounge area that leads to the kitchen. There are stairs in one corner and a large flat-screen TV on the wall, but no chairs for some reason. Jim has closed the curtains and the air inside is heavy. There's a smell of onions and garlic, which I think is coming from Jim.

Jim hasn't told me how to get to Mercury but has told me how important a good passport is, how I will actually need two passports, how his passports are quality passports, that they are in fact real passports, and on and on . . .

He wipes his nose on the back of his hand before sniffing a large amount of snot back into his chest.

"There's more work in these than a bespoke suit, more skill, more everythin'. These passports will get you through the strictest checks. These passports may save your life."

I don't even want a passport. I just want the directions to Mercury. But I'm guessing I shouldn't fall out with him. "Well, I'm sure you're right, Jim."

"You'll see I'm right, Ivan. You'll see."

"So that's two thousand then, for two passports and the directions to Mercury."

"Oh, I'm sorry, Ivan, if I've not been clear. It'll all come to three thousand pounds." He wipes his nose again, this time with the palm of his hand.

"Look, you said a thousand for one passport."

"Oh, Ivan, you're new to this, aren't you? Let me explain. It's the problem of the foreigners. I'll get you a British passport at a thousand, but it's best to get one from somewhere foreign as well. The States is a possibility, but I favor New Zealand these days. A lot of people got grudges against the Yanks for one reason or another, but no one's got a grudge against a Kiwi, 'cept maybe a few sheep . . ." And he sniffs and swallows deeply. "Course, foreign stuff is dearer."

I don't know. I've no idea if a thousand pounds is a good price or not. It sounds a lot to me. Two thousand sounds ridiculous.

"Mercury will want to know that you're being careful. She likes people to take all the precautions."

And I've no idea if he knows the first thing about Mercury, but . . . "Fine. When?"

"Great, Ivan. Lovely to do business with you. Lovely."

"When?"

"Okay, son. I know you're keen. Two weeks should see us right, but let's say three to be on the safe side."

"Let's say two weeks, one passport and a thousand pounds."

"Two weeks, two passports, three thousand."

I nod and back away from him.

"Brill . . . Half now, of course."

I can't be bothered to argue more so I pull out three wads that I have made up of five hundred each. I saw that in a film and I'm pleased I've done it. Everything with Jim feels like a cheap gangster movie.

"Pick the directions up at the same time in two weeks and follow them. It'll be a different meeting place. Never use the same place twice. You bring the money etc. etc."

"Are the instructions part of a spell, Jim?"

"A spell?"

"The instructions to get to the meeting point. A spell to ensure Hunters can't follow."

Jim smiles. "Nah. Though I do always check out my customers as they wait for buses and trains and if I saw a Hunter I'd be long gone."

"Oh."

"But mainly they're directions. Don't want a customer getting lost. You wouldn't believe how thick some people are."

Jim goes to the door and switches the light on. "Blimey."

We both blink and shield our eyes in the glare. "Just need a photo of you."

While he's doing that I wonder what Gift he has. It's considered rude to ask, but this is Jim so I do.

He says, "The usual. Potions. I hate 'em."

He continues, "And I thought . . . we all thought that I was goin' to have a strong Gift. From childhood I had this special talent, and my mother, bless her, said, 'My son will have a strong Gift.' See, already from age three or four, I could tell witches from fains. Could tell it easy, and that's rare, that is."

"Yes. Rare, for sure. So how do you do it, Jim?"

"Well, you're not going to believe this but it's all in the eyes . . . I see little glints of silver in White Witches' eyes."

My mouth must have dropped open.

"You don't believe me, do you?"

"Jim, I'm just . . . amazed. What exactly are these glints of silver like?"

"Oh well, like nothing else, really. The nearest I can say is that they are thin slices of silver and they move around, twistin' and turnin', like bits in one o' them snow-shaker toys. That's what it's like."

"You see it in your own eyes when you look in the mirror?"

"I do. I do."

"Amazing."

"Yes, it is. Beautiful, really. Witches have beautiful eyes."

"And what do you see in my eyes, Jim?"

"Oh well, your eyes . . . you've got interestin' eyes for sure."

"Do you see silvery sparks?"

"Ivan, if I'm honest, I'd have to say, not so much silvery . . ."

I sit on the floor and lean back against the wall.

"Do all White Witches have silvery bits in them?"

"As far as I've seen they do."

"Have you ever met any Black Witches?"

"A few. Their eyes is different." He looks worried. "Not silvery."

"Like mine?"

"No. I'd say yours are unique, Ivan."

No. They're like my father's.

Jim gives a huge sniff and swallow then sits next to me.

"I can tell Half Bloods as well."

"You can?" I don't think I've ever even seen a Half Blood, someone who is half witch and half fain. They are despised by witches.

"They've got real pretty eyes. Weird, though . . . like flowing water."

There's a knock on the door and I'm on my feet behind it, looking at Jim. He's smiling at me.

"All right, Ivan, all right. It's just Trev." Jim looks at his watch. "He's late, though. He's always late, is Trev."

"Who's Trev?" I whisper.

Jim gets up and stretches his back before wandering to the door.

"Trev's the brains. He's got skills, has Trev"—and here Jim lowers his voice to a whisper—"not a lot of magic but a lot of skills. He's goin' to take a look at them tattoos for you."

Trev looks like an expert, but I'm not sure in what. He is exceptionally tall, balding, with wispy gray hair growing from below the level of the top of his ears to his shoulders. He's wearing a worn brown suit, thick beige shirt, and rust-red knitted waistcoat. Trev is expressionless in every way. His body seems to float along with hardly any arm or even leg movement. His voice when he says, "Hello, Jim," is flat and toneless. He shows minimal interest in me and hardly looks at my face, which is fine. He is, however, brought to life by my tattoos.

"I'll have to take samples," he says, peering at me and pulling my skin around and moving from my neck to my hand and then my leg. "Of the skin and bone."

"The bone?"

"I'll take it from your ankle."

"How?"

Trev doesn't answer but kneels on the floor and opens a scuffed, black leather bag. It looks like an old-fashioned doctor's bag.

I notice that Jim is grinning.

"Are you a doctor, Trev?" I ask.

Trev possibly hasn't heard as he doesn't reply. Jim sniggers and sniffs heartily.

Trev pulls out a plastic bag, rips it open, and lays a blue surgical sheet on the floor. Next out of the bag is a scalpel; it too is in a plastic bag that is quickly ripped open and thrown to one side. Soon there is a glinting row of surgical implements, most worryingly a small hacksaw.

By this stage Jim is hopping around with glee.

Trev lays another blue sheet beneath my leg and then starts to clean my ankle with a surgical wipe, saying, "It's better if I don't use anesthetic."

"What?"

"Except the patient usually jerks around too much. Think you can hold still?"

"Probably not." My voice has gone higher.

"Shame." And he turns to his bag and removes a hypodermic needle and some clear liquid. "I need to analyze the skin, tissue, and bone. If there's some anesthetic in there it may skew the results."

I don't know if he's making this up and just wants to make Jim's day.

Jim looks expectant.

"Okay. I'll hold still." And I wonder at what stage I can change my mind.

"Jim can help . . ."

"No, I don't need him." I don't want his snotty fingers anywhere near me. They're more terrifying than the hacksaw.

"Don't do any healing until I say I've finished. I'll be quick."

To give Trev his due, he doesn't hang around.

I don't jerk. I'm rigid, watching it all. I don't make a sound either, no screaming or moaning, though my jaw and teeth ache, I'm clenching them so tightly. I'm drenched in sweat by the end of it.

Jim watches me heal and says, "Blimey! You're quick."

Trev then asks how the tattoos were applied and while I talk he pops lids onto the four small, round plastic trays that contain the bits of skin, blood, flesh, and bone. Then he stacks the trays and puts a large elastic band round them, holding them together. He carefully places them in the corner of his bag. Next he rolls up the bloodied plastic sheet with the surgical tools into a large bundle, gets Jim to hold open a bin liner, and slides the lot in, then screws up the sheet that was under my leg and tosses that in as well.

He peers at my ankle and nods. "I took the '0,' but you can see it's already reappeared on the scab. That's very clever. It's all very clever. I'll take a few photos." He gets out his phone and clicks away.

"Interesting scars," he says, looking at my hand. "Acid?"

"You're studying the tattoos," I say.

"Just professional interest."

"How soon will you be able to tell me the results?"

Trev looks at me totally blankly. "I need to analyze what chemicals are in the tattoos. That should be straightforward, but there'll be magic involved, which makes it a thousand times more complicated."

"How soon will you know if they're tracking me?"

Trev doesn't answer. He snaps the lock on his bag and stands up to go. He says to Jim, "The tattoos are unlikely to be used to track him." And Trev picks up his bag and walks out.

Jim shuts the door. "No manners. That's 'cause he's too bright for 'em. Still wouldn't do 'im any 'arm to try." He sniffs, swallows a mouthful, and then says, "He never rushes neither. Never. I'll give you the latest when I see you in two weeks."

"He didn't mention money."

"A sad failin' of our Trev, that is. Thinks he's above all that. 'Course he's got to eat, ain't 'e? Like anyone."

"I'm guessing he isn't cheap."

"He's an expert, Ivan. Experts ain't cheap. Experts in passports, experts in tattoos, experts in anythin' ain't cheap. He charges by the hour. I'll let you know what sort of region he's goin' to be in when I see you next time."

Jim and Trev (Part Two)

•·•··•

Early one morning two weeks later Jim and I are in the changing rooms of a village tennis club. I'm not sure if the odor is Jim or the changing room, but I can't imagine the tennis-club members would put up with this smell for long.

"You're looking a lot better, Ivan. A bit fuller round the ol' cheeks. Gaunt, that's what you were, gaunt." He is glancing to the door behind me all the time as he speaks.

"Is there a problem, Jim?"

"There shouldn't be. Shouldn't be. You did follow the instructions all right?"

"Of course."

"It gives me the willies this place. Let's make it quick, eh?"

I take the passports and look through them. They seem fine to me. I have two different names and dates of birth, but I'm eighteen in both, which is plausible.

"That's it then," Jim says as he finishes counting the money. He puts it in his jacket pocket and I grab his arm.

"The directions to Mercury, please, Jim."

Jim shakes his head sadly, but is still smiling, professional that he is. "Ivan, me ol' mate, I'm real sorry but I can't divulge any details till we have the results in from Trev. I'd love to help, course I would. Course I would."

"And how is Trev doing?"

"Oh, Trev's havin' a great time, Trev is. I went round to see him the other day and he's lovin' it. A giant puzzle he said. A big, giant puzzle."

"And how soon will he have the answer to the big, giant puzzle?"

"He didn't know. He hardly spoke. Quiet even for Trev. But he did say he'd leave directions in the usual spot on a Tuesday at ten in the mornin'. You've just gotta check every Tuesday."

"I'm guessing it won't be this Tuesday from the size of the puzzle."

"You never know, Ivan. Our Trev is a genius. He might be having his 'reeka moment right now. You just check every week and one Tuesday it'll be there."

"And money?"

Jim's face sours so much that his mouth puckers and seems unable to form words for a few seconds before he shakes it off to say, "He says he'll discuss things with you and only you." Jim wipes his nose with his fingers and then rubs them on his trousers.

The first week I don't expect anything to appear on the locker. I've got a decent stash of money now and I can't face stealing any more. I buy some new boots and clothes. I keep training. A hundred push-ups are easy now. But I need to get out of the city. I've not seen any Hunters, and I'm moving around every night to sleep in a different doorway, but I'm on edge all the time. I decide that after I check the locker on the following Tuesday I'll go to Wales or maybe Scotland, somewhere remote, and come back the following Monday.

But the next Tuesday I find an envelope on top of the locker. I walk away slowly, looking around. A young boy no more than five years old is holding his mother's hand and staring at me. I freeze and look around again and then clock him again. He is still staring at me. I don't know why, but I run.

I've been way too complacent. But even if they aren't tracking me—and I'm beginning to believe that they aren't—then they *are* looking for me. They could get lucky and see me wandering around the streets. They underestimated me and I escaped, but I mustn't underestimate the Hunters. As Mary said, "The clue is in the name."

In the envelope there is a train ticket and a note. With a bit of help I discover that the ticket is for tomorrow, leaving at six a.m. The journey to Liverpool can't be more than a few hours, so it will leave me time to find my way to the meeting point which is indicated on the note:

11 o'clock
42 Mill Hill Lane

Liverpool is a place with few witches, because there's a gang of fains there that are on to them and don't like them one bit. Gran told me White Witches try never to go there because there's a sort of agreement: the Scouse fains won't out the witches as long as the witches keep away from Liverpool.

I tell myself that this is a good plan. Jim is looking after me, sending me to a place with no White Witches, no Hunters, but later in the day I get jittery and can't keep still. It bothers me that this is a change to the plan. Jim never mentioned train tickets. He only ever talked about instructions.

I'm walking back to Cobalt Alley. I think Bob will have left weeks ago—I hope so, but something makes me want to check. If the train ticket is because the Hunters are on to Bob—or worse, if they have captured him—I want to know.

Before I reach my previous vantage point across from the Council building I can see that something is happening in the alley so I keep moving slowly along the opposite side of the road. There's a large white van parked outside Bob's place and another vehicle to the far side of it that I can't quite see, but I think it's the same 4x4 that came to Scotland for me. I risk one last look and see a man come out of Bob's door holding a painting. The man is Clay.

I don't sleep that night. I go to the train station only a few minutes before the train is due to leave and find my reserved seat.

The carriage is less than half full; it's an early train. I try to see each person's eyes as they come past me. I see no Hunters.

I'm dog-tired and doze on the journey. There's a judder and an announcement. We are arriving in Liverpool.

It's 11:15 and Mill Hill Lane feels increasingly unwelcoming with every minute that passes. The street is empty of people. Number 42 is a derelict house in a terrace of derelict houses. Broken glass and graffiti seem to be the norm, but inside it's relatively untouched: the floorboards are bare and the only broken window is the one I broke to get in.

I've stashed my rucksack in a back alley half a mile away. My passports and money are in the zipped pockets of my jacket. I am wearing an Arab scarf and sunglasses, though it's not sunny. Fingerless gloves are more practical than ordinary gloves and they hide the tattoo and the scars on my hand, but not the tattoos on my finger, which I've taped over.

I tell myself that at the first sign of anything odd I'll go. But I'm kidding myself; the whole thing is odd, and I need to see Trev.

I'm standing upstairs looking up the street when Trev turns the far corner, walking quickly and carrying a thin plastic shopping bag. I stay still, a little back from the window, and watch. There's a kid on a bike at the far end of the street, and he's watching Trev too.

I go downstairs as Trev comes to the front door and I pull him inside, telling him that this is not a good place to meet.

"I normally leave all the directions to Jim. That's what he's good at." Trev looks out of the window and then back at me. "Jim's gone."

"Gone? Gone where?"

"Abroad, I think . . . I hope. I don't think the Council got him, but they're on to us. That's why I moved up here. Jim told me that even Hunters don't like coming here."

I don't tell him about seeing Clay at Bob's place but ask, "Are you going abroad too, Trev?"

He tries to smile but looks sick as he pats his breast pocket. "Got the tickets and I'm off this evening."

"Good. And what about me?"

"Ah yes, glad you asked. The tattoos on your little finger are the clue. As soon as I saw them I had an idea what they were up to. You see, the three little tattoos mirror the tattoos on your body. The one by your nail reflects the one on your neck, the middle one is the one on your hand, and the lower one the tattoo on your ankle. They planned to make some sort of witch's bottle."

I look at my finger.

"Witch's bottles are extremely hard to control. I think they're working on a sophisticated version. A very sophisticated version. So instead of putting some of your hair or skin or blood in the bottle, I think they were going to amputate your finger and use that. They would probably cut your finger into the three sections and make three witch's bottles. They would do something to the tattoo on your finger and you would feel it, suffer the pain, on the larger tattoo on your neck, hand, or ankle."

"To force me to do things for them?"

"That's what I've been wondering. Not sure how it would work. They could inflict so much pain you'd want to comply."

"Comply or die."

"Comply or suffer. Suffering is their speciality."

"But they could use it to kill me?"

"Well, yes."

I rip the tape off my finger and look at the three tiny tattoos. They all go through to the bone. I take out my pen-knife and prick the tattoo by my nail, wondering if I will feel anything in my neck.

"Nothing?" Trev asks.

I shake my head.

"It has to be in a bottle, with the correct spell."

"How soon would they have amputated?"

"I would think they would want to check the tattoos were deep and had healed fully. A few days, no more than a week. Then they would test it. And, of course, if it didn't quite work, you've got nine other fingers."

"They could still do it? I mean if they caught me, chopped off my finger?"

"Oh, yes. It's permanent. A permanent problem. You can't remove them."

"I thought they were some sort of brand or a tracking device."

"They aren't for tracking," Trev says. "But, yes, they are a brand. I think that the tattoo will show whatever you become . . . I mean if you have the Gift to transform, the brand will still be there."

"And there's definitely no way to remove them?"

"You could cut off your leg and your finger, but you'd still be left with the problem of your neck."

There's shouting from outside. Fains.

Trev glances to the window and pulls a piece of paper out of his pocket and stuffs it in my hand. "How to get to Mercury is on there."

I push the paper deep into my pocket saying, "Thank you, Trev. Thank you for everything."

Trev holds the shopping bag out to me, saying, "These are all your skin and bone samples. You must destroy them. Burn them. If the Council get them they could make a witch's bottle with them. A crude one . . . but still."

I peer into the bag. There are the plastic dishes with bits of blood in them.

He adds, "Just so there's no doubt. Ever. From anyone . . . that I kept anything of you."

I think he's worried about my father.

Glass smashes in the room above.

We drop low and freeze.

Another smash . . . but farther away, from a different house. Shouts.

I peer out the window.

"Shit!" I duck down and tell Trev, "Hunters."

I raise my head again to look. A Hunter is walking down the street, and there's a gang of three fains throwing stones at her. She doesn't look that bothered. They only work in pairs, though, so there'll be another in the back-streets somewhere.

I drop down again, saying, "We've got to go."

We run to the back of the house. The door is locked and bolted. The bolts won't budge. I smash the window with my elbow and kick through the glass and we're climbing out. At the back wall I give Trev a lift over the gate, which is nailed shut, and I scramble after him, looking left and right at the top.

Nothing. No one.

We run.

A few roads away we slow down, though I keep check-ing behind.

Trev looks like he's going to be sick. He's beyond car-ing what I owe him, so I give him most of my cash and say, "Thanks, Trev. If you ever need anything . . . I mean . . . you know . . ."

We shake hands and he leaves in one direction and I go in the other.

I feel for the piece of paper in my pocket. It's still there.

Then I realize I haven't got the plastic bag.

I can hardly believe that I have been that stupid, but I have. I'm sure I didn't drop it. I think I put it down when I was giving Trev a lift over the wall.

Hunters

•··•·•

I could leave without the plastic bag, hope that it just looks like rubbish, but . . . but, but, but. Never underestimate the enemy. If White Witches get that stuff, the bits of me, they won't need my finger; they might be able to make a witch's bottle with my skin and blood and bone.

I retrace my steps to the house. There's no plastic bag in the alley, in the backyard of the house or in the house itself. There is no sign of the Hunters either.

Shit!

From the front room of the house I can see both ways up the street. It's empty. I sit on the floor to try to work out my next move.

The Hunters were on to Bob, and now Jim and Trev, but I'm not being tracked. If they knew that I was here there'd be twenty Hunters, not two. They probably don't know what's in the bag, but they might know that Trev had been carrying it.

There's shouting outside. I scramble over to the window to peer out, and duck down a second later to get my breath and to get my head into gear. The Hunter is back, as are the three stone-throwing fains. The Hunter is carrying the plastic shopping bag. She must still be looking for Trev.

I scoot upstairs to get a better view of the Hunter. She's slim and tall and picking up stones to throw back.

"She a friend of yours?"

I turn round.

A big girl in a hoodie is standing at the back of the room.

"No, but she will have a friend. She won't be alone. There's bound—"

"Her mate's around the back. Seen her already." The girl folds her arms and looks me up and down. "I thought you were one of them, but you're different. What are you?"

"Different."

"Well, I don't like them and I don't like you."

The shouting has stopped and I turn back to the window. One of the fains is on the ground, flat out, unconscious or dead. The big girl is next to me, and she's looking too.

"Is she here because of you?"

I'm looking at the Hunter. She's backed up to the house opposite and whistling a signal for her partner.

"No." That is technically true, as I think they must have been following Trev. "Look, I'm leaving . . . soon. I just need to get that plastic bag back."

"So, it *is* you they're after? Should I give you to them?"

I keep watching the Hunter, and I grin but don't turn round. "You could try."

The other Hunter appears and more stones are thrown.

I shake my head. "Throwing stones won't get rid of them."

"My brother's on his way. He's got a gun."

"They've got guns."

The fain lad is lying in the street, not moving. I say, "Do you think you should call an ambulance for your friend?"

"If I thought it'd turn up I might."

Two more fains have appeared, but they are all hanging back. Both Hunters are standing close to the kid on the ground. They actually look quite nervous. They won't want a lot of fain attention. If anyone gets a phone out to film them, they'll be out of there. I can't let them run off with my stuff.

I pull my scarf on tight and am out of the front door in seconds. I grab two bricks as I march toward the Hunters. The Hunters are by the prone fain. I hope I look like his pissed-off friend.

"What've you done to my mate?" I add a few swear words.

The Hunters stand still, watching me, like they can't believe I'm going to do anything serious. But I keep on coming. The farthest one pulls her gun and I speed up as she shouts, "Stop!"

As if that's going to stop me.

I hit the first one with a brick on the side of her face and use her body to shield me as I charge the other one.

A shot, another, and then I'm kicking the gun out of her hand and it's sliding across the road. The bricked Hunter is out of it on the ground. I'm in a crouch. The other Hunter is too, and now she has a knife in her hand.

It's only now that I realize how good Celia is. This girl is a Hunter, a top fighter, but she seems slow, and I can read what she's going to do, easy. I get the knife out of her hand on my second move.

I don't stab her but break both her arms, like Celia has taught me. I've got her on the ground, my knee in her back and could break her neck easy enough. I pull her head round. I hate Hunters. I'm breathing hard, but her hair is silky in my hands and I don't want to kill anyone.

"Nice moves!" The big girl is holding the plastic shopping bag in one hand and the gun in the other. She's pointing the gun at me.

I stand, arms out in surrender. There are fains all around me, and none of them look friendly. "They're yours." I nudge the Hunter on the floor with the toe of my boot and glance over at the other one who's still unconscious.

There's two fains bent over the lad who's sitting up now with a cut on his forehead. There are seven fains around me, ranging from a skinny teenage kid to two big, tattooed blokes. Another is coming up the road with two white bull terriers straining at their leads. The girl's brother with his gun is probably not far away.

"That's my stuff." I nod at the plastic bag.

She hesitates but holds the bag out to me. "You've no reason to stay, no reason to come back."

I take the bag, saying, "Not now."

I wonder what will happen to the Hunters, but I'll leave that up to the fains. I have to push past the gang that have gathered round. I head in the opposite direction to the lad with the dogs, walking fast and then breaking into a jog.

I don't stop until I get back to the train station. That's where I'd left Nikita.

Arran

•˙•⋅•˙•

Nikita had been watching Bob's place when Clay was there. She saw me and followed me. I didn't notice her until she was standing in front of me. I bought her a hot chocolate.

Nikita's real name is Ellen. Her eyes are amazing, like a sea, a clear, turquoise sea, currents of blue and green moving through them. She's a Half Blood. Her mother was a White Witch and her father is a fain. Since her mother died, Ellen has been outside the witch community and pretty much ostracized by them. Her nearest relative on the witch side is her grandmother, who pretends she doesn't exist. She lives with her father in London and says she goes to school "half the time." She also says she's sixteen, but I'm not sure, she looks younger.

She told me that Jim went to France and that she wanted to go with him but he said no. I told her a bit about myself. And about Arran, Deborah, and Gran, and Annalise. She agreed to help me get a message to Arran.

Ellen is waiting for me as we agreed. While I was meeting Trev she has searched the internet for information about Arran. There isn't much, but his old school website has a small article about him winning a prize and going on to study medicine at Cambridge. We get the first train out of Liverpool that's heading in that direction. It's late by the time we arrive in Cambridge, and I tell Ellen she has to stay in a B&B for the night. She doesn't look too happy when she realizes I'll be sleeping rough, but the good thing about Ellen is that she quickly gets that there are some arguments she's not going to win.

The next morning we meet up at nine. The B&B landlady has given Ellen a leaflet about Cambridge and a small map. Ellen says she's going to suss the college out and see how many Hunters are around. She's convinced there will be some watching Arran. We agree to meet up again in the evening.

"I saw one Hunter. She swapped over with her partner at four o'clock, so it looks like they're watching Arran twenty-four seven, doing a twelve-hour shift each. If they believed you'd try to see him they'd have many more than that."

I nod. I'm not going to try. I don't want to give him any more trouble than I already have.

Ellen thinks the best time for her to see Arran is in the college dining room at breakfast. She thinks she'll be able to sneak in and sit with him as his guest. The Hunters hang around outside the building, and Arran isn't in their sight most of the time.

I give her a small picture that I've drawn. "He'll know it's from me."

"Okay. But I'm going to take a photo of you as well."

Oh.

"I'll just show it to him on my phone. So he can see you. What you look like now. We could do a video."

I shake my head. "A photo."

"You could speak to him on the phone."

I shake my head. I couldn't.

I wait in a park where we have arranged to meet. I feel sick.

Ellen's bright. She won't mess up.

But I still feel sick.

It's midday when I see her walking toward me. She's smiling. A big smile.

"It worked fine. He looked a bit confused at first, but then I showed him your drawing and he was so happy. He kept smoothing his hand over it. He wanted me to send the photo of you to his phone but I said that was too dangerous. So he looked at it while we talked.

"He's enjoying studying. He's found his Gift, which is healing, but it's not very strong. He misses home and Deborah. Deborah is living in Gran's house. She has a boyfriend called David. They want to get married."

"Married!"

"She wants children. Arran says David is great. He's nothing to do with the Council or Hunters. He's a White Witch, from Wales. He works as a carpenter. Arran said that you'd like him. Deborah has an office job in town. Arran says she's happy there. He says to tell you that she has an amazing Gift."

"What is it?"

"Well, I don't really get it but it's something to do with being good at paperwork. I'm not sure if he was joking."

I don't think he'd joke, but paperwork doesn't make any sense.

"He said that your gran died three months ago, when Arran was home for the holidays. He said she went to bed saying that she was tired. She died in the night."

"You asked him, didn't you? Was it suicide?"

"I asked him. And he said he didn't know. He said Deborah thought she might have taken one of her own potions."

I know Deborah is right.

"Arran said that after you were taken the Council often called your gran down to London for questioning. He said she refused to answer anything."

"They never questioned Arran?"

"He said not, but he's not very good at lying."

"And Deborah?"

Ellen nods.

"He said Hunters searched the house a few months ago. Deborah overheard them saying something about the 'incompetents at the Council.' They had a feeling that you had escaped.

"He asked what they did to you and where you were

kept. I told him that I didn't know. I told him you were well."

"Thank you. You didn't tell him about the tattoos?"

"No. You said not to." She takes a breath and tries to smile. "I asked about Annalise too." Ellen's tone isn't promising. "He's never spoken to her since you left. Even at parties and weddings, he and Deborah aren't allowed near her. He heard that she had a small Giving ceremony."

She was seventeen last September. "She still goes to school, doesn't she?"

"I didn't ask that. I got the feeling he didn't like talking about her."

"Yeah, well. He disapproves of me and her."

"Why?"

"He thinks I'm asking for trouble. Her family are very White, brilliant White. Pure as they come. Involved with the Council . . . Hunters."

"She doesn't sound your type."

"She's not like them."

And she is my type, very much my type.

"You're not thinking of going back to see her?"

I think about it a lot, though I know it would be stupid.

Ellen says, "I told Arran where I live in London. He said we should meet up, maybe. I thought that I could get messages to him for you. I'd be like the go-between."

I don't know. It might be better if I never contact them again. But if anyone could do it Ellen could.

I say, "Ellen, I don't want to get you into trouble with the Council."

"Ha! Too late for that."

She gets out her mobile phone. "I took a photo of Arran. And a short video."

I tell myself I'm not going to cry, not in front of Ellen, and I'm okay at first. Arran looks a little older, but his hair is the same. He's pale, but he looks good. He tries to smile and doesn't quite manage it. He tells me a little about what he's doing at university, and about Deborah and David, and then he tells me how he's missed me and wants to see me but knows it's impossible. He hopes I'm well, really well, not just physically but inside myself too, and says he's always believed in me and knows I'm a good person, and he hopes I can get away, that I must be careful whom I trust and that I must leave them all behind, how he and Deborah will be fine and will be happy knowing I am free and that is how he'll think of me, happy and free, always.

I have to walk away for a bit after watching it. And I so want to see Arran for real and be with him, and I know I can't. I can't ever do that.

Later I thank Ellen for helping me. I'm not sure what else to do. I offer her some money, but she doesn't want any, so we have fish and chips and sit in the park eating them. I tell her she has to go back to her dad, and she complains, but not much.

She selects a chip and asks me what I'm going to do next.

"Get three gifts."

"You're going to find Mercury, then."

And I wonder about Ellen. "What do Half Bloods do, Ellen? Do they have Givings? Do they have Gifts?"

"They don't have Givings unless the Council allows it, which only happens rarely and also means working for them in exchange for them allowing the ceremony. I'll never work for the Council; they despise us. All witches do. But I've heard of a few Half Bloods in the past who have had Givings from their witch parent and have found their Gift. My gran's too terrified of the Council to even see me; she'll never help me."

"So? What are you going to do? If you can't get three gifts from your gran or the Council?"

"I don't know yet. There's always Mercury. But she's the absolute last resort."

"What do you know about her?"

"She's a nasty piece of work. You shouldn't trust her. Rumor has it she makes slaves of little girls. So I'm not racing over for her help just yet. You shouldn't trust her." Ellen picks a fat chip.

"I'm not a little girl."

"She doesn't make slaves of little boys, she eats them." Ellen pops the chip into her mouth.

"You serious?"

Ellen nods and swallows. "That's what I heard." She selects another chip and looks up at me. "Not raw. She cooks them first."

PART
FIVE

GABRIEL

Geneva

•˙•˙•˙•

Geneva Airport. The journey here was stressful: working out how to get a flight, flying, and worst of all standing at Passport Control. Though my passport worked fine.

The instructions on the piece of paper Trev gave me say to be at the revolving glass doors at 11 a.m. on Tuesday. There are people walking in and out of the glass doors. People of all ages: business people with mini wheeled suitcases, air hostesses with micro wheeled suitcases, pilots with black-leather wheeled cases, holidaymakers with huge wheeled cases. Everybody is moving quickly, not really rushing, not in bad moods, just getting to where they are going.

And then there's me, wearing sunglasses, a cap, an Arab scarf, fingerless gloves, a thick green army jacket, jeans, and boots, carrying my battered rucksack.

I don't know what time it is but I've been here ages: it's way past eleven o'clock.

A movement in the cafe to my right catches my eye. A young man in sunglasses waves me over.

I pick my way through the narrow gaps between the tables and stand opposite him. He doesn't look up but swirls his half-full coffee cup around and drains it. He puts the cup in the saucer as he stands, grabs hold of my arm, and, moving fast, guides me through the revolving doors and into the next building, the train station.

We go down an escalator to Platform 4 and straight onto a train. It's gloomy in here. The train's a double-decker and we go upstairs, where he lets go of my arm. We sit on a sofa-style seat with a little round table in front of us.

My contact looks a year or two older than me, Arran's age, I guess. His skin is olive, and he has shoulder-length wavy hair, dark brown with lighter streaks in it. He's smiling, lips together, like he's just heard a really good joke. He's wearing mirrored aviator sunglasses with silver frames, almost identical to mine.

The train starts, and a few minutes into the journey a ticket inspector appears at the far end of the carriage. My contact goes downstairs and I follow. We stand by the doors. He's slim, a tad taller than me and he doesn't have the hiss of a mobile phone to him.

I think he might be a Black Witch. I want to see his eyes.

The train stops a minute later. It's Geneva Central Station. My contact sets off fast, and I walk a step behind him.

We walk for an hour or so, always fast, but going back on ourselves quite a bit; I come to recognize a few shop windows and glimpses of the lake. We finally enter a residential area of tall apartment blocks and stop at a door in an old building much like all the others we've passed. The road here is quiet, a few parked cars, no traffic, and no other pedestrians. My contact pushes a number code into the entry system, saying to me, "9-9-6-6-1 . . . okay?"

And I say, "9-9-6-6-1, okay."

He lets the door swing back hard in my face so that I have to stop it with a slam of my palm. I stride after him up the stairs, up and up, and up, and up, and up . . .

We continue to the sixth floor, the top floor, where the stairs come to an end at a small landing. There is one wooden door.

Once again there isn't a key but a number code. "5-7-6-3-2 . . . okay?"

And he goes in and lets the door slam behind him.

I stand looking around. The varnish on the door is peeling, the landing is bare, the plaster is cracked, an old blackened cobweb hangs loosely in the corner. An empty silence hangs around too. There is no hissing.

He opens the door. "5-7-6—"

"I know."

His smile has gone, but he still has his sunglasses on.

"Come in."

I don't move.

"It's safe."

He holds the door wide open with his back and repeats, "It's safe." He speaks quietly. His accent is strange. I think it must be Swiss.

I walk over the threshold and the door clicks shut behind me. I feel him watching me. I don't want him there, behind me.

I wander around the room. It's large, with a kitchenette in the right-hand corner: a few cupboards, a sink, an oven. Moving around I pass between the fireplace and a small, old sofa. There's no carpet, but wooden floorboards stained dark brown, almost black, and three rugs of different sizes, all a sort of Persian design. The walls are painted a creamy color but there are no pictures or anything else, apart from a long smoke stain on the chimney-breast over the fireplace. It looks like a fire might be the only source of heat, and the slate fireplace contains a metal grate and some blackened logs. Next to it is a large pile of wood, a newspaper, and a box of matches. Moving left, I come to a small window that looks toward the lake and the mountains beyond. I can see blue water and a section of green-gray mountains. In front of the window is a wooden table and two old-style French cafe chairs.

"I left the window open when I went out. The fire keeps filling the room with smoke."

He goes to the fireplace and starts to build a fire.

I watch.

He lights the pile of newspaper and it goes out.

"I want to see Mercury."

"Yes. Of course."

But he doesn't stop messing with the fire.

"I don't get the feeling that she's here."

"No."

I go to one of the other two doors and open it. I can tell he's stopped with the fire and is watching me. Inside the small adjoining room is a bed, a chair, and an old-fashioned wooden wardrobe.

"That's my room," he says, and walks past me to close the wardrobe door. There isn't much to see. He hasn't made his bed. There's a book on the chair.

I lean against the doorway and say, "Good book?"

He gives me one of his smiles as he passes out of the room and goes to the other door.

"This is the bathroom." He says it precisely, as if he has been practicing it. It's bigger than his bedroom, with a central freestanding bath, a large white basin, and a toilet with a cistern above and a chain. Black and white tiles cover the walls and floor.

I look back at the apartment and say, "Am I supposed to stay here or something?"

"Until Mercury is ready to see you."

"Which will be when?"

"When she thinks it's safe." He never sounds confident, but I think it might be because of his accent. Everything sounds like a question.

"I need to see her soon. There's a deadline."

He doesn't answer.

"Do you work for her?"

He shrugs. "She asked me to meet you and stay with you until she's ready to see you."

I rub my face with my hands and look around the room, "I can't sleep here, inside."

"I'll show you the terrace."

He walks around the bath to a sash window and slides it up. I stick my head out and then climb through it. There is a small terraced area surrounded by four steep gray-tiled roofs of the building. It's a private haven. The flat area is about the size of my cage, and I find I'm saying, "I'd like sheepskins."

He nods and smiles, like he knows just what I mean, and says he thinks that he can get some.

I'm alone in the apartment. My smiling friend has gone out. I poke around all the cupboards and in his room, but there's nothing much to see.

I check out the roof, scrambling up the steep slope to one side of the terrace. The roof descends precipitously on the far side and nothing would check a fall to the street six floors below. I walk along the ridge of the roof. To the side the gap to the next building is narrow, but it would be impossible to leap across to the roofs of the neighboring buildings, as they are taller. The back of the building is like the front. There is no fire escape. The terrace is a trap.

But I don't have many options. It's less than a month until my birthday, and I've nowhere else to go. I have to get three gifts or I'll die, I'm sure of that now. I need Mercury.

The terrace turns out to be a good place to sleep, cut off from the wind and the road noise. I've pulled out two of the rugs to sleep on, and with my sleeping bag as well I'm warm. The sky is clear and the moon is full, so there's no way I'm going back inside until morning.

The moon is high when my contact wakes me. He's brought sheepskins. Six of them. They're thick and clean and just about perfect when they're laid out.

My contact sits on his haunches on the opposite side of the terrace from me. His legs are long, but I can see his thigh muscles are thick. His arms are folded and his head slightly on one side. He still has his sunglasses on, and his hair is tucked behind his ears.

I close my eyes. When I open them a few minutes later he has gone. He moves silently. I like that about him.

Morning. I lie here and get to know the place, see how the sky lightens with the dawn and deepens with the day. The sounds of the city are an inconsistent, muffled grumble. There's a faint hiss from the building. My stomach starts making noises, and I can smell bread.

In the kitchenette my contact is leaning with his back against the unit, sunglasses still on.

"Breakfast?"

This is not what I expect from a Black Witch.

"I have croissants, brioche, rolls . . . jam. Orange juice. I'm making coffee, but I have hot chocolate too."

"What's your name?" I ask.

He smiles a huge smile, lots of regular white teeth. "What's yours?"

I wander over to the chair and look out of the window. He lays the food on the table. The coffee is strong and milky, and he serves it in a bowl. He sits opposite me and dips his croissant in his coffee, and I copy. I've never had a croissant before. It's okay. Celia wouldn't approve.

He's watching me the whole time, though all I see is myself in his mirrored glasses. His fingers are long and bony, pale really, considering his skin is olive. When he's finished his croissant he rips a roll in half and from that rips a smaller piece. He cuts a section of hard, cold butter and puts it on the piece of bread. A perfect oblong of butter on a ragged piece of bread. He puts it in his mouth and chews, lips together, and all the time it's as if he's trying not to smile.

"You look pleased with yourself," I say.

"I'm pleased to meet you." He puts his hand up to his glasses and takes hold of them as if he's going to take them off, but he doesn't. "That sounds very English, doesn't it? I'm very pleased to meet you, Nathan."

And instantly I'm pissed off.

He laughs. "You're funny, though. Very funny. I like you. You scowl like . . . it's a proper scowl." He laughs again.

I cut an oblong of butter. Then another. Then another.

"Why do you keep your gloves on?"

"Why don't you take your sunglasses off?"

He laughs. Then he takes one of my pieces of butter and puts it on his bread. When he has finished eating he says, "I'm Gabriel." He pronounces it funny.

"Gabrielle?"

He laughs again. "Yes, Gabriel."

I put a section of butter on some bread and try it. It's good, creamy.

"How come you know my name?"

He smiles. "Everyone knows your name."

"No, they don't."

He sips his coffee and swirls it around and sips it again. "Okay. You're right, not everyone. But all Black Witches in Europe, some Black Witches in the States, most White Witches in Europe . . . most White Witches everywhere. Few fains, though, very few fains." He shrugs. "So . . . no, not everyone."

And I see this famous person in his mirrored glasses looking back at me, not scowling but looking pretty miserable. I look away, out of the window to the distant section of mountains.

"Is it that bad, being Nathan?"

Every White Witch I have ever met has known who I was. One look at me and . . . it's like I've got a big sign on my head. It seems it's going to be the same in the world of Black Witches.

I turn back to him. "I'd prefer to be anonymous."

"It won't happen." He's pushing his hair back off his face but at least he's stopped smiling. "Not with your father being who he is."

And his father and his father and his father and his father . . .

"Who's your father?" I ask. "Anyone I'd have heard of?"

"No, definitely not. And my mother . . . no again. Two very fine Black Witches, but not famous. When I say fine I mean . . . respectable . . . for Blacks. My father is living in America now. He had to leave after he killed my grandmother—my mother's mother." He shrugs. "I should explain that it was self-defense; my grandmother was attacking my father. It's complicated . . . She blamed him for my mother's death." He swirls his empty coffee cup. "Anyway, they are not famous."

"Violent, though."

"In both violence and fame, your bloodline outdoes mine."

Gabriel

•·•••·•

I am not supposed to leave the apartment except to sleep on the terrace. I'm sleeping okay. The usual nightmares.

I sleep inside on the sofa some afternoons. Most of the time I'm alone. In a way this is worse than the cage. At least there I could run. Here I just lie around.

Every day I ask, "When can I see Mercury?"

And every day Gabriel replies, "Maybe tomorrow."

I've told him that I need three gifts and that it's less than a month until my birthday. He keeps asking me other stuff, though, stuff about me: where I've been the last few years, if I've had contact with the Council, with Hunters. I don't tell him anything, all that is private.

I see Gabriel in the mornings. He brings shopping, eats breakfast with me and then we wash up. Sometimes he reminds me of Celia with her chores. He always washes and I dry. Every day he says, "I will wash today. You mustn't get your gloves wet." He says it with a look of deep concern. When I give him the finger he just laughs.

I haven't taken my gloves or scarf off. I sleep in them . . . live in them. If Gabriel saw my tattoos or the scars on my wrist I'd get a load of questions and I don't want that.

After washing up he hangs around for a bit then leaves

the apartment and I only see him the next morning at breakfast. I don't think he's slept in the bedroom since I've been here, but I can't be sure. He never makes the bed; sometimes he lies on it reading.

Gabriel starts after breakfast on the first day with his questions, but I just concentrate on drying the crockery. When it dawns on him that I'm not going to tell him my life story, he tries different subjects: first off it's books. He's reading a really good book, Kerouac, whatever that is.

"Do you have a favorite?"

I'm busy drying a plate, slowly, round and round, getting it really dry, and I don't reply. So Gabriel lists his top books. He can't pin down one favorite. He lists a few French ones I've never heard of, and then some English ones I've never heard of—though I have heard of *Wuthering Heights*—and then he's on to American authors. I'm not sure if he's showing off or if he's always like this.

When he finally shuts up I put the very dry plate on to the top of the pile of very dry plates and say, "I've never read a book."

His left hand is in the washing-up bowl, suds around his wrist. It has stopped washing.

"I do have a favorite though. Solzhenitsyn. *One Day in the Life of Ivan Denisovich*. You read that one?"

He shakes his head.

I shrug.

"How can it be your favorite . . . if you've never read it?"

And I want to yell at him, "'Cause the woman who kept

me chained up in a cage was a Russian-loving lunatic, you stupid, spoiled Swiss idiot." I want to scream and shout. And next thing the plates are all smashed on the floor and I don't know how I got so angry so quickly. I'm breathing hard and Gabriel's standing there, with suds dripping off his fingers.

Next day at breakfast, on new plates, Gabriel isn't talking; he's reading Solzhenitsyn.

I eat the bread, drink the coffee, look out of the window.

I say, "Can you read all right with your sunglasses on?"

He just gives me the finger.

When we're washing up, and he's put the book down, he has another go at me, about art this time. He goes on and on about Monet and Manet and stuff like that. I don't know what he's talking about. All Black Witches can't be like this, can they?

I tell him, "I don't need a lecture about art. I need to get out of this stupid apartment and see Mercury. There's a deadline." I throw a few swear words in there too.

When he's gone I remember a book Arran gave me once. It had sketches in it by da Vinci. I'd almost forgotten about that book. They were good sketches. I find a pencil in a drawer but there's no paper, so I rip a blank page out of Gabriel's book.

After I've finished the drawing I burn it. But the fire smokes badly.

* * *

At breakfast on day three he says he's finished *One Day in the Life of* . . . and he likes it. Then he asks me why I like it.

And of course there are a million reasons. Does he expect some fancy reply or something?

"So," he asks, "why do you like it?"

I say, "Because he survives."

Gabriel nods. "Yes, I'm glad about that too."

While we wash up he talks about climbing. He really likes climbing. He stops washing and starts to climb up the kitchen cupboards. He's good . . . precise and fast. He says his favorite place for climbing is Gorges du Verdon, which is in France.

He asks me where my favorite place is.

I say, "Wales."

When he goes I rip another blank page out of his book and draw him climbing up the kitchen cupboards.

Day four and Gabriel's on to poetry. I've got to give him ten out of ten for trying, but if he's attempting to piece together the story of my life, poetry isn't going to add much. I mean—poetry! Then I start laughing. Really laughing. We're Black Witches, hiding out from Hunters, White Witches fear us . . . and we're washing up and talking about poetry. I bend over at the waist I'm laughing so much. My stomach aches.

Gabriel watches. He doesn't laugh with me. I don't think he knows what I find so funny, but he smiles. I manage to calm down, but I keep sniggering like a kid every now and then while Gabriel is talking about some great poet. He even recites a poem. It's in French, so it's rather lost on me, but I don't laugh at that.

I ask about his accent. His mother was English and his father is Swiss. Gabriel was born in France and lived in America with his father and younger sister for a year. His English is excellent, but his American is better, and he speaks English with a weird French-American accent. He says that he came back to Switzerland after he got his Gift. He hasn't said what his Gift is, and I don't ask.

That afternoon I've had enough. I sneak out, go down to the lake, and then head out of town toward the hills. When I get back I can't find the right road and have to go down to the lake to get my bearings. People are hurrying home or into bars and cafes. They each have a phone hiss to them and the city is a low engine rumble in my head. I walk along the road that skirts the lake. The mountains are now hidden in low cloud, and although I know they are there I can't see them; even the huge lake is diminished to a pond edge by a bank of mist over it. The boats on the quay-side are vague shapes in the fog. I can hear two voices, men speaking French. They go quiet.

I turn and see a figure in black watching me, and as slow as I can make myself do it, while a gallon of adrenaline is urging me to flee, I saunter away. A whistle sounds: a Hunter's call to her partner. Now I run.

I keep to the backstreets and find an entrance to a bar and hang around in the corner where I can see into the street through the window. The street is busy with fains. Eventually I step out and make my way cautiously back to the apartment, but I don't see the Hunter again.

I'm back just before dark and go straight on to the terrace.

I know they saw me. I'm sure I lost them, but they know I'm here now. Somehow they knew it was me.

I dream. I'm still running in that blasted alley, but now it's different; for the first time in the dream I remember to look at the end of the road. I look and look and there are the ordinary buildings and ordinary fains and a bus and some cars, but I still can't reach them. I hear Hunters behind me, shouting, "Get him! Rip his arms out!" And I panic and run faster and they're shouting so close behind me and I can't run any faster . . . and then I wake up.

Gabriel is on his haunches watching me.

I tell him, not in a nice way, to leave me alone and then lie back down and close my eyes. I'm not sure I should tell him what happened today. I'm not supposed to leave the apartment, but maybe if I tell him about the Hunters he'll take me to Mercury. I decide to tell him. But when I open my eyes Gabriel has gone.

Day five. I'm building up to tell Gabriel about the Hunters while we're washing up. He passes me a cup to dry and as I take it he holds onto it for a moment before releasing, so I have to pull it a little from him, and he says, "Switzerland is a great country. There are few White Witches, none in Geneva, and the Black Witches here can be trusted. But there are Half Bloods who will sell you out if they see you. Hunters use them."

That's Gabriel's way of saying that he knows I left the apartment.

I dry the cup.

He says, "Geneva is a wonderful city. Don't you think?"

That's another way of him saying he knows I left the apartment.

I swear at him.

"You're not supposed to leave the apartment." And that's the final way he has of saying he knows I left the apartment.

"Then take me to Mercury."

"How do I know you're not a spy? How do I know you didn't go to meet some Hunter?"

I just stare at him. In his sunglasses I see this lone figure staring back.

"How do I know, if you won't talk to me?"

I swear at him again and go out onto the terrace.

When I come back into the apartment Gabriel has gone.

I don't know what to do about Gabriel, but I'm not about to share my life story with him, that's for sure. I decide to mark time with five-bar gates like they do in prison movies. I cut short vertical lines into the wall near the window and scar in a deep gouge diagonally across them.

I stare out of the window for a while and do some push-ups. Then I stare out of the window. Then I do sit-ups and a few more push-ups. More staring out of the window and after that it's time for a bit of shadow-boxing. Then back to check out the view.

I don't think me telling Gabriel anything will make any difference anyway. It could all be lies. He must know that.

I flop on to the sofa. Then get up. Then throw myself back down.

There's no way I'm going to tell Gabriel anything real about me.

I get up. I need something to do.

I decide to sort the fire out, which means standing in the fireplace with my head up the chimney. There needs to be more draw, but I don't know how to create it, so I just tidy up in there, cleaning the soot out as much as I can, finding a slate that is sticking out of the bricks and jiggling it around a little, and then finding a loose brick and a large, flat tin hidden high in a narrow gap above it.

With the chimney cleared and the slate back in place the fire blazes, but I am black with soot. I need to wash everything. I get in the bath with my clothes on. The bath is an old-fashioned tub on ball-and-claw feet; it's deep but not very wide. As soon as I get in the water turns gray. I peel my clothes off and throw them onto the terrace to sort out later. I have a change of clothes. I even have two pairs of socks.

I run another bath. There's a little nailbrush and I scrub at my feet and hands, but the dirt is in the skin and won't budge.

I submerge myself and hold my breath. I can do it for

over two minutes, nearly three if I get the breathing right beforehand. But I'm not as fit as I was under Celia's regime.

I dry myself and put clean jeans on, and check out my tattoos. They are the same. The scars on my back seem worse but they're not. How thick they are always surprises me. The line of scars on my right arm is faint, white on the paler skin there, but my wrist can only be described as an ugly mess. My hand works fine, though, and my fist is solid.

When I lean over the basin and look in the mirror, my face looks the same, only more miserable somehow, grayer. It looks old. I don't look sixteen. There are gray circles under my eyes. The black, empty pieces that move around in my eyes seem to be bigger. The blackness of my eyes is not like the darkness up the chimney; it's a blacker black than that. I move my head to the side, wondering if I can catch any glints, but instead I see Gabriel standing in the doorway staring at me, mirrored glasses reflecting back.

"How long have you been there?" I ask.

"You've done a good job with the fire." He takes a step farther into the bathroom.

"Get out." I'm surprised by how angry I am.

"Did you find anything?"

"I told you to get out."

"And I asked if you found anything." For the first time he sounds like a Black Witch.

I turn and stride to him; my left hand is around his throat, and I'm pushing him by the shoulder against the wall. He doesn't resist. I hold him there and say, "Yes, I found something." And all I see is myself looking back at me. My eyes are black with silver reflected in them but it's just from the bathroom light. I don't want to hurt him. I manage to loosen my grip on his neck and then walk back to the sink.

"Did you read them?" He is coughing a bit as he speaks.

I lean forward over the basin, grabbing its sides. I'm concentrating on looking down the plughole at the dirt and the blackness, but I can feel his eyes on my back.

"Did you read them?"

"No! Now get out!" I shout and look up in the mirror.

Gabriel says, "Nathan," and he steps forward again and takes his sunglasses off. And his eyes are not those of a Black Witch.

He's a fain.

A fain!

So what was all that talk about being the son of two very respectable Black Witches?

And I'm shouting, "Get out!" as I hit him and he's on the floor, blood on his face, and I'm swearing and using all the worst words I can think of and he's lying on his side, curled up, and I stomp on his knees and I hate it that he lied to me and I hate how I was thinking he was okay but he's just some lying fain and I have to walk out to the kitchen before I really hurt him. Then I walk back and lean over, grab his hair and shout at him. Properly shout, 'cause I can still see him staring at my back. And I hate it that he was staring. I hate that. And I bang his head on the floor and I don't know why I'm doing that, except I'm so angry. I'm still shaking when I walk out of the bathroom again.

I pace around the sofa, but I have to go back and get my shirt.

Gabriel's groaning a bit. He looks a mess.

I slide down to the floor next to him.

We're sitting at the table, by the window. Gabriel is wringing out a cloth into a bowl of water that's pink with his blood. His left eye is swollen shut. His right is a light brown with a few flecks of golden-green in it but no sparks. Definitely a fain eye. But he has told me that he wasn't lying: he is a Black Witch but he has a fain body.

"So you can't heal at all?"

He shakes his head.

He says that his Gift is that he can transform to be like other people. It's the same Gift as Jessica's, but he is different from her, opposite to her. He explains, "I like people. They're interesting. I can be male or female, old or young. I can find out what it's like to be different people. The only problem is once I became fain, to see what that was like, I couldn't transform back."

"You're stuck then?"

"Mercury thinks I'll be able to become myself again. She says it's more than physical, or at least more than just my body, that makes me able to transform. She says she'll help me find the route back. . . . But she's in no rush." He puts the cloth in the water and swirls it around then wrings it out again and puts it back on his eye.

"I've been with her for two months." He looks at me. "She wants to meet you." He pats the cloth against his cut lip, which is also swollen. "But she's suspicious. And rightly. You have spent all your life with White Witches." He shrugs. "You are half White and the perfect bait, just the sort of thing the Council or Hunters would use."

"But I'm not sent by them."

"And you're not likely to admit it if you are."

"So how do I prove to her that I'm not?"

"That's the problem. It's impossible to prove." He dabs at his mouth with his fingertips. "Someone once said that the best way to find out if you can trust somebody is to trust them." He carries on dabbing his mouth. But he's smiling a little.

"Do you trust me?" I ask.

"Now I do."

"Then take me to Mercury."

He swirls the cloth in the water again.

"I can't stay in this apartment any longer. I'll go mad . . . or kill you."

He puts the cloth back on his eye.

"Tomorrow."

"Yes?"

"Yes."

"Not today?"

He shakes his head. "Tomorrow."

I get the tin and put it on the table in front of Gabriel and sit back opposite him.

"I didn't read them."

He pulls the lid off and carefully takes out the top letter, which has my sooty fingerprints on it. It's folded over once and there is one word written on the outside in large curly writing. He pulls out the next letter, which is smudged with my black sooty marks too. He shakes his head.

"What are they?" I ask.

"They're just love letters from my father to my mother, before . . . when they were in love."

"So why do you hide them?"

"There's something else in here. If Mercury succeeds in helping me, she'll want payment. That is what I'll pay her with."

I don't ask what it is. The words of a spell, perhaps, or maybe instructions for a potion.

He puts the letters back into the tin and gently presses the lid down, using the weight of his shoulders and chest but so gently.

"I didn't read them . . . I can't read."

He waits for me to say more.

"I can't sleep inside . . . or if I do I'm ill . . . sick. I'm not very good at staying inside at all any more. Electric things give me noises in my head. But I can heal fast. And I can tell if a person is a witch from their eyes."

"How?"

I shrug. "They look different."

He strokes his hand across the tin but then pushes it away. "So . . . my eyes? Are they witch or fain?"

"Fain."

He doesn't respond straightaway but eventually shrugs and says, "My body is fain now."

Slowly he reaches over to my hand and touches my tattoo with his fingertips. "What are these?"

And I tell him about the tattoos. He hardly moves, doesn't speak, just listens. He's good at listening. But I tell him the tattoos are a brand, nothing more. I want to tell him more. I want to trust him, but I remember Mary's warning: "Trust no one."

Gabriel says, "Mercury said that you wouldn't be able to sleep inside. And she told me to wear the sunglasses."

So she knows Marcus and assumed I'd have the same abilities.

The Roof

Gabriel says we will go to Mercury in the morning. He says that he spotted two Hunters in Geneva and wants to see if they are still in town. I tell him that they are, and they saw me and I think they recognized me. He doesn't say much about that, but he wants to have a look around for himself and insists I wait in the apartment.

When he's gone, the apartment feels like a prison and the terrace isn't much better.

I wake up in the night. It's raining but not heavily, just spitting. I expect to see Gabriel in his usual spot where he watches me from. He's not there. I fall back to sleep again and have my usual alley dream. I wake drenched in sweat. It's well after dawn. The sunlight is trapped on the terrace. Steam rises off the damp roof. There's a smell of coffee and bread.

Gabriel is sitting at the table surveying me as I survey breakfast. He has laid out the usual array.

I want to go to Mercury, and I don't want breakfast. He puts butter on bread, chews, swirls his coffee. I pace around.

He says, "I saw a few Hunters."

I stop pacing. "A few?"

"Nine."

"Nine!"

"I watched one and followed her for a few minutes. Then I saw another. And another. They didn't pay any attention to me. I'm just another fain to them. But you, I think, they must have recognized. Nine Hunters can only be for someone important.

"I skirted around town, went to see a contact of Mercury's. Pilot. She didn't know anything. I came back this morning and saw another Hunter on my way here. I thought I'd test something out and bumped into her shoulder. I apologized. She apologized back in poor French."

He laughs.

"They don't recognize witches by their eyes, like you do. Mercury says that Hunters are trained to detect Blacks. They notice the little differences, the way we walk, the way we stand, how we move in relation to other people. But I must have lost that."

"I guess if you saw nine there are probably more you didn't see."

"Definitely."

And yet Gabriel seems relaxed: he saunters around, bumps into a Hunter, and then wanders off for a leisurely breakfast.

He glances up at me, saying, "Don't worry. If they knew about this place we'd have been bloody messes on the floor of some cell hours ago." He drains the last of his coffee and says, "However, I think we should go to Mercury's now."

I try to sound coolly ironic, saying, "Take your time. Have another croissant."

He gets up, smiles at me. "No. I don't want to be late. Mercury's expecting us, not you. She's looking forward to meeting you."

He beckons me onto the terrace then takes my hand, interlocking our fingers, and leads me to the spot where he always hunkers down.

"Keep hold of my hand. Tight."

He slides his other hand, his left hand, through the air, as if he's feeling for something.

"There's a passageway here. You have to find the entrance—it's like a slit in the air. We go through it and down the drain. It's hard to breathe in there so it's best if you hold your breath until you're out the other end."

At the base of the roof tiles is a narrow metal gutter running around all four sides, and in the corner is a drainpipe. Gabriel seems to find the cut and lowers his hand down into the drainpipe.

And down.

My body already feels different, light, and I slide up through the gap, following Gabriel, and then spiral down the drainpipe with him. It's swirling blackness. We go round and down like going down a plughole, speeding up as the spiral narrows until I'm spinning so fast that I'm afraid I'll lose my grip on Gabriel, but his fingers are solid, bound around mine. Then we're spiraling upward and slowing and I can see past Gabriel's body above me to light, and I feel myself being sucked out and my body stops.

I'm heavy again and gasping for breath, sprawled on my front on a hard slope. I'm glad I didn't have breakfast, as my stomach is not happy with that experience. I roll over to sit up. I'm sitting on a roof of unevenly cut black slate. In front of me is a small expanse of grass, and beyond that a tree-covered mountainside rises so steeply that I have to tilt my head back to see the blue sky. My head and body feel like they are moving in circles at different speeds.

"We must stay on the roof until Mercury comes."

Gabriel has scrambled up and is sitting astride the rooftop. I join him, moving cautiously.

The cottage is high on the side of a wide U-shaped valley passing down to the right. The valley is lined with trees, forest. At the top of the valley, to my left, there is snow and a glacier. The mountaintops that teethe the valley wall are snow-covered, and across the valley another glacier hangs in them. The whole valley is a huge fortification.

There are no bird sounds, but there is a chirping of crickets and beyond that is a constant, distant roar. The sound is not in my head, and there is no hissing of electrical equipment. The roaring is relentless and I realize it's the river in the valley bottom. I smile. I can't help it. The river must be big, powerful.

The roof is made of thick slabs of slate. There's a stone chimney with smoke curling out. The cottage is at the top end of a meadow area that's surrounded by trees. The only other thing in the meadow, much farther down the slope, is a huge, splintered tree stump.

"This is Mercury's cottage. There's a trespass spell to protect it. You must step off the roof only when you are touching her."

"Where are we?"

"Another part of Switzerland. I sometimes come here by train or I hike. Or I use the cut. I can go back through there." And he indicates a space above the drainpipe. "Mercury made the cut. Her Gift is control of the weather. It's a strong Gift. It's her only one, but she has learned other things and been given other things from the people she helps . . . that's how she learned how to make the cuts."

The latch of the door rattles. We both turn and are met with an icy squall as Mercury steps into view.

She is tall and thin, and her skin is translucently pale, almost gray. Her eyes are black holes but with sheets of silver passing over them. I think she's looking at me but can't be sure.

"I thought I smelled something good," she says. The breeze becomes warm now. Humid and heavy. "Nathan. At last."

Her voice almost doesn't belong to her but to the weather; it's as if it's coming out of the breeze that's passing around her body to mine. She walks to the back of the cottage. It's built into the hillside so that the roof is only a foot from the ground on that side. She holds her hand out to me, beckoning me with her fingers. The wind picks up and is now swirling round me, pulling me to my feet and jostling me down the roof toward Mercury.

I reach for her.

At last!

It's like holding hands with a skeleton.

PART
SIX

TURNING SEVENTEEN

The Favors

•.•••

I blink my eyes open. It's still night. Gabriel is asleep near me. We're in the forest above Mercury's cottage. The cottage is special; I can sleep inside it, but I've only tried it twice. I'm too claustrophobic in there at night, though I don't get sick. Anyway, I prefer it here in the trees. Rose sleeps in the cottage. I don't know where Mercury sleeps, if Mercury sleeps.

The first night Gabriel said, "The cottage is the guest house. I think Mercury's real home is far away."

"A stone castle on top of a craggy outcrop?"

"That is more her sort of thing. I've seen her walking up toward the glacier. I guess there is another cut up there that leads to her real home. I've seen Rose go in that direction a few times as well."

Rose is Mercury's assistant and is in her early twenties. She is dark and curvaceous and beautiful but she is not a Black. She is a Shite—her name for White Witches—but she has been brought up by Mercury. Rose has the Gift of being a forgettable mist, according to Gabriel, which makes no sense to me, and he says it is best experienced rather than explained. Rose uses her Gift to acquire things for Mercury.

I've hardly spoken to Mercury. I've been here over a

week and she hasn't been back to the cottage since the day I arrived.

I told her that I needed her help. I explained that my seventeenth birthday was just over two weeks away. I was polite. And all I got in return was nothing.

Nothing.

Gabriel says she will see me in time.

But every day . . . nothing.

I know it's some kind of game she's playing. And—

"You awake?" Gabriel mumbles.

"Mmm."

"Stop worrying about Mercury. She will give you three gifts."

Gabriel always seems to know what I'm thinking, and I always try not to let him know he's right.

"I'm not worrying. I was thinking about what I'll do after I get my Gift."

"And what will you do?"

Look for my father. If he wants to be found, I'm sure I can find him. And then I will somehow prove to him that I won't ever kill him. But I don't think he wants me to find him, and I don't see how I can prove anything.

"Well?"

I haven't told Gabriel anything more about myself: not more about the tattoos, not about my father's vision or about the Fairborn.

I say, "I'll develop my Gift. I don't want to get stuck as a dog."

"Yeah, being a fain is bad enough. And what else?"

"What makes you think there's something else?"

"The way you go all . . . there's an English word—mopey? Yes, I think that's it. You are mopey sometimes."

Mopey!

"I think you've got the wrong word. Thoughtful is more like it."

"No, I think the right word is mopey."

I shake my head. "There's a girl I like."

"And?"

"And it's probably really stupid of me. She's a White Witch."

I'm expecting him to say it is really stupid and I'll get killed and probably get her killed, but he doesn't say anything.

The next morning we're sitting on the grass by the splintered dead tree trunk in the meadow below Mercury's cottage. The sun's warmth seems magnified here.

"We could go for a hike," I say, squinting up the valley.

"Okay."

We don't move.

"Or we could go climbing," Gabriel suggests, and takes the long piece of grass out of his mouth but does nothing more.

We hike and climb every day.

"A swim?" he asks.

There's a small lake, but today I don't want to hike,

climb, or swim. I want Mercury to come and tell me that she will give me three gifts.

"You know it's only just over a week until my birthday."

"You know, I may have said this before: 'Stop worrying.'"

"And if I don't get three . . ." I stop speaking as Rose has appeared from the woods below and is walking toward us, taking long, slow strides. Her thin dress clings to her curves. When she reaches us she drops on to the grass close to me.

She says, "Hi."

"Hello, Rose."

Rose giggles. She doesn't seem to be the giggly type, but she does it a lot. She blushes a lot as well, and she doesn't seem the blushing type either. It's a bit baffling.

Rose looks at Gabriel. "You have to go to Geneva, see Pilot, assess how many Hunters there are, and report back to Mercury tonight." That's more the type Rose is.

She then plucks at some grass and says, "Nathan, Mercury says that she would be delighted to give you three gifts on your birthday."

At last.

"She says it would be an honor."

An honor!

"Will she expect some kind of payment in return? Or is the honor enough?"

"Not a payment," Rose replies. "A favor. A mark of thanks and respect. It's only natural to thank the giver. It's polite."

"And what favor does she want from me?"

Rose grins and blushes. "She wants two favors from you."

So the honor definitely isn't enough.

"What two favors does Mercury want?"

"She will tell you this evening."

"Will she want the favors first? Or after the Giving?"

"She said one should be given before the ceremony."

So one must be relatively easy, but I don't know what it could be. I don't have anything I can give her.

"The other is to be given afterward, as soon as you can provide it."

"And what if I don't ever provide it?"

Rose giggles but draws a finger across her throat.

Gabriel goes back to Geneva through the cut, and I go for a long hike to keep myself occupied. When we meet up again at the cottage in the evening, I have got myself psyched up. This is Mercury I'm going to meet. I have to be a Black Witch. I have to be the son of Marcus.

Mercury greets me formally with three kisses, but she gives them so slowly it's as if she is inhaling me rather than kissing me. Her lips don't touch me, but I can feel the chill off them. She says, "You always smell so good, Nathan." Then she ignores me and asks Gabriel what he has seen in Geneva.

The Hunters seem to be using Geneva as a base, and Pilot says they are scouting the area, looking for clues, looking for the son of Marcus. Mercury seems satisfied that the cottage is far enough from them and the apartment is still safe.

After we eat she says, "You see my eyes differently, Nathan?"

"I've never seen eyes like yours before." Looking into her eyes is like looking into hollowed-out sockets, completely black but with distant lightning flashing occasionally.

"You haven't met many Blacks?"

"No." I turn to Rose. "I've met White Witches, though."

"Yes, Rose is a rare White Witch. Unusually talented and very able."

Rose blushes on cue.

Mercury continues. "By birth Rose is a White Witch, but she is like a daughter to me now. She is at heart a true Black Witch. You, though, Nathan, are physically very much a Black Witch but I wonder about your heart. Is it that of a true Black Witch?"

"How can I judge? As I said, I haven't met any Black Witches before."

Mercury shudders and makes one wild laugh that sounds like an echo in a cavern. "We are a good mix here tonight."

I lean back in my chair and look at Mercury. She is horrifically thin. But not weak, nothing about her is weak. Even her gray, almost transparent skin looks like it is bulletproof. She is thin like an iron bar, and brittle, and maybe flaking here and there, but as cold and heartless as an iron bar too. Her hair is a mass of wiry gray, black, and white in a swirling pan-scrubber pile of knots and plaits, all held up by long hairpins, which she occasionally pulls out to spin on her fingers.

She wears a long gray dress made of silk or rags, it seems, but parts of it float out when she moves or for no reason at all, as if she is underwater and they are drifting in the current.

I'd love to find out what she knows of my father, but tonight I stick to my Giving. I get it started by offering up, "Thank you for your kindness, Mercury. For looking after me, providing me with a place to stay," as polite as polite can be.

She inclines her head a little in acceptance. Her dress dances around a little more.

"And thank you for your offer to give me three gifts."

Again she inclines her head but as she raises it she says, "It's your birthday soon."

"Eight days."

She nods.

I press on with my speech. "I would like to present you with a token, to show my gratitude. Perhaps two tokens, one before the Giving and one after?"

"That is appropriate. Yes. A small token before."

"It would be a pleasure. Is there anything . . . ?"

Silence.

She loves playing these games.

A bit more silence before she says, "Some information."

I wait a bit. Give her some silence back. Then finally: "Any particular information?"

"Of course."

Mercury has her elbows on the table, her fingers rub together, and a long hairpin appears, twirling between them.

"Leave us. You two get out." She doesn't look at Gabriel and Rose as she gives her orders but keeps her hollowed-out stare on me. After they have gone outside the wind begins to rattle the door and the windows.

Mercury twirls her hairpin on the tip of her finger.

"The first favor is simple . . . a mere trifle. I'd like you to tell me all you know about those tattoos of yours."

"And the other favor?"

"Slightly more difficult . . . but perhaps not for you."

She stabs the hairpin into the table and moves it backward and forward until it comes free again.

"I can't agree unless I know what the favor is."

"There aren't many other options open to you, Nathan."

Mercury stabs the table again.

I fold my arms and wait.

Her mouth muscles tighten further, and then I struggle not to jump back as she lets out a wild cry, her laugh. The wind howls and Mercury leans across the table to me. Her hands raise and the pin reappears, spinning in her fingers. She speaks, and her breath is ice on my face.

* * *

"Why do you want him dead?"

I'm curious rather than angry.

Mercury leans back in her chair and looks at me, I think, though her eyes are just black chasms in her skull. "He has taken a life from me. The life of someone precious. And I intend to take a life from him. And as the only life he holds precious is his own, that is the one I will take."

"Whose life did he take?"

"My sister. My twin sister, Mercy. He killed her, viciously. He ate her heart."

Mercy wasn't on the list of people my father has killed.

"I'm sorry about your sister, but killing Marcus won't bring Mercy back. And Marcus is my father."

"Is that a no?"

"I get the feeling that if I say yes but then fail to fulfill my obligation there will be consequences."

"Of course. For you, your family, your friends. I detest those who break a deal. They must pay the highest price."

"Then I think your price may be too high."

She reaches over me with a finger and strokes the tattoo on my hand. "Your father is no hero, Nathan. He is vain and cruel and . . . if you were ever to meet him you would realize that he cares nothing for you."

I slide my hand away and get up. I move to stand by the fireplace. "Perhaps there is something else you might accept instead."

She surveys me. "Perhaps." She gets up and comes to me and strokes her finger over the tattoo on my neck. "Yes, perhaps there is something else. Your services for a year."

"Services?"

She screeches her laugh out again. "I am always in need of assistants."

I don't know if I can stand being with her for a week, never mind a year. I don't like this at all, but what did I expect? I've nothing else to give her.

"I won't kill people, if that's what you want."

She steps back and spreads her hands out a little. "Well, I understand you feel like that now." Her dress flutters. "But in time . . . your attitude will change." And as she says it I look in her eyes and I see Kieran on his knees in front of me, a gun in my hand. I blink and look away but I've already felt my finger pull the trigger.

She screeches her laugh again. "Killing is in your blood, Nathan. It's what you are made for."

I shake my head at her. Besides, if I'm going to kill people, I'll choose who they are.

"Perhaps you don't want three gifts after all."

"I'll work for you for a year. I won't kill people."

"I shall be delighted to remind you of those words in a year's time."

"Do. And I'll tell you what you want to know about my tattoos on the morning of my birthday."

A chilly gust slaps my face. "We are alone . . . now is a good time."

"I'm sure we can find time to be alone on my birthday."

There's a lull, no wind, nothing but chill in the air. I wonder if she could freeze me to death—probably.

And I'm not going to tell her all I know about my tattoos and certainly not about Mr. Wallend. But I need to work out how much I can reveal to satisfy her.

She goes to the door and without turning to look at me says, "Pass a message on to Gabriel. There is another young person seeking my help. Gabriel must go to the meeting point in Geneva tomorrow."

The Eagle and Rose

•·•·•·

It's a week until my seventeenth birthday. I've found Mercury and she will give me three gifts. Why do I not feel good?

Gabriel has gone to Geneva. He said he'd be back in the late afternoon. It's hot. The sun is dazzling. A great day for a swim. The hike to the lake takes an hour, but I stop along the way to sit and look at the valley. I'm trying to work out what to tell Mercury about my tattoos but I'm not making any progress.

I lie back and look at the sky. The roar from the river seems loud. High above, a bird soars. It's an eagle. A big eagle. I watch it for a long time then get up and run to the lake. I'm dizzy, almost stumbling on the path. A swim will wake me up. The lake is nothing more than a large pond really, surrounded by forest and a patch of tall grass on one side. I strip and plunge in.

I swim out a few strokes and am numb. The lake water comes from the snow melt. I roll on my back and look at the uninterrupted blue of the sky and see the eagle again, not so high now.

I watch it for a while, circling higher and higher and then dropping down lower, and then circling higher again, dropping down much lower so that I can see the individual feathers at the ends of its wings. It looks black with the sun behind it. And I sink beneath the surface and realize I'm cold inside, really cold. It's murky underwater and there's mud and weeds. I can see the surface above me. I can see it but it seems way above me . . . farther and farther away. I've stayed down too long . . . I fight back up but swallow some water.

I'm at the surface again. Water in my nose but gulping air.

"Relax." It's Rose. She's behind me in the water. "Relax!"

I look up to the eagle. He's back, low, still there hanging above me. I spread my arms out, floating.

"You've been in here too long. I'll tow you in." Rose pulls me back to the shore, rhythmically and slowly, by my hair.

By my hair!

"I don't think that's the right technique."

"Stop complaining. I've always wanted to do this . . . to rescue someone."

I smile and water goes in my mouth but I spit it out. I'm numb but I can feel Rose's body with my shoulder. A small patch of warmth.

"You can stand now."

"No, take me all the way in."

She yanks on my hair, towing me a bit farther and then splashes a few drops of water onto my face. "I think that's far enough."

I find my footing in the mud and stand up. The water is below my waist.

Rose stands too. Her dress clings transparently to her curves and I have to look away.

She giggles. "Are you blushing, Nathan?"

I walk out of the water and let her guess.

I drop down on the grass on my stomach, but I'm shivering.

"You need to get dry. Can I use your T-shirt?" But she is already using it to brush the water off my back.

I wait for the comments about my scars, but she doesn't say anything. The sun is strong still, but inside I'm bitterly cold. I shiver and can't stop.

Rose lies with me to warm me. It's strange, being so close to someone else. I'm sure Rose would slit my throat if Mercury told her to but Rose hasn't been told to do that. She has been told to look after me. I roll away from her and dress.

Rose has some bread and cheese in her bag and we eat it together.

I thank her for rescuing me even though I didn't need rescuing.

She giggles. "I only did it to make Gabriel jealous."

"Of me?" I didn't think Gabriel was interested in Rose.

"No." She giggles and shakes her head.

I've no idea what she's scheming.

"He would love the chance to rescue you. To show you

how much . . . you know . . ." Rose giggles again. "To show you how much he loves you."

"*What?*"

"He's in love with you. Totally in love with you."

Rose is just winding me up. "He's my friend."

"Totally. Desperately. Madly. And, alas, it seems, hopelessly too."

"He's my friend."

"Oh, he wants to be so much more than your friend, Nathan."

I shake my head. Gabriel is Gabriel. He likes being with me for sure. I like being with him. We climb and swim and talk. That's what friends do, I thought.

He gave me a present a few days earlier. A knife. I take it out and look at it. It's beautiful. A black, leather-bound handle and black plaited-leather sheath. The blade is shaped like a bowie knife. He seemed nervous about giving it to me. I could tell he really wanted me to like it. I do.

"Love is strange," Rose says. She takes the knife and looks at it. "Gabriel would die to show you how much he loves you."

Rose looks at her reflection in the blade.

"And who would you die for, Rose?"

"I've not met that person yet." She gives me the knife back. "Have you?"

I think about it but don't reply.

She says, "You're like your father."

"You've met Marcus?"

"Once. Ten years ago, when I was twelve. You look like him. Exactly. You sound like him. Even your silences are like his."

"You remember that from when you were twelve?"

"He was memorable . . . and I'm not your average thick Shite."

"No, you're certainly not, Rose. Did you go to see Marcus or did he come to see Mercury?"

"He came to Mercury. He asked her for a favor. She refused, of course."

"Because Marcus had killed Mercy?"

Silence. She's letting me work it out.

"What was the favor, Rose?"

She giggles. "Maybe I'll tell you . . . maybe not."

She lies on her side to look at me.

"I love teasing you, Nathan. You get so wound up so quickly. It's fun to watch."

"Was Marcus like that? Quick to get angry?"

"I didn't see him for more than a few minutes. He seemed quite calm to me. Mercury was rather more full of fury at the time."

"And the favor was?"

"Can't I drag it out a bit more . . . make you wait a little longer?"

"I'm sure you can."

She giggles again. "The favor he asked of Mercury was that she should bring up his son. You. She refused. She doesn't like little boys much."

"Except in stew."

Rose giggles again.

Mercury had said my father cares only for himself. She lies about everything. But Marcus must know that too, so . . .

"Why did he ask Mercury for her help?"

"I think she considers she made the wrong decision now. She would like to have a hold over Marcus. But at the time she was too angry about Mercy."

"But why did he ask her?"

"He thought Mercury should help. You are related, after all."

"Mercury is my relative?"

"Her twin sister, Mercy, was the mother of Saba."

What?

"Marcus killed his own grandmother?"

"Not that unusual. But not something that Mercury is ever going to forgive. She loved Mercy. There can be no getting over that. Mercury might not die for the person she loved but she'll kill for her. It makes me laugh. Black Witches are always killing their relatives, wives, lovers. Shites should just leave them to it and there'd soon be no Blacks left."

I look up to the sky again. No eagle. Mercury is my great-great aunt . . . And my father has been watching me, watching out for me all my life.

Trusting Gabriel

.•·•.•.

I go back to the cottage and wait on the grass for Gabriel.

I'm excited about my father, pleased—elated even.

I want to tell Gabriel. But late afternoon turns into evening and then night. I forget my joy and think about Hunters. Geneva is crawling with them and Gabriel is too casual. He could easily make a mistake or be betrayed by the person he is supposed to be meeting or by one of the Half Bloods he keeps warning me about.

It's nearly midday the following day when Gabriel appears on the cottage roof. He doesn't smile; he looks like he hasn't slept.

I tell him he looks terrible.

Now he smiles. "So do you."

I leap up on to the roof and sit by him.

He says, "There's a perfect English word for how I feel." He flops back. "Knackered."

"You didn't try bumping into more Hunters?"

"No, but it got complicated. We had to make a detour . . . a serious detour. I wanted to spend the night with Pilot—she lives farther out of Geneva—but she took one look at the girl who was with me and said no. The girl's a White Witch, as pure as they come, says she's fleeing from the

Council. But I don't know what to believe. The girl was freaking out as well, which didn't help. Basically it was a mess."

"So where is the girl now?"

"In the apartment. Though I wasn't sure about taking her there. I don't trust her at all." Gabriel shakes his head. "She won't talk to me, says she will only speak to Mercury and, as you know, I can't help her until she tells me more. She won't. I won't. We went round in circles for a long time. Physically and verbally."

"It all sounds rather convenient that someone is fleeing from the Council and needs Mercury's help when they are searching for me. Do you think she's been sent by the Council or the Hunters?"

"I don't know. I can't work her out. She's exhausted me. I need to forget her for a while and relax. I have some news from Pilot for Mercury. Then we can go for a swim."

We wait for Mercury on the roof. I tell him what Rose told me about Marcus killing Mercy and then I tell him about the eagle. And that is when Mercury appears. She must have been listening to everything.

Mercury wants to know more about the eagle. Like me, I think she wonders if it's Marcus.

I don't answer but instead ask her, "Do you think Marcus watches me?"

I expect her to laugh. I feel ridiculous as soon as I say it.

She says, "He cares only for himself, Nathan. If he watches you it is for his own ends."

And I can see that if Marcus thinks I'm going to kill him he would want to keep an eye on me. But I'm his son, his only son. And if I had a son I would watch him, and I would want to meet him too. I would want to see him in the flesh, to touch him as a child and hold him. But Marcus hasn't ever come to see me, to hold me and—

"And you met the girl, Gabriel?"

"Yes. She's at the apartment. I don't trust her, but it's the only place I could leave her. Pilot gave me another message for you. She told me that Clay was in Geneva. She said, 'Clay has the Fairborn.'"

Mercury laughs her howl of a laugh, practically skips on to the roof, and grabs our hands. Roof tiles fly up and we seem to hover in the air on an upsurge of wind before she lowers us to the grass.

When we land Mercury strokes my cheek. "I've heard of a vision about the Fairborn and you, Nathan. And I think you have heard it too." She pinches my chin and looks into my eyes. "Definitely."

She strokes my cheek again before turning to Gabriel and saying, "It will be interesting to see how Nathan changes with that knife in his hand."

Gabriel looks confused.

"Nathan can explain to you about the vision. And tonight we will discuss how the Fairborn can be taken from Clay and put into my—no . . . *Nathan's* hands."

*   *   *

We lie on the mossy bank of the small lake. We have run there, swum, and now we are letting the sun's rays dry and warm us. But my head's in a different place.

Gabriel says, "This morning I went to the house where Pilot said Clay was staying to check it for myself. Pilot gets things wrong sometimes. But she wasn't wrong. Clay is there."

"How do you know it's him?"

Gabriel shrugs. "They have that look, don't they? Arrogance. He's the most arrogant of them all. The king of arrogance."

It's him.

"He has a girlfriend," Gabriel says.

"You serious?" I remember his truncheon and being on the ground, trying to protect my head with my arms.

"Even more surprising . . . she's attractive. Tall and slim and young . . . young for Clay, you know what I mean. Some women go for looks, some go for money, some go for power. She obviously goes for"—he shrugs—"arrogant old men."

Gabriel's trying to make me laugh, but I can't see anything funny about Clay.

I say, "He's not that old. He's powerful. Has a certain position in society. He's cunning . . . intelligent." And brutal.

"So, a good catch for a White Witch."

I sit up and look at the lake, the deep blue surface reflecting the sky, lime green underneath from the weeds growing in the water. It reminds me of Ellen. I tell Gabriel. "I met a Half Blood in London. She had amazing eyes. A bit like the lake, that mix of blue and green, only hers had turquoise and . . ." I run out of things to say. Clay's eyes were like ice.

Gabriel sits up too. "What's wrong?"

"I've met Clay. Twice." I remember his breath on my neck.

I want to tell Gabriel about the Fairborn and my tattoos and Celia's training and Mary's warning. But I don't know what the first word is . . . where to begin. . . . Where do I start with all this stuff?

He says, "Tell me about this Half Blood. She sounds interesting."

"She is. You'd like her. She's smart."

And once I start to tell him about Ellen it gets easier and I explain about Bob and Mary and then the assessments and Clay and all of it.

When I've finished Gabriel says, "Mary said you should trust no one. But you trusted Ellen and you're trusting me."

I shrug. I do trust him, though.

He leans over and hugs me. It feels a bit awkward.

Gabriel is convinced that Mercury will want to steal the Fairborn. Then she will pair me up with it and set us against Marcus. He says that if I work for her for a year she will use all her powers to manipulate me to kill Marcus. He thinks that is part of the pleasure she will have, setting me against Marcus, having power over his son. He says, "You're right to believe in your father."

He says he no longer wants Mercury's help.

I remind him. "But I need her help. It's only six days to my birthday. I need three gifts."

"Yes, that's a problem," he says. "We need a plan."

But a plan is hard to find. We agree that we need to destroy the knife, or throw it into the lake where it can never be recovered, but Mercury will be furious and out for revenge if we do that. And anyway my father may not believe what we have done. We could try to give the knife to him, but clearly this has the twin dangers of both getting it to him and giving it to him when he doesn't trust me.

We decide to go along with any plan Mercury comes up with to steal the Fairborn as it's better in her hands than the hands of the Hunters. We can only hope that after I have three gifts and I'm working for Mercury I will get an opportunity to destroy it. It's not much of a plan.

That evening Mercury is in a celebratory mood. Rose has been to Geneva and is back. She tells us what she has seen: the same as Gabriel. Clay is staying in a house in the suburbs of Geneva. There are at least twenty Hunters in the area around the city, which is nothing to celebrate in my opinion. Pilot has left for Spain.

Mercury doesn't sit, she stands and paces, but the fabric

of her dress is dancing around in glee. She doesn't seem to care how many Hunters there are. She wants the Fairborn and thinks Rose can steal it.

Gabriel says, "If Clay has it. Pilot has often been wrong."

Rose says, "Pilot told me there's a rota of people who guard the Fairborn. It's Clay's turn at the moment. Wherever he goes, the Fairborn goes."

"Getting it from Clay isn't going to be easy."

"No, not easy," Mercury agrees. "But quite within the capability of my wonderful, darling, genius Rose of a White Witch, who has the talent to take anything, however securely it is kept."

Rose blushes and giggles.

Mercury says, "Tomorrow, Rose, you and Gabriel go to the house, find the Fairborn, and bring it to me."

Just like that.

"And how—?" I begin.

Gabriel puts his hand on my arm. "It's fine. We'll be careful. Mercury is right. Rose is very good. Even Hunters are fooled by her mist. But we won't take any chances. If the house is protected by trespass spells we won't try. It would be impossible, even for Rose."

Rose adds, "But Shites don't like to use them in case fains get hurt. They wouldn't want to kill a fain burglar. It can bring them into the limelight too much. Cleaning up after fains is a chore."

I say, "So you'll just walk into a house full of Hunters, pick up the knife, and walk out again."

"They won't see me," Rose says.

"It's too dangerous," I say to Gabriel.

"You are becoming more fain than me," he says. "We'll be careful."

Mercury laughs again.

"Then I'll come too," I say.

Mercury says, "No. You stay here."

I curse her and she laughs. There is a clap of thunder above the cottage and hairpins spin around the room.

"And the girl?" Rose asks.

"Ah yes. The girl . . ." Mercury looks to Gabriel. "What did you say her name was?"

"Annalise. Annalise O'Brien."

And when Gabriel says her name, it doesn't make sense. Annalise can't be trying to find Mercury. She can't need Mercury's help.

Gabriel asks me what's wrong.

When I don't answer he stares hard at me. "You know her?"

I don't know what I say.

"She's the one you . . . like?" And I can see the disgust on his face.

I say to Mercury, "I need to see her. She's a friend."

"How lovely." Rose blushes.

Mercury stares at me too, her eyes flashing wildly. "A

friend? Who arrives just as your birthday approaches, just as Geneva fills with Hunters?"

Mercury says to Rose, "You are going to get the Fairborn tomorrow night." She stands to leave and goes to the door but then turns back and says to Gabriel, "Make sure Nathan doesn't see the girl. Not yet. I need to think about her."

To me she says, "If you go, Gabriel will pay for failing to stop you." And then Mercury's gone.

Rose looks from Gabriel to me and blushes, saying, "The course of true love never did run smooth." She giggles and reaches out to hold Gabriel's hand. "But I'm on Team Gabriel."

Gabriel snatches his hand away from Rose and looks at me. "I knew there was something wrong all the time I was with her, Nathan. She's a spy. She's working for the Council."

I shake my head. "She isn't."

"She's come to capture you or spy on you or kill you. They are using her to get you."

"You're wrong."

"Am I? She's a White Witch. Pure White. I bet half her family are Hunters or Council members."

"That doesn't mean she's like them."

"Oh, of course not. She's *different*." His voice is mocking. "And she thinks you're special, she understands you, she knows you're not bad really, she doesn't mind that your father is the most wanted Black Witch, she's not interested in him, just in you. She sees the real you. The kinder, gentler you. And she swishes her blonde hair and smiles her bright smile and—"

But I'm out of there.

I run. It feels like the only good thing to do, running until I can't run any more. I sleep in the forest, badly, even though I'm exhausted. I stay there for most of the day, walking, staring at the sky. It's only five days until my birthday, and I feel like everything is spinning out of control. I can only imagine Annalise is here because things have got bad back at home with her family. And for her to risk coming to Mercury, it must be really bad. But she is not here for her Giving; she was seventeen in September.

Late in the afternoon I go back to the cottage. Preparations are underway for stealing the Fairborn from a house full of Hunters.

As I walk in, Gabriel continues what he's doing, which I'm surprised to see is cleaning a gun.

"Do you know how to use that?" I ask. I can't stop myself from sounding angry, even though I told myself not to be.

"I lived in the U.S. of A. for more than a year, didn't I?" His voice is soft, joking.

"But have you ever actually shot anyone?"

He stops cleaning the gun and looks up at me but doesn't answer.

And I almost see the Black Witch in him.

"Who did you kill?"

He keeps his eyes locked on mine and says, so I can only just hear, "A spy."

"That's your speciality, is it? Killing spies."

"Nathan, don't." He starts cleaning the gun again.

"I've known Annalise a long time. She's not a spy. I trust her."

"Those are the ones they choose."

"So that's it? There's nothing she can do to convince you otherwise? Everything she does will be suspicious because of who she is."

He doesn't reply, just carries on cleaning the gun.

"And if Mercury told you to shoot Annalise, would you do it?"

He doesn't look up from the gun but at least he's stopped cleaning it.

"Would you?" My voice is quiet but unsteady.

He shakes his head but looks me in the eyes as he says, "If I was certain she was betraying you I'd kill her, whether Mercury told me to or not."

"So you're not certain?"

"Not one hundred percent. But Nathan, if there's one thing I'm good at it's reading people, and there's something not right about her."

"Or maybe you just want to see that, but you can't actually find anything wrong with her, because there isn't. Because she won't ever betray me. Because she's actually a good person. But you don't want to believe that. You want her to be a spy!" And I realize I'm shouting and shaking with anger.

"Nathan. I know this is difficult for you." He comes to me and puts his arms around me. I don't hug him back, but I don't hit him.

Rose appears from her bedroom, sees us, and blows me a kiss.

I swear at her and go sit in the corner.

Rose is dressed as inappropriately as ever in a long, swirly, figure-hugging gray dress a bit like Mercury's. Her hair is immaculate, piled on her head in a sleek twisting knot. She looks like she is going to a Halloween Ball, except that her feet are bare. She shows Gabriel her hairpins, which are decorated at their ends with skulls. Small black skulls are for picking locks of doors, small red skulls for opening safes or more complex locks, and the large white skull is . . . she blushes . . . for killing Shites.

Mercury blows in. She is smiling in her own way.

"Before you go for the Fairborn, Gabriel, I'd like you to bring Nathan's friend to us."

Gabriel looks uncertain.

"If she's been sent to spy on us I want her in my hands and unable to give any warning."

And I know she really wants Annalise in her hands so that she has another hold over me.

"When you and Rose are ready to go, bring her here. Give her no chance to do anything."

Gabriel and Rose go through their plan. Then we eat in silence. Even Rose looks serious.

At sunset Gabriel goes on to the roof and through the cut.

I wait on the grass.

I don't have to wait long.

Gabriel and Annalise appear, holding hands. Gabriel drops hers as if she is plagued. Annalise is sprawled across the roof, her eyes closed.

Gabriel calls to Rose and she appears, comes to me, kisses me on the cheek, steps on to the roof, over the body of Annalise and into Gabriel's arms, but Gabriel's eyes are on mine all the time. I hear Rose giggle as they disappear through the cut.

Annalise

Annalise and I are sitting together. Close. She always seemed so much more mature than me, but now she seems much younger. Her face has changed, become longer and thinner, even more stunning. She is dressed in jeans and a T-shirt and a pale blue jumper, but her feet are bare.

I wonder when Mercury will come. She is letting me have some time with Annalise. There will be a motive behind it.

I take Annalise's hand in mine and ask her what happened.

She blinks and tears run down her cheeks.

"I'm in such trouble, Nathan."

I wipe the tears with my fingertips, hardly touching her skin.

"After Kieran attacked you, he told my father about us. My father was angry, but he said I wouldn't be punished. I just had to regain their trust. I had to do as I was told in every little detail. And I didn't have any other options, so I tried to be good. But they never trusted me, however good I was. My father or one of my brothers was always with me if I left the house. I wasn't allowed to see any of my old friends. I was lonely but it was bearable. But then, after my Giving, the Council asked to see me. They questioned me about you. My uncle Soul was there. He treated me like I was a traitor. I didn't answer their questions about you, I said I'd forgotten. But it was frightening. I was summoned again that day I saw you in the Council building. Then a few nights later my uncle came to our house, and I overheard him telling my father that you had escaped and that I would have to go back for more questioning. I wasn't sure what to do, but I knew I couldn't face any more of it. I thought that if you'd escaped then maybe it was possible for me too. So I ran away."

She looks into my eyes and the silver in hers twists slowly. "I thought that if I could find you . . . Well, I didn't think much beyond that. But I wanted to find you. I've always wanted that. And I heard that Mercury helped White Witches for a price. The only thing I did have was money. I can't believe that I've found you . . . that you really are here."

I wipe her tears away again, this time tracing my fingers over her cheek, feeling the smoothness of her skin. She tries to smile, and reaches over to brush my hair back from my face.

"Your eyes are how I remembered them. They haven't changed." And her fingers are on my cheek now and before I can think about it I turn to kiss them, and then I press her hand to my mouth and kiss her palm.

She strokes her fingers over the tattoo on my hand and looks at my neck and strokes that tattoo as well. But she doesn't ask about them. And the silver in her eyes tumbles and catches the moonlight and more tears come into her eyes.

We sit together and still Mercury doesn't come.

"I'll help you, Annalise. But they think you're a spy. They don't trust you."

"But you do?"

"Of course." And I hold her; she's so fragile and shaking. "I'll speak to Mercury . . . convince her."

Annalise nods.

"We have to wait for her here on the roof. You mustn't step off the roof unless you are touching Mercury."

"Or else?"

"Gabriel told me that you fall into a deathlike sleep."

"Gabriel doesn't trust me. He doesn't like me."

"You're a White Witch, he's a Black—"

"Pilot wouldn't have me in her house."

"Mercury is more . . . business-minded."

Annalise nods. "I heard Pilot say that Clay is in Geneva."

And with that a warm breeze blows over us.

I wait for Mercury to appear, but she doesn't. I think she's hinting that she wants to know more.

"Do you know anything about a special knife called the Fairborn?" I ask her. "I think Clay may have it."

Annalise frowns. "Yes, I've heard my father talking about it with Kieran. It's important, but I don't know why. Different people take turns to look after it. Only those most trusted by the Council. My father had it for a time last year.

My uncle has had it too, and Clay is also one of the ones who guard it."

Annalise grips my hand; hers is damp now. "You're not thinking of trying to get the knife, are you?" She turns to look at my face.

I shrug.

"It would be madness. There will be Hunters everywhere."

"If someone was . . . invisible, say, and could sneak into Clay's headquarters."

Annalise shakes her head. "There will be trespass spells to protect the building."

"Like the one on the roof here?"

"Yes, Clay will have a spell to protect the house. The spell won't kill you; it will just make you incapable. Kieran told us a story about a fain who tried to break into a Hunter's bunkhouse once and was found wandering around in a drunken stupor. They did things to him . . . laughed at him . . ."

"All the doors and windows will have the spell?"

"There will be one door that his Hunters use; that's the only door that will be safe. If you use a different door or break in through a window, you'd be caught by the spell."

The warm breeze kisses my cheek. I guess that Rose will be able to work this out.

"I've also heard Kieran telling Niall and Connor about other spells Hunters use. The entrance door, the one the Hunters use, will have a password spell. You say the password before you cross the threshold and the trespass spell is lifted for a short period of time. There may be different words to go in and out. I'm not really sure . . ."

The breeze has gone cold. Rose doesn't know about these spells. Perhaps they will realize . . .

The breeze gets stronger and colder.

I stand as Mercury appears. She doesn't look happy. The wind picks up more so that I'm pushed backward up the slope of the roof.

Annalise is on her knees, her hair blowing wildly.

"Annalise. What a charming child you are." Mercury's voice is cold. "Come, let us get better acquainted."

Mercury stands on the grass near the roof and holds her hand out to Annalise. Annalise looks back at me and I try to move to her but the wind holds me back. Annalise rises and takes hold of Mercury's fingers. But just as she steps off the roof another gust blows Annalise sideways. Her fingertips reach out but Annalise is not touching Mercury as the wind blows her on to the grass. And the wind is holding me back, holding me still, though I fight against it and I try to reach for Annalise, but it's too late.

I can't hear what Mercury says because I'm shouting and the wind is blasting in my ears. Annalise is lying on the ground; only her chest is moving, heaving, and her mouth is open and gasping for breath.

Mercury stands over Annalise, watching her. And I'm shouting and shouting.

And Annalise's chest is not heaving now. She is completely still. Her eyes are open and I'm screaming at Mercury.

Mercury slides her hand down Annalise's face, closing her eyes.

Annalise's body is pale on the dark ground.

The wind is relentless, pummeling me as I scream curses at Mercury.

Mercury's voice is part of the wind in my face. "You must warn Rose and Gabriel about the password spell. There is still time to help them."

"What about Annalise?" I shout, pointing at her body.

"She's asleep. Not dead. Return safely and I'll wake her."

She's not dead. She's not dead. Gabriel said it was a deathlike sleep.

"If she dies, Mercury . . ."

"Enough of this. Go."

The Fairborn

•∙•∙•

Mercury has been as businesslike as ever. She has drawn a map to show me how to find Clay's house. I've heard all the plans, so I know that the house is an hour's walk from the apartment. I run it in just over twenty minutes. Assuming Rose and Gabriel didn't dawdle, they're over an hour ahead of me but they should still be watching the house, waiting for it to go quiet.

I have to concentrate on them, because if I don't, all I see is Annalise's body lying on the grass. She looked dead; her chest was still, her eyes were open.

I'm nearly there. I've got to concentrate.

The house is in a quiet suburb on a back road with large houses sitting in their own spacious gardens. Behind is a wooded hillside. I scout out the roads round the house and through the woods at the back.

There's someone at the edge of the woods. His back is to me. He's watching the house.

And all the training I did with Celia comes back to me. It's easy, second nature, the way reading is to Gabriel. I tread slow and quiet, taking my knife in my hand. The figure begins to turn as I take my final step and grab his body, the blade at his throat. Poetry in motion.

Gabriel's body is stiff against mine. I keep the knife pressed against his skin.

"Not good enough," I hiss in his ear.

"Nathan? What are you doing here?"

"Where's Rose?"

"Watching the front. What's going on?"

"Mercury sent me. I need to tell Rose something about the spells on the house. Something useful that Annalise told me."

He doesn't reply, so I release him and push him away from me.

"What did she say?"

I tell him and he nods. "Let's tell Rose then."

We work our way around to the front of the house. It's still early, before midnight. Rose is in the garden of a house across the road. She doesn't giggle as I explain the situation, but she doesn't want to give up either. She thinks she can work it. All the Hunters enter and leave through the front door. She'll shadow the next Hunter to arrive and listen for the password.

Now I'm at the back of the house again, leaning against a tree on the edge of the woods. There's no fence, but there is a lawn that stops just before the trees.

Rose and Gabriel are round the front.

The house is divided into two apartments: the upper one on the first and second floors is occupied by several Hunters; the lower one by Clay. From what I can make out, Clay has an office and a bedroom at the back. I can see several Hunters moving around in their apartment; if they are going in and out they're not using the back door or the windows for that matter.

The weather is warm but overcast, and a fine drizzle has started to fall.

I asked Rose what to do if something goes wrong.

She smiled. "Escape if you can. Run. If you can't run, kill as many as you can. They killed your ancestors and they will do everything to kill you, Nathan. Kill them all." She kissed my cheek and said sweetly, "When you've killed them all, then you won't need to run any more."

I don't want to kill anyone. If it came down to kill or be killed, I'd fight for sure but I'd try not to kill. But then again if it was Clay or Kieran . . .

What was I thinking about?

Rose appears beside me. She has come through the garden using her mist, her Gift. She evaporates like mist and so does my memory of her. Even as you watch her, you forget about her. It's strange . . . confusing. But if she touches you, skin on skin, the confusion goes, and while she's touching you she's visible. It's hard to work with her because of the mist, and you can't keep hold of her hand all the time. Gabriel says that the best way to work with her is not to watch her at all but to know what she will do and look away while she clothes herself in her mist so that your thoughts remain clear.

Rose asks, "How many Hunters are in there?"

"Four upstairs." And none of them have Kieran's bulk. "I think Clay's in his office."

"I'll wait here until he goes to bed, then I'll go round the front and in. I listened in and heard the password. 'Red rain.'"

Nice!

"By the way, I think there's a cellar," I tell her. "There's a grate in the ground to the left of the house. A light came on earlier. I think Clay was down there."

"A good place to keep weapons."

"Maybe. If I was Clay . . ." What would I do? "I'd keep the Fairborn near me. But he has guns to store for his troops, I guess; guns, bullets, whatever. So maybe . . ."

"Anything else?"

"If I'm at the back, how will I know that you are out of there?"

"Don't wait here. When I go in, you go round the front and wait with your boyfriend."

"Do you know how irritating you are, Rose?"

She giggles softly.

I nudge her and nod to the house. The light in the office has gone out. A few seconds later the light from the cellar comes on.

"Is he putting his weapons away for the night?" Rose wonders.

And I know the answer. "No. He's a Hunter. He never sleeps without them."

"Under his pillow then."

"I have the feeling he sleeps with his boots on and the Fairborn strapped to his thigh."

"I like a challenge."

The cellar light goes off and the bedroom light comes on. A shadow. Two shadows. Clay and his girlfriend move around, come together, kiss, separate, Clay's shadow goes. The office light comes on again.

"And I thought it was going to get romantic," Rose says.

I watch the shadow in Clay's bedroom, the way it moves, and how familiar it seems.

It's much later when the office light goes off. Clay moves to the bedroom and that light goes out too.

"See you the other side," Rose says, and she skips lightly up the garden in full view of the house. A mist covers her, and I'm wondering if I saw her at all. I tell myself that she has gone to the front of the house and is slipping in.

I go into the woods to work my way around to the front in a wide circle, cutting between two houses way up the road and heading back to Gabriel. I move slowly. There's no rush, though really I've no idea how long Rose will be. But I want to be sure that I don't make any stupid mistakes. I get the feeling that the Hunters are relaxed near the house. They've switched off or at least lowered their guard a little, never imagining anyone—any witch—would attempt to break in.

Gabriel is in the garden of the house opposite Clay's. He

doesn't speak but glances at me as I move next to him. He watches the house. I watch behind us.

Nothing happens.

No cars, no Hunters coming or going. It must be two in the morning by now.

Then Gabriel nudges me. I turn to see the front door opening and two Hunters leaving the house. I get that confused feeling, wondering what's happening, and I can't work it out, but I tell myself to look away and find I'm looking at Gabriel's profile and he turns and looks at me, smiles, and then murmurs, "Rose is with them."

I nod. Rose has done well to get in and out without being spotted. But I can feel my heart thudding now. Does she have the Fairborn?

"Let's go."

But before we take a step there's a shout from the house. From inside. I can't make out what it's saying but I think it's Clay. And then I hear, "Find whoever's got it—NOW!"

We hunch down low and run fast through the garden to the back of the house, over the fence, and into an alley.

Gabriel runs left to the corner. "This is where I said we'd meet."

I keep watch to the right while Gabriel looks down the side street.

I hear a soft giggle and turn around.

Rose is leaning against Gabriel. They are both smiling. As excited as kids who've stolen sweets from a shop. Rose holds up a long knife. Black handle, black sheath.

"Easy for someone so talented," Gabriel says to Rose. "But I think Clay has noticed the Fairborn is missing . . ."

"Let's go," I say and head back along the alley.

We're sprinting when a Hunter steps out of the road ahead of us. She seems as surprised as we are. She stops, hesitates, then shouts, "They're here!"

I'm nearest to her and in that time I've closed in on her. She's taking her gun out of its holster and I'm three strides closer. She's raising her gun as I launch myself at her, my right arm going for her throat and my left for her gun. I hear a shot and I land on her and we seem to fall in slow motion but my hand is on her throat and she's looking at me. And she's so young, not much older than me, and the glints of light in her eyes are twisting frantically and then I hear a crack and it's the sound of her skull and the glints in her eyes have gone.

I'm sitting astride her.

There's a metal grille behind her head and there's blood oozing over it. As I get up I see that her neck is at a strange angle. I want to believe the metal grille killed her, but I had my hand on her neck and her neck is broken and I still can't believe she's so young and I killed her. I manage to get up but it's hard. My side hurts.

Then there's a shot and another and another. I drop down to a crouch and turn to see Rose lying on her stomach on the ground and Gabriel kneeling by her, his arm stretched out, gun pointed at the body of another Hunter lying on the ground farther back down the alley. Nobody moves.

Rose is very still. As still as the Hunter by me.

Gabriel bends down and takes the Fairborn out of Rose's hand. He has to unfurl her fingers and he lays her hand back down on the ground and by then I'm next to him. Rose's head is turned to the side; her eyes have no glints in them and her back is a mass of blood.

Gabriel pulls me away and we're running round the corner and there's more shots. There's another Hunter up ahead and Gabriel is shooting at her and we're in some gardens and over a fence and then I have to stop.

I've killed a woman. I didn't mean to but her neck is broken and Rose is dead too and I'm shaking. There's blood all over my hands, the girl's blood, and I'm rubbing my hands on my shirt but there's more blood. There's lots of blood.

Gabriel says, "Oh no, Nathan."

And I look up at his face and see then that he's staring at my stomach and he pulls my shirt back and my knees are like jelly.

"Shit, Nathan."

I look down. My T-shirt has a spreading, dark stain on it. The blood looks black.

"I'm okay." I'm saying it without thinking anything about it. I don't feel okay.

"I can heal it," I say. I get a buzz and straighten up. Take a breath. Calm down. "I'm okay."

She shot me in my left side, lower ribcage. "I'll be fine." My hands are still shaking. For some reason I can't heal that.

"You sure?" Gabriel sounds so worried.

"Yes. Let's go."

And we go and I'm okay for five minutes but then the pain in my ribcage comes back. I've healed it and it has come back and the pain is crippling. This isn't normal. I have to stop again.

Gabriel says, "It's a Hunter bullet, not a fain bullet. Is it still in you?"

"I think so."

"We've got to get it out. It will be magical, poisoned."

"There's no time. I can heal it for now. Get it out when we're at Mercury's."

"It's bad, Nathan."

"I'm fine. At the moment I'm more concerned about getting a bullet in my back."

And I set off, but I can tell I'm slow. I'm struggling to keep up with Gabriel. In fact, I'm not keeping up, he's slowed right down. We turn the corner and a jeep is coming toward us. A Hunter jumps out, shooting, and Gabriel shoots back and then we're running and I can't keep up with him. I know Gabriel must have hit the Hunter, because I'd be caught by now if he hadn't.

We go through more gardens to reach a back alley. Gabriel waits for me, then scoots me over a high wall.

He jumps down to stand in front of me and I have to lean against the wall for support.

He speaks quietly. "Nathan, you can't run fast enough. They'll catch you if you try to run. I'm going to draw the Hunters away and keep them occupied so that you can make your way back to the cut. But you must be careful. Don't take any risks. Don't wait for me at the apartment. Just go through the cut and back to Mercury's."

And I know he's right; I can't outrun Hunters. But I have a bad feeling. I remember what Rose said: that Gabriel would love to have the chance to save me. But leading Hunters away, so many Hunters, is suicide.

I shake my head.

He says, "It's the only way," and he gives me the Fairborn. It hangs from a leather strap that he puts over my neck.

"Gabriel. It's too dangerous."

"I'll be careful."

"You don't know how to be careful."

He smiles, then he kisses me on the cheek and says some words, and even though they are in French I know what they mean, and I grab him to me.

He says, "How many days to your Giving?"

"Four. You know that."

"I won't miss it."

And then he's climbing over the wall and is gone.

I wait and wait before I dare set off. I hear something that might be another shot or maybe a car backfiring but it's distant. I know it isn't a car really. And then I hear police sirens. The Hunters won't like that. They're distant too, but there are lots of them.

I've got to head to the apartment.

Back to Mercury

•ׁ•●•ׁ•

I don't know where I am. I can't even find the lake. I keep seeing Rose's body and feeling the Hunter's neck and her warm blood, and it's all wrong and shouldn't have happened. The plan was hardly a plan; it was lunacy. And I should have reached the apartment ages ago.

I'm on my knees on the wet cobbles again. My legs keep giving way.

I rest with my forehead on the wet stone and try to heal, but my healing is hardly working and there's no buzz. It's like it's used up.

It's light now but still early. Quiet. No people. The rain has stopped.

I get up. I need sugar. Food and drink are my first priority, then I'll heal better and think better, then I can find the apartment and Gabriel.

On the street a man is rolling up the security blinds on his small tobacconist's shop. He goes in and I follow close behind and move in on him until he is pressed up against the wall. I don't know what to say in French so say it in English and put my hand over his mouth so he can't make a noise. He looks into my eyes and I know he understands. I can't mess around with tying him up. Celia told me the real thing wasn't like training. She taught me to control my breathing. Focus on what I have to do. Do it properly. I knock him out. I've done it properly.

I stand by the fridge and drink an energy drink. Then another. They help. I can heal better already.

I grab the man's small battered backpack and fill it with drinks and sugary sweets.

Now I have to find the apartment. I head downhill, toward the lake. When I find that, I can find the apartment. My legs feel stronger.

At last I find the corner of our road. The apartment block is across from me. There's no one around but something feels wrong.

Parked on my side of the road is a blue car and also a rusty red one that I've seen before. On the left, up from the entrance to the apartment, is a van. I think I've seen that van before but where? It's not a Hunter van . . . so why am I hesitating? There isn't anything unusual. If I run I'll be inside the apartment in a minute and at Mercury's in two. But something seems different.

I stand in a doorway, well back. The rain has started again. There's the sound of distant traffic.

I wait.

Nothing happens. Nothing. And it's killing me. Gabriel's not here and Rose is dead and that girl's neck was so thin. And I can't think that they've caught Gabriel and what they'd do to him. I can't think about that.

More rain.

A car driving down the street.

Someone comes out of one of the apartments, puts her umbrella up, and, heels clacking, walks quickly away.

I'm sweaty. It's warm and the rain is still falling. There's the sound of a car in the street behind me. And then I see it . . . a movement, a shadow in the doorway down from our apartment entrance.

All is back as it was before except now I know what's wrong. I know what the shadow is. I can see that it is a Hunter, gun raised, motionless again. Her mobile phone is buzzing, faint but there. That is what I could sense.

There's nothing I can do except hope. Maybe they followed Gabriel here and he had no option but to go through the cut with Hunters close behind. They wouldn't have been able to work out how to get through unless they saw exactly where it was, and even if they did get through the cut Mercury would pick them off while they were stuck on the roof. That would mean that Gabriel is safe at the cottage and couldn't risk coming back to warn me.

But he said he'd lead them away.

How else could they know to come here?

If they've captured him and tortured him . . . how quickly would he tell them about the apartment?

A car swings into the street from the far end. A black jeep, the one I saw at the Hunters' house. Clay parks the jeep in the middle of the road and gets out. He doesn't look pleased. He goes to the hidden Hunter and then to our apartment building and in. The Hunter gets into Clay's jeep and reverses it fast up the street and away. A minute later she is running back to her position. The road is quiet again.

I have to leave.

I'm covered in blood; fains will stop me if they see me.

I need to find somewhere to rest and get clean. I set off, although I don't know where to.

Twenty minutes later I spot her. She's at the end of an alley, partly hidden by a small van, but I can tell it's her straight away. And I know I should walk on by, but there's Rose and Gabriel and a whole bunch of other stuff that stops me from doing the sensible thing. I don't know where her partner is but I'm not going to hang around for long.

I heal before I approach her, sneak up as quiet as can be, and draw the Fairborn out of its sheath.

And, in that instant, things change.

The Fairborn is almost alive in my hand. It's part of me, but I'm part of it too.

I reach the Hunter and pull her round, the Fairborn at her throat.

"Looking for someone?" I ask.

She flinches. Even now she hates my touching her, but she gets over the surprise in less than a second and starts transforming into a huge man. But I'm her little half-brother and I'm ready for her tricks, and so is the Fairborn. We stab Jessica's shoulder and slam her half-morphed body into the wall. We stab her other shoulder and she squeals. If her partner is nearby, she'll be here in less than a minute.

Jessica is fully changed into a man but her arms are useless and I have the strength and the Fairborn to hold her back against the wall.

Jessica transforms quickly again, into Arran.

Arran's voice pleads with me, "Please don't hurt me, Nathan. I know you don't want to hurt me."

"Shut up."

"I know you're a good person. I've always known that. Please. Don't hurt me."

And I know I should run. But seeing Arran is so amazing. I just want to look at him. But it's not Arran; it's Jessica, and she's an evil witch. I'm holding the point of the knife to Arran's eye. And the Fairborn wants to cut it out.

"Nathan, please. You're a good person."

And I know it would be a good plan to cut out her eye. She'd never be able to disguise that. But I can't do it. I don't want to. Not to Arran, even though I know it's not Arran and I'm telling myself it's Jessica but I don't even want to do it to her . . . but the Fairborn wants to cut . . .

I'm shaking again, trying to get the knife in the sheath. And Jessica pushes me back, weakly but it's enough, and I raise the Fairborn and then it slashes down across her face.

I've broken into a small house in the suburbs. There's no alarm and no one around. I think they've gone to work. I shower. My body keeps shaking, shivering.

My gunshot wound is a neat round scar but if I touch anywhere near it I feel like I might faint. I'm not even tempted to try to get the bullet out. Besides, the energy drinks and sweets seem to be working well enough.

I help myself to a huge bowl of cereal and a banana and then another while I think how to get back to Mercury. I've a vague idea where her cottage is. Gabriel said that he sometimes went by train and sometimes hiked. Hunters are bound to be at the train station and also watching the roads, but maybe I can get a bus. There must be one that can take me out of Geneva to somewhere that I can get a train. It's four days until my birthday. Caution is more important than speed.

I need a map.

There's a computer, but I've no idea how to use one. In the drawers I find a road map of Switzerland, but I need a walker's map so I can find Mercury's valley. I'll have to buy one. The one good thing that's happened is that the small battered rucksack I took from the shopkeeper had his wallet and till money in it. Normally I wouldn't steal money from someone like him but I didn't mean to, I didn't know the money was there, and this isn't normally.

I look in the mirror before I leave. The house must belong to a middle-aged couple. His clothes are a bit big. I can't find any sunglasses so I'm wearing his red baseball cap with a white cross on it and her paisley scarf wrapped twice round my neck. Gloves! I find a pair of leather ones and cut the finger ends off them.

Before I leave I want to look at the Fairborn properly. I want to feel it too. As soon as I slide it out of the sheath it seems to want to cut something. The blade is unusual, not shiny metal but a dull gray, almost black. The knife feels alive but looks dead. I really don't want Mercury to get her hands on this knife, I don't want Hunters to get it, and I don't want it. I could leave it at the back of a cupboard here and it would probably be safely lost forever. But I take it with me. I'll bury it somewhere. I can't give it to Mercury, can't let her know I have it. But she has Annalise. One thing at a time. Leave here. Find a place to bury the Fairborn. Get to Mercury. Get my three gifts.

I make my way to the main road and a bus stop.

The bus was a good idea. It stopped at a train station in a town half an hour outside Geneva. I've bought a map at a climbing shop near the station. The map is wonderful. Switzerland is full of valleys but Mercury's valley is unique, with the glacier and the villages strung along the river east to west, so it's easy to spot on the map. The train will take me so far and then it's another bus and a hike but I'll be back at Mercury's late tonight. I buy a bag of energy drinks, sweets, and fruit and get on the train. It's busy. I find a seat and keep my head down.

Shit! Shit! Shit!

A Hunter's walking up the platform. She's scanning the train. She's getting on. I get off. Casually.

Early morning, but it's still dark. I'm in a woods somewhere. The Hunter can't have seen me or I'd be a prisoner or dead by now. There's no way I could outrun them like this. I can't run. I'm covered in sweat, shaking and shivering, and my side has swollen. An egg-sized lump has grown on my rib. At least I have the energy drinks. I can't risk going back to the train station. I could hitch, but if I stand at the side of the road for more than ten minutes the Hunters will pick me up. Anyway I couldn't make myself get into a car, I'd feel trapped. Besides, I have a map. I know where I'm going and I have the time to get back. It's two days' hike to Mercury's valley and my birthday is three days away. I can do it. I can get back to Mercury, get my three gifts, and somehow help Annalise.

It's getting light. I've covered a lot of ground. Steady pace. Sticking to the woods not far from the road. I can rest now. I'm as stiff as an old man. But I can let myself have a couple of hours' rest.

It's twilight already. The whole day has gone, I've just slept through it. But I'll be stronger now it's night and I've had sleep. I've only got two energy drinks left but I hope I can buy more. I can relax in the trees. I change my pace, walk fast past five trees and walk slow past five. The egg-sized lump is now a fist-sized lump.

It's getting light and I can't walk at all any more.

Rest a bit. Don't go to sleep.

Shit! What time is it? Midday, maybe. Keep falling asleep. Got to get going.

Keep on going. Feeling dizzy.

There's a village. I'll buy some drinks. I need sugar.

I need to check what day it is too.

What day is it?

Feeling odd . . . dizzy . . .

I'm back in the trees. I walk at a steady pace. Sugar's done me good. It's my birthday the day after tomorrow.

Is that right? I checked. Didn't I? Someone checked.

Or did I imagine that? No, I had a drink. I checked. I saw a newspaper. Yes, that's right.

I've forgotten again.

It's a good day for a walk. Sunny.

I'm a bit slow. It's sunny, though.

If I walk through the day and the night I'll be back at Mercury's before my birthday. I think that's right.

Just keep walking.

What day is it?

I'm wet. Sweat.

The lump is still there.

My chest aches. Everything aches.

Don't touch it, just walk.

I'm slow but sunny.

Sunny. Sunny. Sunny.

What's that? Someone's in the trees up ahead. I saw someone.

Who is it?

A girl.

Sunlight. Long blonde hair. She's running like a gazelle.

"Annalise! Wait!"

I run but have to stop almost immediately.

"Annalise!"

Lean against a tree, rest for a minute.

Annalise has gone. I sink down to the ground.

I wish she would come back for me.

"Annalise!"

A giggle comes from the other side of the tree trunk.

Rose?

I crawl forward to look and Rose is lying on the ground, giggling, and then I realize she can't giggle because she's dead and, even though I know I shouldn't, I try to lift her head up to check. I can't stop myself, and she's changed into the Hunter and I feel her blood and her broken neck in my hand.

I wake up, panting. Sweaty. Shaking again.

It's dark. Got to get going. I've slept too much. I get up and my legs collapse.

It's light already. The sun is shining through the trees. And I hear Rose giggle again.

"Rose?"

She peers from behind a tree and says, "Happy Birthday tomorrow, Nathan."

Is it my birthday tomorrow?

Hey, everyone, I'm nearly seventeen!

But where is everyone?

Where's Gabriel?

"Rose, where is Gabriel?"

She doesn't even giggle.

It's silent again.

And where am I?

My map! Where's my map?

And I had some drinks, didn't I?

I have the Fairborn, though. Yes, I have the Fairborn.

And I have a stream. Don't need drinks. I have a stream. This was a good place to stop. A good place.

Let's have a look at the lump.

Not good.

Yellow, very yellow, with a little scar and lots of red veins.

Not good. Not good.

If I touch it . . .

F***!

Rose is back. She's dancing around me. She bends over and looks at the lump on my side. "Yuck! You really need to cut that out."

"Where's Gabriel?"

She blushes but doesn't reply and I shout, "Where's Gabriel?"

Silence.

It's getting dark.

I look at the lump. I think it's still growing.

I'm just going to be one big lump soon.

What day is it?

I can't think. Can't think.

"Rose, what day is it?"

No one answers. Then I remember Rose is dead.

The lump is full of poison . . . Gabriel said it was poison . . . it's poisoning me . . .

It has to go.

Just cut it out.

I hold the Fairborn. It wants to do it.

It's light. I'm lying on the ground by a stream. I'm aching but not as bad as before.

Did I cut into the lump?

I can't remember.

I look down and my shirt is open and covered in dried blood and dried yellow stuff. Lots of yellow stuff. There's no lump, though.

The stream water tastes good and I'm feeling better. My head's clear. I've drunk lots of water, a stream-full. My wound isn't too bad now I've cleaned the last of the yellow pus out. There's still a bit of swelling but nothing much. My body doesn't ache so much. Maybe the poison has gone but the bullet's still in there so maybe more poison will come out. The worst must be over though as I'm feeling so much better.

I'm not sure what day it is but I think it's my birthday.

It must be. I'm seventeen.

I AM SEVENTEEN!

And I'm feeling good. I can make it. Don't need a map now. I recognize the mountains.

I set off and then realize I don't have the Fairborn. I have the knife that Gabriel gave me, but not the Fairborn.

I run and stumble back to the stream to look for it.

There's where I cut myself. There's all the pus. The Fairborn has to be here. I cut myself with the Fairborn. I was by the stream and I stabbed my lump and . . . when I woke up the Fairborn had gone.

I don't have time for this. I have to go to Mercury's. Forget the Fairborn. I don't want it. If I maintain a steady pace I'll get to Mercury's just after it gets dark.

The rain is back, heavy drizzle and feeling cooler now. I'm walking up the valley along the road. It's quicker on the road and I need to be quicker. Only a few cars pass by, their headlights dazzling me, but I stick to the road through three small mountain villages and then cut up the mountain itself. I know the trail but the going is slow as it's sodden and slippery. Still, I'll be there in less than an hour of hiking.

I have a pain in my ribs but it's not as bad as before. I don't heal it. Maybe the healing made things worse. I don't know but I can put up with this. I'm going to make it. I will get my three gifts and I will help Annalise.

As I get higher the rain turns to sleet and then to snow. Thick snow. The flakes are huge and seem to parachute slowly. I'm high in the mountains but even so this is far too cold for June. The snow is thick on the ground, up to my knees, and it is slowing me but only a little as it's so light and powdery that I don't take huge steps but just brush through it. I look back at the trail I'm leaving but it's not obvious:

the snow is light and collapses on to my tracks, almost as if it's smoothing itself over. I keep thinking I must be near the cottage but there are no lights anywhere except behind me.

I reach the broken tree trunk, its fractured, splintered ends so sharp and thin that little snow has settled on them. I should be able to see the lights from the cottage.

I speed up and then slow down for the last twenty meters. The cottage is in darkness and I go along its side wall and down the far side to the door. As I am about to go in there is a flash, small and distant below and to the left in the valley. Then sound arrives. A shot. And another. Then lightning followed by thunder. Mercury is fighting the Hunters.

The Hunters must have found the cut, but they wouldn't have been able to get off the roof if they came through that way. They will have worked out where the cottage is, though; they'd be able to do that. And then they came up the valley. They must have only been a bit ahead of me. And then another thought hits me: if they captured Gabriel and tortured him he would tell them where the valley was . . .

I can't think about that. I have to find Mercury. I have to head to the shots. Mercury must be there. There's a swirling cloud in the valley below me, toward the glacier. A flash of lightning shoots out of it. It's her.

But first I have to see if Annalise is here. I don't know how much time I have left. Not long.

In the cottage everything is neat and tidy. My things are as I left them. So are Gabriel's. He's not been back.

I check the bedrooms.

I don't know what I expected but I was hoping Annalise would at least be here. She's not. Mercury must have taken her to her castle, and I don't know where that is. Is she still asleep? Maybe she woke her . . . but I know she won't have done.

I put on my jacket and look at the clock in the kitchen. I can work out the time if I try hard enough.

It's later than I thought. Just a bit more than ten minutes to midnight. I think that's right.

Or just a bit less. I'll reach Mercury in time if I run.

I dash outside and take two steps in the direction of the shots. Then I am stopped; I can't move forward.

The snow is falling around me but the flakes are slowing too . . . and then they stop. The snowflakes hang in the blackness of the night air.

Everything around me has stopped, and all I can do is drop to my knees in thanks.

Three Gifts

•··•·•

My father.

I know it's him. Only he can make time stop.

And I'm kneeling in stillness and silence. There are snowflakes hanging in the air, veils upon veils, and the ground around me is snow-covered and gray in the gloom. I can't even see the forest ahead of me.

And then there's a gap.

Him.

A darker figure in the darkness, flakes of snow hanging in front of him.

He comes closer, flicking a snowflake out of his way with his finger and blowing another gently as he breathes out. He comes closer still, walking not flying, the snow up to his knees.

He stops in front of me, sweeps the snow away with a sideways kick, and comes down to my level, sitting cross-legged a few arm-lengths away.

I can't see his face, only his silhouette. I think he's in a suit.

"Nathan, at last."

His voice is calm and sounds like mine only more . . . thoughtful.

"Yes," I say, and my voice doesn't sound like mine but like a little boy's.

"I've wanted us to meet. For a long time I've wanted that," he says.

"And I've wanted it too." Then I add, "For seventeen years."

"Is that what it is? Seventeen years . . ."

"Why didn't you come before now?"

"You're angry with me."

"A little."

He nods.

"Why didn't you come before?" I sound pathetic but I'm so exhausted that I don't care.

"Nathan, you are just seventeen. That's very young. When you're older you'll realize that time can move differently. Slower sometimes . . . faster occasionally." He circles his arm round now and swirls the snowflakes until they form a strange sort of galaxy that drifts up and up until it disappears.

And it's amazing. Watching my father, his power. My father, here, so close to me. But still, he should have come years ago.

"I don't care how time moves. I said, why didn't you come before now?"

"You are my son, and I expect a certain amount of respect from you . . ." He seems to breathe in and then out with a long exhalation that disperses a few more snowflakes hovering low to the ground in front of him.

"And you are my father and I expect a certain amount of responsibility from you."

He makes a sort of laugh. "Responsibility?" His head inclines to the right and then straightens again. "It's not a word I'm used to dealing with . . . And you? Are you familiar with respect at all?"

I hesitate but say, "Not that much up to now."

He waits, picks up some snow and sprinkles it from his fingers.

He says, "Mercury was going to give you three gifts, I assume."

"Yes."

"What did she want in return?"

"Some information."

"That sounds cheap for Mercury."

"She wanted something else as well."

"Let me guess . . . it's not hard: she wanted my demise. Mercury is very predictable."

"I've no intention of killing you. I told her that."

"And she accepted it?"

"She seemed to think I'd change my mind."

"Ah! I'm sure she would have fun trying to change it."

"You believe me then? I won't kill you."

"I'm not sure what to believe yet."

And I'm not sure what to say. You never ask someone to give you three gifts. Never. And I cannot ask him, but if he has come now, on my seventeenth birthday, then he must be here for that. Surely?

"What information did she want?"

"Stuff about the Council and my tattoos. I haven't told her anything."

"I'm not fond of tattoos."

I stick my hand out, show him the one on my hand and the one on my finger. They are a blue-black and my skin looks milky white in the darkness. "They planned to use my finger to make a witch's bottle. To force me to kill you."

"Lucky for me that you still have your finger. Lucky for you that you didn't tell Mercury. I think she would have taken your finger."

"She wanted the Fairborn too."

"Ah, yes . . . where is the Fairborn?"

"Rose stole it from Clay but . . . things went wrong. She was shot by the Hunters. I lost the Fairborn."

Silence.

He looks down, pinches his nose between his eyes. "And inevitably this is where I find things a little harder to believe. Where exactly did you lose it?"

"In the forest on the way here." And the pain in my side stabs me so that I shiver. "I was poisoned or something."

"What's happened? Are you hurt?" he asks, leaning toward me. He sounds concerned. Concerned! And I want to cry with relief.

"A Hunter shot me. I heal it but it keeps coming back. The bullet's still in there."

"We need to get it out."

"It hurts."

"No doubt." He sounds amused now. "Show me."

I open my jacket and shirt.

"Take them off. Lie on the snow."

As I take my shirt off he gets up, walks around me, and picks up the knife Gabriel gave me.

"What are these?" And he traces his fingers over my back. The touch of his skin on mine is strange. His hands are as cold as the snow.

"Scars."

"Yes." He laughs again but I can only just hear. "Who made them?"

"Kieran O'Brien, a Hunter. A long time ago."

"Some think a millennium isn't a long time." He runs his rough palm over my back and his touch is strangely gentle.

"So . . . Lie back. Keep still."

He doesn't hurry.

I clench my jaw; my flesh feels like it's being ripped off my rib, like pulling chicken meat off a bone. The meat is attached surprisingly strongly.

I start to count. After nine the numbers become swear words.

Then the pain stops.

"The bullet was lodged behind the bone. It was hard to reach. You can heal now."

I do and I can tell he is watching how quickly my skin knits together.

I'm buzzing; already my healing is better with the bullet out of me.

I start to push myself up and my father grabs my hair, pulling my head up and forcing me onto my front. His knee is in my back and the knife is at my throat. He strokes the flat of the blade over my skin, then turns it so the edge is pressed against my neck. I'm not cut yet.

"Your life is mine, Nathan."

The blade is so close that I daren't swallow. I'm arching back so far I could snap.

"However, I'm in a giving mood, so please accept your life as a gift from me today."

He lets my hair go and my head and body drop forward. And I'm on my hands and knees in the snow wondering, Is he going to do it? Does that count as a gift? What time is it now?

I turn and he's sitting cross-legged near me. He's in a suit but he isn't wearing a tie; his top button is undone. His face is darkness.

I put my shirt on and sit cross-legged opposite him.

He holds the bullet out to me. "For you . . . another gift. Perhaps it will remind you to be more careful around Hunters."

The bullet is round, a metallic green, with markings cut into it.

"Fain science mixed with witch magic. Not elegant, but like so many things, it can still kill you."

The way he says it I know he's talking about me.

"I won't kill you. Mary told me about your vision. I won't kill you."

"We'll see." He leans toward me, his voice low. "Time will tell."

"Mercury won't give up, though."

"She thinks I wronged her. And I suppose I did. And she will think I led the Hunters here, but you can tell her I didn't. I wouldn't do that to her. The Hunters are very good, Nathan. They don't need me to help them. Tell her that they have found a way of detecting her cuts in space. She will have to be more careful in future."

"I'll tell Mercury, if I see her. But . . ."

Doesn't he want me to go with him?

Silence. Stillness. Snowflakes waiting.

"What now?" I ask.

"Between me and you?"

I nod.

"I'm not a great believer in prophecies, Nathan, but I am a cautious man. So I suggest you keep away from Hunters and take care not to lose your finger, as you say that you have lost the Fairborn."

"But . . ."

And I can't ask him if I can go with him. He's my father. But I can't ask. He would say if he wanted me.

"Why did you never come for me?"

"I thought you were doing fine. I caught glimpses in visions. You did well enough on your own. I saw nothing after they took you away. They had you well hidden, even from visions. But you escaped. I'm pleased about that, Nathan, for both our sakes."

He looks at his wrist but I don't see a watch there.

"It's time for me to go."

He pulls a ring from his finger and takes my right hand, slides it on to the index finger.

"For you, my father's ring, and his father's before him."

He takes the knife and cuts his palm and holds his hand out.

"My blood is your blood, Nathan."

And his hand is there, his flesh, his blood. Carefully I take his hand with both of mine. His skin is rough and cold, and I raise his hand to my lips and drink his blood. And as I suck and swallow I hear the strange words that he whispers in my ear. His blood is strong and sweet and warm in my throat and my chest and stomach, and the words curl into my head, intertwine with my blood, making no sense but wrapping me in what I know, and I smell the earth and feel its pulse through my body, through my father's body and from his father before and his father before that, and at last I know who I am.

As I let his hand go I look up and see his eyes.

My eyes.

Marcus gets to his feet and says, "I take my responsibilities as a father seriously."

And as he moves back, the snowflakes begin to slowly, slowly fall again. The wind strengthens, buffeting me and picking up the snow from the ground. I can only just hear Marcus say, "I hope we meet again, Nathan."

And the snowflakes are falling more thickly, and the wind has built to a gale, and the snow is a white blur around the two of us.

The snowflakes fly in my face and he's gone.

The ring is heavy. It is thick, warm. I can't make out the shapes on it in the poor light. I turn it around my finger and feel its weight and then I kiss it and whisper thanks. I am a witch.

I have met my father. Too briefly, but I have met him. And I think he must know that I don't mean to kill him. He would not have given me three gifts if he believed that. My head feels clear, good. It's an unusual feeling. I realize I'm smiling.

Then the sky above me fills with lightning and thunder drums the air.

Running

·•·•·•

I turn back to the cottage door and Mercury is there, in gray chiffon, her hair only slightly more wild than normal, but she is in a fury and she swirls and crackles with lightning.

"I get the feeling that you have met your father." Her voice has lost its slow measured pace and is screeching at me.

"Yes."

"He gave you three gifts?"

"Yes."

"And led the Hunters here."

"No. The Hunters found you without any help from him. Marcus said that they have found a way of detecting your cuts. He wanted me to warn you to be more careful."

A bolt of lightning hits the ground near my feet. "You should be more careful too. Where are Rose and Gabriel?"

"I don't know where Gabriel is. Rose was killed by the Hunters."

Mercury screams.

"You knew it was dangerous. You sent her in there."

"And yet you survived. Do you have the Fairborn?"

Her eyes are black hollows.

"No."

"But Rose got it from Clay?"

"Yes."

"Where is it? Does Marcus have it?"

I hesitate but then say, "Yes, he took it."

She screams again and a small whirlwind swirls around her and then stops abruptly.

"It seems that all I have is Annalise."

"Where is she?"

"Safe. For now. Do you want her back?"

"Of course."

"Bring me your father's head. Or his heart. I'll accept either."

Mercury spins around in a cloud of gray, a mini tornado, her face appearing and disappearing in its calm center. The tornado flies up the valley in the direction of the glacier.

The air is calm again, the snowstorm over. It's quiet.

Will the Hunters be able to find the cottage in the dark? Of course, they're Hunters.

Then I hear the buzz of their phones. They're here.

A shot, and another.

But I'm already running. And running is even better than before. I'm stronger, faster, more in tune. The night is black but I can find my way with ease. And I know where I'm going. I'm going to find my friend. Gabriel.

Acknowledgments

I started writing rather late in my life, not very long ago in 2010, and did my best to hide this new obsession (as it quickly became) from my friends and relatives. I certainly had no intention of making myself the object of ridicule when the most I'd ever written before was a note to the milkman. However, it didn't take long before my husband noticed that I was up to something in our little office room until 2 a.m. every night. I decided to be brave and come clean.

"I'm writing a novel."

I waited. Would he laugh? Tell me I was being ridiculous?

"Oh! Okay. Sounds good."

Not the reaction I expected, but just what I needed. I could not have written *Half Bad* without his support and quiet encouragement.

After that I became a little bolder and confided in a couple of friends, who then had to bear the brunt of my tedious conversations about writing. Lisa and Alex were (and still are) amazingly good listeners, never yawned to my face, and always managed to say, "Really?" in the right places (and were early readers of my manuscripts).

Thanks as well to my other readers. I'm so grateful for their time and honesty. David gave me lots of advice on my original novel. Mollie was the first teenager to read *Half Bad*—that she chose to spend her time with Nathan I take as the perfect compliment. My Open University buddies, Gillian and Fiona, have been stars, giving me full and frank feedback.

I sent *Half Bad* to Claire Wilson at Rogers, Coleridge and White in January 2013, hoping she would be interested in acting as my agent. She was. She has championed *Half Bad* wonderfully and advised and guided me through the strange world of publishing. Claire had rejected my first novel, saying it wasn't edgy enough, and I am so grateful, as without that kick *Half Bad* would not have been written.

I have an impressive array of people working with me at Puffin, all of whom have been a joy. Ben Horslen, my editor, should win an award for enthusiasm (and tact) and with him are a great bunch of people: junior editor Laura Squire; Tania Vian-Smith and Gemma Green and the Marketing and Publicity departments; designer Jacqui McDonough; and Zosia Knopp and her fantastic Rights team (along with The Map). Thanks to everyone at Puffin.

I also feel incredibly privileged to have Ken Wright as my editor at Viking in the United States, along with his associate editor Leila Sales. He also has a great team of people but in particular I have to thank Deborah Kaplan and her designers for the gorgeous cover art.

While writing *Half Bad* I revisited some of the literature from my teenage years (before Young Adult was invented), notably Aleksandr Solzhenitsyn's *One Day in the Life of Ivan*

Denisovich, which reassured me that Nathan's time in the cage was bearable.

The someone who said, "The best way to find out if you can trust somebody is to trust them," was Ernest Hemingway.

I was searching for a name to give the Fairborn and was inspired by the Fairbairn-Sykes knife, information about which I found on Wikipedia.

I haven't seen the film *Lawrence of Arabia* for years, but the scene with the matches is one of the many that have stayed in my head.

As for *Hamlet*—well, if I'm honest I read it many years ago and have never seen the play on stage (I have watched a film version), but the line "There is nothing either good or bad, but thinking makes it so" was a key element in the forming of my story. While Shakespeare hasn't taken up a huge amount of my time over the last ten years, being a mother has, and I often watched my son and pondered the nature vs. nurture question: "Why does he do that?" "What makes him him?" "What makes any of us the way we are?" These questions undoubtedly influenced my writing.

The mountains of north Wales were an inspiration as I scrambled up, down, and around them, as were the Sandstone Trail in England and the Lötschental valley in Switzerland. If you saw a woman walking there, muttering to herself (and sometimes a luckless friend) about fains and three gifts it might have been me.